THE CRYPTIC CIPHER

Also by Denver Acey

The Quantum Breach
The Quantum Deception

THE CRYPTIC CIPHER

DENVER ACEY

BONNEVILLE
BOOKS

An Imprint of Cedar Fort, Inc.
Springville, Utah

ISBN 13: 978-1-4621-1840-3

Published by Bonneville Books, an imprint of Cedar Fort, Inc.
2373 W. 700 S., Springville, UT 84663
Distributed by Cedar Fort, Inc., www.cedarfort.com

LIBRARY OF CONGRESS CATALOGING-IN-PUBLICATION DATA

Names: Acey, Denver, author.
Title: The cryptic cipher / Denver Acey.
Description: Springville, Utah : Bonneville Books, an imprint of Cedar Fort,
   Inc., [2016]
Identifiers: LCCN 2015045950 (print) | LCCN 2015049512 (ebook) | ISBN
   9781462118403 (softcover : acid-free paper) | ISBN 9781462126354 ()
Subjects: LCSH: Hackers--Fiction. | Murder--Investigation--Fiction. | Code
   and cipher stories. | Political fiction. | GSAFD: Suspense fiction. |
   Adventure fiction. | Mystery fiction.
Classification: LCC PS3601.C488 C79 2016 (print) | LCC PS3601.C488 (ebook) |
   DDC 813/.6--dc23
LC record available at http://lccn.loc.gov/2015045950

Cover design by Rebecca J. Greenwood
Cover design © 2016 Cedar Fort, Inc.
Edited and typeset by Melissa J. Caldwell

Printed in the United States of America

10 9 8 7 6 5 4 3 2 1

Printed on acid-free paper

To my wife, family, and friends.
Your support, encouragement, and unending
enthusiasm made this book possible

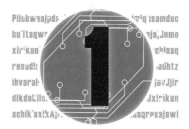

OCTOBER 23
MESA VERDE NATIONAL PARK, COLORADO

THE BRIGHT OCTOBER sun warmed the high mountain plateau, reinforcing the exact reason why the Anasazi Indians had originally inhabited the region. Even at an elevation of seven thousand feet above sea level, the afternoon temperature climbed to a comfortable sixty-two degrees. It was the best time of year to visit Mesa Verde National Park. The sparse crowds and pleasant weather attracted tourists who preferred a slower and more intimate experience of the natural landmark.

Tanner Stone leisurely walked along a dirt trail that was flanked by juniper and pine trees. His family had just completed the one-mile hike to the Square Tower House. Built by the Anasazi Indians over a thousand years ago, the Square Tower House was an impressive site. It was just one of nearly six hundred ancient cliff dwellings that covered the large mesa.

The strenuous hike had taken its toll on Tanner, and he intentionally slowed down, falling behind the rest of his family. Alone with just a sleeping baby, Tanner enjoyed the quiet of the moment.

The calmness of the national park was a welcomed contrast to the frenzied atmosphere of his top-secret job.

Tanner didn't resent working for the National Security Agency. In fact, it was just the opposite—he loved his job. Nevertheless, he eagerly anticipated the week-long vacation he took every year to decompress and recharge his battery. Moving among a world of spies was daunting and demanding, even for a thirty-six-year-old systems analyst who tirelessly worked to keep government secrets out of the hands of nefarious people.

Tanner took a deep breath of the pine-scented air as he completed the last part of the trail. On the opposite side of the parking lot, his family was waiting for him to unlock the car. Few tourists came to the southernmost part of Mesa Verde this time of year, and Tanner's minivan stood alone in the large parking area. Looking at his white Honda Odyssey, he shook his head in disbelief, overwhelmed by the fact that he was now a "family man."

Sara Nicole Stone was Tanner's first child. Barely two and a half years old, she was a nonstop bundle of energy. The newest addition to the family was currently sleeping in a baby carrier attached to Tanner's chest. Amber Lynne Stone was born six months ago, and she was part of the reason for his slow ascent up the trail.

"Hurry up, Daddy!" Sara shouted. Her little voice carried out across the vacant parking lot.

Tanner waved back to his daughter, but he didn't say anything. Although he wasn't considered old by any calculation, he had increasingly felt his age, especially over the past two years. He had gained twenty pounds since Sara's birth, and the extra weight had slowed him down a bit. Fortunately, Tanner's six-foot-two-inch frame concealed the fact that he now tipped the scales at two hundred pounds. While he knew that he needed to lose some weight, he often rationalized away his lack of exercise, claiming the added bulk wasn't his fault.

It was due to a bad injury.

Tanner paused at the edge of the parking lot to catch his breath. His mind raced off momentarily, thinking about a petite female assassin named Reina. Nearly three years ago, she had broken Tanner's lower leg with a well-placed karate kick. The assault was retribution for his discovery of an ingenious computer virus created by the Chinese. The sinister scheme would have succeeded if Tanner hadn't stopped the malware at the last second. Except for a handful of people at the NSA, nobody fully understood how close the computer virus had come to wiping out the financial data for every person in the United States. But Tanner remembered every part of the horrible ordeal with sharp clarity, especially when his reconstructed tibia ached like it did after the one-mile hike.

"Are you okay?" Megan Stone called out. At age thirty-four, Megan was in significantly better shape than Tanner. The hike hadn't fazed her at all.

"Yeah. I'm just taking it slow so I don't wake the baby," Tanner shouted back. Suddenly, he realized that yelling was probably more disturbing to the infant than walking too fast. On cue, Amber woke up and started to cry. Tanner quickly reached for the pacifier and coaxed his baby daughter back to sleep.

"Daddy, hurry up! I'm hungry," Sara shouted.

Tanner continued his casual walk across the parking lot while checking his watch. It was 1:14 p.m. The expensive timepiece came from the director of the National Security Agency. It was given to Tanner for his excellent work in uncovering the Chinese cyberattack against the United States. He had received the watch just before he was awarded an even greater honor—the Presidential Medal of Freedom. Unfortunately, Tanner's classified work at the NSA had necessitated that the award ceremony with the president be a private affair. Only Tanner, his wife, and his former boss attended the intimate event at the White House last year.

"We thought you wouldn't make it," Glen Holland joked as Tanner finally arrived at the family's minivan. He reached out and patted his son-in-law on the back.

Tanner got along well with his father-in-law, and he took the teasing in stride. He pointed to the sleeping infant strapped to his chest. "Hey, I'm carrying an extra thirty pounds here," he said.

The baby actually weighed just fifteen pounds, but the added bulk seemed to amplify Tanner's own personal weight gain.

"Yes, but we're carrying an extra thirty years," Julie Holland said, pointing to her husband. Glen and Julie were both in excellent health for being in their early sixties. They had completed the hike with only mild difficulty.

The idea to visit Mesa Verde National Park came from Tanner's in-laws, who had returned home the past summer after serving a religious mission in Guatemala. Having lived among several native groups, Glen and Julie now had an appetite for anything associated with Native American culture. Glen had been especially excited to visit Mesa Verde. It had been a lifelong dream of his to see the ancient Anasazi cliff dwellings.

Megan pulled her shoulder-length blond hair back into a ponytail before helping Tanner remove the baby carrier from his chest. "Should we eat here or go back to the lodge?" she asked.

"Let's eat over there," Tanner said, pointing to a picnic table under a large ponderosa pine. The group grabbed their lunch supplies and headed toward the table. A few minutes later, little Sara was tearing into her peanut butter and jam sandwich.

A soft breeze rustled through the trees. "It sure is peaceful here," Julie said.

"I'm so glad we did this trip," Megan said. She took the bottle from the baby and starting the burping process.

"Well, Dad, what do you think about the Square Tower House?" Tanner asked.

Glen adjusted his eyeglasses. "Fantastic," he said. "I can't believe those ruins are over a thousand years old."

Tanner nodded, empathizing with his father-in-law's astonishment at the ruins. "And they built that without power tools or machines."

"The guidebook said that the Anasazi lived here between AD 600 and AD 1000. That means they arrived just about the time the Mayans were disappearing from Central America," Glen said. He quickly moved into one of his mini-lectures on the native culture of Guatemala, but Tanner didn't mind. He had never traveled outside the United States, and he enjoyed hearing how people lived in other parts of the world.

Everyone ate their lunches while Glen described the different Mayan dialects of Guatemala. He rattled off a half-dozen languages that Tanner had never heard of, like Kaqchikel, K'iche', and Mam. When it came to foreign languages, the Holland family definitely had the advantage over Tanner. They had all learned basic Spanish after living in New Mexico most of their lives. Glen and Julie further refined their Spanish skills on their Mormon mission to Guatemala. They even managed to pick up parts of the more common Mayan dialects while they lived there.

Megan also took three years of Spanish at the University of New Mexico before graduating in computer science with a minor in music. Unfortunately, Tanner wasn't as well versed. Besides some basic high school Spanish courses, the only other language he really understood was computer code.

As Glen continued talking, Tanner noticed a faint sound in the distance. At first he thought it was just the breeze in the trees, but the sound didn't fade. He stood up and walked away from the picnic table to listen better.

"Where are you going?" Megan asked.

"Do you hear that?" Tanner asked over his shoulder. He might have lost a step or two over the past couple of years, but his hearing was still perfect.

"I hear it too, Daddy," Sara said. She got up from her seat and ran over to her father. Tanner took his daughter's little hand, and they cautiously moved closer toward the edge of the cliff. They stopped about fifteen feet away from a large drop-off. Tanner listened a moment longer before recognizing the faint "whump-whump" sound of an approaching helicopter.

He glanced back at the others seated at the picnic table. They now heard the noise and looked around in various directions to see where it was coming from. Unfortunately, the steep canyon surrounding the mesa caused too much echo for anyone to get a good fix on the origin. Then, like a dark flash of lightning, a black object shot up from beyond the edge of the drop-off. The fast moving helicopter clearly frightened the family, but not Tanner. His mind quickly recalled the events of a crazy night five years ago when he had taken a ride in a similar aircraft.

The helicopter briefly hovered overhead and then landed in the empty parking lot in a smooth and efficient manner. The blades slowed down a bit, but the downdraft was still powerful enough to scatter some of the picnic supplies about in a white cloud. Tanner picked up his daughter and raced back toward his family, who were trying to contain the mini blizzard of white napkins and paper plates.

"Stay with Grandma," Tanner said. He passed his daughter off to Julie. "I'll be back in a second," he told the rest of the group.

Tanner trotted toward the waiting helicopter. The clearly marked letters *F-B-I* on the side of the aircraft were obvious to everyone.

"That's an FBI helicopter," Tanner heard Glen yell. "What are they doing here?"

Tanner barely heard Megan's response. "They're telling us that our vacation is over," she conceded.

OCTOBER 23
STATE OF TABASCO, MEXICO

Two thousand miles away, Javier Soto watched a helicopter on its final approach. The aircraft touched down on a pristine private beach, just a hundred yards from his enormous mansion overlooking the Gulf of Mexico. Walking out of his hacienda, Javier recognized that his residence could have easily been mistaken for a luxury resort with swimming pools, waterfalls, and white-sand beaches. The large villa had all the indulgences of modern life, including satellite TV and high-speed Internet. Javier demanded the best in his life. And as the leader of the Chiapas drug cartel, he never settled for anything less.

Javier's growing drug empire stretched across southern Mexico and into Guatemala. Despite his vast wealth, he kept a low profile. Few people knew about his hacienda's existence just fifty miles east of the capital city of Villahermosa. Isolated at the end of a dirt road, Javier made sure his property was obscured by the large trees and plants that grew abundantly in the tropical climate. If a visitor ever

7

happened to pass through the overgrown vegetation and stumble upon his mansion, Javier's small army of private guards would make sure that the intruder never mentioned its location to anyone.

The drug lord moved across his patio, past an immaculate swimming pool, and out on the vacant beach. With a *guayabera* shirt, khaki pants, and flip-flops, Javier knew he looked more like a tourist than one of the most feared men in southern Mexico.

"Amigo, cómo te va?" he shouted to the man who had just jumped out of the helicopter. He was returning from his trip to Panama.

"I told you, I don't like speaking Spanish," the visitor said. In his late thirties, the tall, skinny man had a serious demeanor. But his stern face quickly faded to a smile, and he shook his boss's extended hand enthusiastically.

"I heard it on the news. Everyone is talking about it," Javier said. He patted his employee's shoulder and directed him over toward a patio set in the shade.

Javier quickly motioned to a waiter. The anonymous servant, who had been standing in the background, disappeared and returned with two drinks. Javier took one bottle and handed the other to his lieutenant.

"We drink to success," Javier said.

"Yes," the other man concurred.

Javier was sure none of his staff knew the visitor's actual name, but everyone at the hacienda called him El Flaco, which was Spanish for the "skinny one." Javier's guest was six feet six inches tall, but even after a large meal, he would hardly weigh 180 pounds. With his fair hair and freckles, El Flaco obviously didn't fit in with the locals. That's because he was a *Norteamericano* from California. He had moved to Mexico two years ago to become the first lieutenant in Javier's increasingly powerful Chiapas drug cartel.

"What's your next step?" Javier asked.

"Rest here for tonight, and then I'm heading up north to take care of the final arrangements," El Flaco replied.

Javier couldn't have been more pleased with his right-hand

man. Before moving to Mexico, El Flaco had spent ten years in the United States Army. After sacrificing his sweat and blood in Afghanistan for no apparent victory, El Flaco decided that he had had enough and quit the military. He took the only real compensation that Uncle Sam had given him—his military training—and decided to become a mercenary. With his leadership skills and army expertise, El Flaco brought a sense of professionalism and dedication to everyone in Javier's organization. In a short amount of time, El Flaco had militarized the group's workings, causing the Chiapas cartel to become a formidable player in the southern Mexico drug trade. Javier stared at his lieutenant with a smile. El Flaco was crafty and cruel, but he was absolutely the best employee on the cartel's payroll. The mercenary demanded a high salary, but Javier didn't care. If the cartel's grand operation worked out as planned, Javier would soon have more money than he could possibly imagine.

OCTOBER 23

MESA VERDE NATIONAL PARK, COLORADO

ANNER WAS STILL thirty feet away from the helicopter when he saw the person in the passenger's seat remove her helmet. He instantly recognized the bright red hair of Nicole Green, the Special Agent in Charge of the Albuquerque FBI office. Nicole's quick stride toward Tanner confirmed that she was just as feisty now as when he first met her five years ago. She walked directly up to him, stopping just a few feet away. She was dressed in a white blouse and black slacks and had a Glock 23 pistol on her waist.

"So an FBI helicopter lands out here in the middle of nowhere, and somehow it just happens to be you that steps out," Tanner said, putting his hands on his hips in mock frustration.

"Hey, I had to come for a visit. I haven't seen your kids yet," Agent Green said. She flashed Tanner a sarcastic smile and then lunged forward, giving him a friendly hug.

Tanner returned the warm embrace. "It's good to see you again, Red." The nickname was in reference to Nicole's fiery red hair, but Tanner wasn't being disrespectful. In fact, he and Nicole had a unique history together.

Before Tanner was married, he had been kidnapped by a group of cyberterrorists. The cunning criminals forced Tanner to hack into Los Alamos National Labs and steal classified information about a prototype quantum computer. Miraculously, Tanner had outwitted his kidnappers and escaped before surrendering himself to Nicole Green of the FBI. Ever since that chaotic time, they had been good friends. In fact, Nicole was such a respected acquaintance that Tanner and Megan named their daughter, Sara Nicole, after the fascinating FBI agent.

"Nicole!" Megan called out in excitement as she approached the helicopter. She gave the FBI agent a quick hug.

"You look great," Nicole said. Almost fifteen years in age separated the two women, but they found common ways to relate to each other.

"Okay, what's going on, Red?" Tanner asked.

"The vice president was assassinated yesterday in Panama," Nicole said.

Megan gasped at the announcement. Tanner and his family had been out of touch for the past three days, staying at an "unwired" lodge just inside the national park. They hadn't heard the news or watched TV since their arrival.

"Who did it?" Tanner asked.

"We don't know, but we found some very interesting stuff that you need to look at. That's why I was ordered to track you down," Nicole said.

"But how did you find us up here?" Megan asked.

Tanner sighed as he held up his arm, showing off his silver watch. "It has a GPS transmitter in it. The NSA always wants to know where I am."

"I guess I shouldn't be shocked at that, considering what you do for a living," Megan said with a sigh.

"I've been ordered to escort you back to the FBI office in Albuquerque. That comes directly from the top," Nicole stated with official emphasis.

"Why not back to the data center in Utah?" Tanner asked.

"Albuquerque is much closer. We can get you up to speed on what's happening there."

"What about us? Are you going to leave us here?" Megan asked.

Nicole smiled. "I figured you'd say that. We've got room for everyone in there." She pointed her thumb over her shoulder to the helicopter.

Just then a national park SUV pulled into the empty parking lot. Nicole turned her gaze toward the oncoming vehicle. "We called ahead and had them grab your stuff from the lodge," she said. "They'll take your minivan back to park headquarters and keep an eye on it there."

Tanner laughed. "I guess you've thought of everything."

"Yep," Nicole confirmed. "The folks back in DC are calling the shots now."

When the helicopter lifted off fifteen minutes later, young Sara squealed with delight. "I'm flying," she said with an enormous grin. She obviously had no idea that the helicopter ride wasn't part of the family's vacation. Like most children, she just enjoyed the new experience with glee.

Tanner and his family rode in the middle compartment of the helicopter while Nicole sat up front with the pilot. Tanner looked at Glen and Julie on the bench across from him, wondering what his in-laws were thinking about the recent events. They seemed to be doing okay, but they appeared rather goofy in their flight helmets.

"The park looks even more impressive from up here," Glen said, speaking into the microphone attached to his helmet.

"You can really see why it's called Mesa Verde from the air," Tanner said. He craved more details about the assassination of the vice president, but he'd have to wait.

The helicopter picked up speed and headed south. "What about our car?" Sara asked. "Will we get it back?"

"Yes, sweetie," Megan shouted to her daughter. Sara wasn't wearing a headset, and it was difficult to hear over the sound of the powerful rotors.

"Is this a normal part of your work routine?" Julie asked through the microphone on her helmet.

Tanner had wondered how long it would be until one of his in-laws asked a specific question about his super-secret job. Before he could say anything in response, however, Megan jumped in to answer.

"Well, you know that Tanner does computer work for the government," she said. "Now you can see just how important his job is."

Tanner was impressed. He had given his wife the "I can't tell you what I'm doing at work" speech over a thousand times. He figured that she just ignored him now, but Megan had concisely summed up the current situation in just two sentences without revealing anything confidential.

"They need your help to find out who killed the vice president?" Julie asked.

"Yeah, I'm going to see what I can do. Unfortunately, I'm always on call, even during vacations," Tanner apologized.

"And bad guys don't take vacation," Megan added reluctantly.

Without saying anything else, the group quietly surrendered the remainder of their trip in the name of national security.

ALBUQUERQUE, NEW MEXICO

The ride back to Albuquerque was also a trip home for Glen and Julie. They had lived in Albuquerque for almost forty years, and they had no intention of moving, even though all four of their kids had left the area. In a way, it was also nice for Tanner to come back to the Rio Grande Valley. He hadn't visited Albuquerque since he got married and moved to Utah five years ago.

It was after 4:00 p.m. when the helicopter landed at the

multistory FBI complex just off Interstate-25 and Montano Road. Tanner gave his wife a quick kiss and then followed Nicole into the building. At that same moment, another female agent came out of the office and walked toward the landing pad. This FBI agent would be the escort for the other members of the family. She would take them inside for a bathroom break before the ride back to the Holland's home.

As Tanner followed Nicole up the stairs, he marveled at the continuing irony of the day. "It was five years ago this month that I was under arrest in this same building."

"I know," Nicole said. She stopped to scan her ID badge at a card reader. "But back then, you were a suspect," she said as she opened the door to the third floor. "A lot has changed since then."

In a former life, Tanner had been a computer hacker. He had been very good at his profession and made millions of dollars from his illegal activities. But a traumatic event caused him to swear off computer hacking, reform his ways, and eventually join the Mormon religion. It was two years after he quit hacking when he first crossed paths with the FBI through the cyber-terrorist situation.

Nicole led Tanner down the hall toward a private conference room. Inside, two FBI agents were already on a top-secret conference call. They paused as he and Nicole entered the room. In the middle of the table there was a cold twenty-ounce bottle of Mountain Dew. Tanner turned and smiled at Nicole.

"I've been trying to quit, but you know my weakness," he said. He opened the bottle and took a refreshing drink before diving into business. "Okay, bring me up to speed," he said, taking a seat.

A refined female voice called out from the speakerphone at the center of the table. "We tracked you down a lot faster than I would have imagined."

Tanner chuckled with delight. It was his former boss, Helen Ripplinger, calling from Washington, DC. "I should have known it was you," he said. "Who else could pull enough strings to make this whole thing happen?"

In many ways, Helen was Tanner's idol. She had convinced him to move to Utah and join her team of hand-picked systems analysts. While he had been a new employee, Helen had taught Tanner all the ins and outs of the NSA. But Helen was more than just an excellent boss—she was a mentor and friend. In hindsight, Tanner now understood why Helen had taken such a personal interest in his career. From the day he had joined the NSA, she had been prepping him to take her position after she retired.

Unfortunately, Helen's departure from the NSA didn't work out as she had planned. Just two months shy of her retirement, she received a phone call that changed everything. The president of the United States personally asked her to serve as his National Security advisor. Patriotism ran deep in Helen's family, and she willingly delayed her retirement to answer the call of government duty. A year ago last August, she left the Quantum Computing team in Tanner's capable hands and headed back home to Maryland to start her new career.

"It's so good to hear your voice," Tanner said. Helen's busy schedule as the National Security advisor kept her from regular communication with her former team in Utah. Except for an occasional email, Tanner hadn't spoken directly with Helen in over three months.

"I know," Helen said. "Life is so crazy here in DC that I often wish I could just go back to Utah. I guess I'm an analyst at heart."

Helen had a charm and refinement that was uncharacteristic of most modern women. In a way, Tanner felt she would have been more at ease in the 1950s, associating with Jacqueline Kennedy. Helen never rushed into business without engaging in casual conversation first, so when she immediately started the briefing, Tanner knew the situation was urgent.

"You'll have to excuse the lack of small talk, but we've got a serious problem," Helen said. "Yesterday at 9:00 a.m., Vice President Torres was assassinated by a group of approximately ten masked gunmen in Panama. He was killed at his hotel as he finished up his morning workout routine."

The vice president's trip to Panama was hardly a secret. It had been in the news for weeks. He was attending a special summit of government officials from both Central and South America to discuss the increasing violence among drug traffickers.

"Was it one of the drug cartels?" Tanner asked.

"That's our initial assessment. You know the vice president was an outspoken critic of illegal drugs," Helen said.

He was more than a vocal opponent. After a couple of states legalized recreational marijuana, Vice President Torres launched a nationwide program to educate children on the dangers of gateway drugs like pot. Despite lukewarm support from the attorney general, the vice president had pushed for tougher laws to prosecute drug crime. He quickly became the nation's leading voice against drug use, and he was making a positive difference.

"So how did the killers get to him?" Tanner asked Helen over the speakerphone.

"Someone told them where the VP would be staying. The terrorists forced their way into the exercise room on the ground level and took out the VP and his bodyguards with AK-47s," Helen said. "It lasted less than twenty seconds. Eight people were killed, including three terrorists."

"Okay, so why call me? This sounds like a job for the Secret Service or CIA," Tanner said casually.

"The CIA found an encrypted message on one of the dead terrorists. They couldn't figure it out, so they passed it along to me. I sent it off to your team in Utah to have them crack it. They've been working on it for over twenty-four hours with no luck. That's when we decided we had to get a hold of you," Helen said.

Tanner was confused. "Is this a handwritten note?" he asked. His team in Utah specialized in cracking digital codes found on the Internet, not messages on normal paper. Cracking codes like that was usually handled by the analyst at Fort Meade, Maryland.

"Nobody has any idea what this code is. The folks at NSA headquarters are completely stumped. I figured that your team might have better luck with QC," Helen said.

QC was the nickname Tanner's team had given their quantum computer—the NSA's ultimate weapon in eavesdropping. Created by the scientists at Los Alamos National Labs, QC was a prototype supercomputer built on the principles of quantum physics. The computer was unspeakably fast, and it could perform 2^{128} or 340 trillion, trillion, trillion simultaneous calculations at once. Because of its phenomenal speed, QC could scan through trillions of permutations every second, enabling the computer to crack even the most complex digital encryption methods. It was a closely guarded secret among the intelligence community that the NSA could read virtually any message sent across the Internet.

"Can you get me a copy of the message?" Tanner asked. "This doesn't seem right. A scrambled note on a piece of paper is much different than encrypted computer code."

On cue, Nicole leaned in and handed Tanner a folder labeled "top secret." Inside was a black and white copy of the message found on the dead terrorist. The bottom corner of the paper had a dark splotch on it, and he assumed it was probably from a bloodstain. Fortunately, he was still able to read the better part of the note. He found the contents fascinating:

PiichwaajpdaajawineldakilSikynJmiq'isamduchu'ltaqwaq'a dnaq'ralawalbojjoyabajajajdumoxirikunChjontadtenuwuqm Reldibalja'sachinaqresadlsojsik'italnbitzindChuyak'walvxeo dhtzíhvaraldubíabejinadmikdxmukurixq'anajoyJjirdikdakil sikynJmiq'isdajjamarInaqmodxirikunachik'axikAjitzavdj'ale ma'sachindaqresajawindelFwaq'anaqwdaq'anaq'Alaxdibach' ekenejdlch'uch'ujirik

The note went on for almost an entire page, but Tanner just concentrated on the first few lines. He analyzed the message for what seemed like an eternity, and then he did something very strange. "Can I get a mirror?" he asked Nicole.

The FBI agent looked back at Tanner with amusement. "What, you don't like your hair?"

"Just trust me on this," he said. Nicole shook her head in disbelief and left the room to find a mirror.

"What's the mirror for?" Helen asked over the speakerphone.

"It's to trick my brain. I'm going to look at the message in the mirror. I know it won't make any sense that way, but it will force my brain to stop trying to English-ize everything," Tanner said.

"When did you learn to do that?"

"It's something that I picked up since you left," Tanner said. "We hired a new analyst last year. He worked cryptology for years at Fort Meade. He showed me this trick to force my mind to see characters in different groups. Naturally, everyone's mind wants to organize letters into their native tongue."

The door to the conference room opened up, and Nicole stepped in with a compact mirror, likely from her purse. "It's small, but it should work," she said.

Tanner took the mirror and held it out in front of him. He then took the paper with the encrypted message and held it next to his face. With three FBI agents watching the process in bewilderment, Tanner studied the note in the mirror's reflection. The trick worked, and he soon determined that he wasn't even looking at encrypted computer code.

"What do you see?" Helen asked. She was eager for information.

"A couple of things," Tanner said. "First of all, there are no numbers in the encrypted string. Usually there are numbers, lots of them. And there are too many apostrophes for any encryption algorithm I've seen before. They're all over the place." Suddenly, Tanner put the mirror down and stared directly at the note.

He was onto something.

"What is it?" Nicole asked.

"Where's my father-in-law?" he shouted with excitement. "Let's get him in here."

TRAVIS BOSTON GLANCED out the window as the plane began its final approach. The flight had been uneventful, giving him plenty of time to contemplate his precarious situation. He was neck-deep in illegal activity, but he never believed that his shady dealings could lead to murder. Travis took a deep breath and leaned back into his seat, accepting the fact that he became a criminal the day he had joined Anonymous.

Travis didn't know exactly how many people belonged to the hacktivist organization called Anonymous. Founded in 2003, the loosely affiliated group of computer hackers represented a wide variety of people. They all joined for different reasons, but the common thread holding them together was dissatisfaction. By uniting with Anonymous, Travis and his fellow hackers discovered a powerful outlet to express their frustration against whomever or whatever was troubling them.

Inside the ranks of Anonymous, however, Travis knew there was disagreement on how the group should proceed. Some individuals joined to rebel against regulation of the Internet. They wanted cyberspace to be like it was originally designed—unfettered and unrestricted. On the other end of the spectrum, some members of Anonymous strived for anarchy. They used their hacking skills to spread hate and discontent all over the globe. They wanted chaos, and they didn't care who got hurt in the process. Travis was somewhere in the middle of the hacktivist spectrum. He wasn't one of those anarchists on the nightly news, wearing a black-and-white Guy Fawkes mask. But he was against government control, and he wanted to see the Feds put back in their place. Ironically, Travis hadn't always been so disenfranchised. He used to be a "white hat," a good guy who kept hackers out of computer systems.

Travis once worked as a computer security professional for a community bank on the East Coast. After the subprime loan implosion of 2008, his bank was on the verge of collapse. His employer accepted the TARP (Troubled Asset Relief Program) bailout and managed to stay afloat just long enough to be bought-out by a larger bank. The bigger bank had also received TARP funds, but Travis knew they didn't really need the money. They grabbed the government handout and used it to fortify their dominance. Travis lost his job, and his faith in government, when the two banks merged. He later joined Anonymous, unifying with other hackers around the world who wanted to curb the government's influence in their life.

Despite his association with Anonymous, Travis wasn't just some twenty-year-old punk who lived in his mother's basement. He was well into his thirties with a wife, two kids, and an upside-down mortgage. A big reason why he joined Anonymous was to protect the future of his kids. He was convinced that the government had become too controlling. If he didn't help push back now, the Feds would soon regulate everybody's life.

Because of his disdain for politicians, Travis was immediately intrigued when a former Army acquaintance had approached him about an unusual hacking job. It was a cyberattack directed against the speaker of the House of Representatives, whose personal involvement had created the monster called TARP. Travis eagerly accepted the lucrative hacking job, believing that it was the perfect opportunity to punish the reckless bureaucrats in Washington.

The 737 landed with a hard bump, jarring Travis out of his hacktivist daydream. He had just arrived at the Dallas/Fort Worth International Airport. Tomorrow was an important meeting with his former Army associate. Travis was getting paid $200,000 for this hacking job, and a good chunk of that cash was going into his carry-on before he headed back home to Orlando, Florida.

TANNER WAITED FOR his father-in-law to join him in the conference room. When the FBI agent returned, he made sure to have Glen wait outside the door until invited in by Agent Green.

"Okay, we've got your father-in-law, but where is this going? You can't tell him anything about the details of the assassination," Nicole said.

Tanner knew that Glen didn't have a top-secret/SCI clearance, and he was positive that he had never endured the stressful polygraph test that Tanner had taken earlier that year. Nevertheless, Glen had some unique knowledge, and Tanner was hoping that his father-in-law could deliver a quick and concise answer.

Tanner spoke as he held up the encrypted note. "I think this just might be a Native American dialect. Specifically, it might be something from Central America."

"What?" Nicole asked.

"It's not computer code because it's too formalized and too deliberate. Encrypted code is much more random. This note looks like there's actually some form and flow to it," Tanner said. "My father-in-law spent the past two years in Guatemala, and he brought back several books with samples of native dialects. The characters in this message look a lot like some of the text in those books. I'm just going to show him the note, without elaborating on anything, and see if he thinks I could be right."

"I'm not sure I buy into your theory," Nicole said. "I don't think we should let him see this note."

Helen called out over the speakerphone. "I trust Tanner. If he says his father-in-law can help, I think we should let him."

Nicole reluctantly shook her head before opening the door and escorting Glen into the conference room.

"Hi, Dad," Tanner said. He motioned for Glen to take a seat at the conference room table.

"What's going on?" Glen asked. He had a concerned look on his face.

"Don't worry. You're not in trouble. In fact, I need your help. Can you take a look at this and tell me what you think it is?"

Tanner slid the sheet of paper across the table to Glen. He didn't give his father-in-law any background information regarding what was happening. He wanted Glen to create his own, unbiased opinion.

Glen studied the note for a moment. Then he took off his eyeglasses and held the paper right up in front of his nose. "Where did you get this?" he asked.

"Sorry, I can't tell you that," Tanner said. He had mastered that phrase over the past five years at the NSA.

"Well, it kind of looks like K'iche' or Mam, but without any spaces between the words," Glen said. He was referring to two of the more common dialects in Guatemala. He studied the note again, and then a look of disappointment showed on Glen's face. "Nope, I don't think it's either of those."

"How do you know about those dialects?" Helen asked over the phone.

Glen was surprised to have a random voice call out from the speakerphone in the center of the table. But Tanner nodded his head toward phone, encouraging his father-in-law to answer.

"Uh," Glen started awkwardly. "My wife and I spent almost two years down there on a mission for our church. I picked up parts of the more common dialects while I was there. I'm definitely not an expert, but I remember enough to recognize some simple phrases."

Tanner probed his father-in-law for more information. "What about another dialect? Could it be something else?"

"Could be," Glen said. "There are hundreds of dialects down there. Some of the more common ones, like K'iche' or Mam, are spoken by tens of thousands of people. But there are dozens of smaller languages, and most of those are only spoken by a handful of the older generation," he said as he studied the note again. "This definitely looks like something that could come from Guatemala, but it's hard to tell for sure."

"Do you know anyone who could translate it?" Tanner asked.

Glen paused as he thought about the question. "You know, I once met a guy down there. He was a really old fellow who understood many of the obscure dialects. I'll bet he could tell us for sure."

"How do we find him?" Helen asked over the phone.

Again, Glen looked confused at who was talking on the phone, so Tanner decided to shed a little light on the mysterious voice. "That's my former boss. She's the one who gave me the copy of the letter," he said.

Glen leaned awkwardly toward the middle of the conference room table and spoke into the speakerphone. "You probably can't. The guy doesn't stick around in one place for very long. He's kind of like a nomad."

"Do you have a name or picture of this person?" Nicole asked.

"We just called him Miguel," Glen said. "We taught him a little bit about our religion, but he wasn't interested. Honestly, he's about one hundred years old and very suspicious of outsiders. But for some reason, he seemed to take a liking to my wife," he said in passing.

"If we went back down there, do you think you could find him?" Tanner asked.

"Oh, no you don't," Helen quickly countered over the phone. "You're not going to Guatemala."

"Wait, hear me out," Tanner replied. "You said nobody can figure out this message. We have some of the best linguists in the world, and if they can't decode it, this Miguel guy might be our only option."

"Tanner, you're an analyst, not a spy," Helen said.

The shocked expression on Glen's face highlighted his obvious concern. He looked directly at Tanner. "You're not a spy, are you?"

Tanner laughed, putting his father-in-law at ease. "No. I'm not a spy, unless you consider figuring out codes like this something that James Bond would do."

Glen visibly relaxed a bit, and Nicole addressed the group. "Let's have Mr. Holland go back to his family while we decide what to do next." Her suggestion was a perfect way to kill the unintended spy-talk.

One of the FBI agents politely escorted Glen back to his family. After he left the conference room, Tanner laughed out loud at his former boss's gaffe. "Well, there shouldn't be much doubt now about what I do for a living."

"I'm so sorry. I completely forgot who I was talking to," Helen said over the phone.

"This might work out for us in the long run," Tanner said. "If we give my father-in-law just enough facts to cooperate, he could help us find Miguel."

"Wait, you're not still thinking about going to Guatemala, are you?" Nicole asked.

"You bet," Tanner said. "This is the best lead we have. If we can find this Miguel guy and get him to translate the message, we might know for sure what the vice president's killers were up to."

Nicole shook her head in disagreement. "Listen to what Helen just said. You're not a spy. We've got professional people to take care of this, right?" she asked, hoping that Helen would endorse her opinion.

The National Security advisor didn't say anything for several seconds. When she did, her tone had changed. "The more I think about it, the more I like Tanner's idea. I think we should send him to Guatemala, and let me tell you why."

For the next twenty minutes, Tanner, Helen, and Nicole discussed the idea of a trip to Guatemala. If Miguel could decipher the message, it made sense that someone should try to contact him. Unfortunately, Miguel was very transient, and it would be almost impossible for someone who hadn't met the old man to track him down. Glen and Julie both knew the mysterious man, however, and it soon became obvious that they would need to make the journey to Guatemala as well.

"I've got an idea," Tanner said. "I'll take the trip with my wife and in-laws. We'll go down disguised as tourists, find Miguel, and get him to translate the message."

"Are you sure you're not just trying to get a free vacation on Uncle Sam?" Nicole said in a half-joking, half-serious voice.

"Hey, you guys just ruined the trip that I was on," Tanner countered in jest before turning serious. "If we want to figure out what this message means, let me go down with my in-laws. They know Miguel and what he looks like. We could probably track him down in less than a week."

"What if you can't find him, or worse, he doesn't cooperate?" Nicole asked.

Tanner had already crafted his defense. "You heard what Glen said. He said that Miguel took a liking to my mother-in-law. I bet you he'd be a lot more willing to talk to her than some CIA goon."

Helen almost laughed out loud at Tanner's observation. He was fully integrated into the NSA now that he was name-calling CIA operatives. As two of the primary intelligence-gathering organizations in the government, the CIA and NSA were often at odds. The NSA never trusted the CIA's human intelligence, and the CIA never really felt confident with the NSA and their high-tech toys.

"I have a meeting with some folks on the National Security Council in an hour," Helen said. "Let me update them with what we discussed here. I'll float Tanner's proposal to the group and call you back at 7:00 p.m. your time."

"That sounds good," Tanner said over the phone. "In the meantime, I'll call my team back in Utah and bring them up to speed." He then turned to Nicole. "Is it okay if my in-laws hang out here for a while longer?"

"That's fine with me. But if you guys do go to Guatemala, who's going to watch your kids?" Nicole asked.

"My parents live close to Las Vegas. We can drop the kids off, and they'll take care of them for a couple of days," Tanner said.

He had planned for everything.

OCTOBER 23
NSA DATA CENTER, UTAH

S ALT LAKE CITY isn't considered a hub for any kind of spy activity. In fact, it isn't even on the radar of foreign govern-ments as a source for international espionage. But the capital of Utah has several unique characteristics, some of which are of special interest to the National Security Agency.

Salt Lake City is the headquarters for The Church of Jesus Christ of Latter-day Saints, or more commonly known as the Mormon Church. Tens of thousands of Mormons in the area have lived overseas, serving foreign-speaking missions for their church. These missionaries return home with a fluent bilingual skill set—something that is crucial for eavesdropping on other nations. The Wasatch Front of Utah is also an exploding high-tech area. Many of its citizens are college-educated and trained with skills to suc-ceed in the modern digital age. Because of these unique cultural advantages, the NSA decided that Salt Lake City was the perfect place to build their state-of-the-art data center.

At the southern end of the Salt Lake Valley is a small piece of government property called Camp Williams. This military installation is the primary training site for the Utah National Guard. On an isolated hillside of Camp Williams, however, is a massive building that has nothing to do with the National Guard. That complex is owned by the National Security Agency, and it is one of the most closely guarded facilities in the United States.

The top-secret building is officially called the Community Comprehensive National Cybersecurity Initiative Data Center. But for the NSA employees who work there, they preferred to use the facility's nickname, "Bumblehive." One hundred and sixteen NSA employees maintain the facility's 24-hour operation. The enormous two-story complex was built with one goal in mind—to collect and store every bit of data transferred across the Internet.

Access to the NSA data center is practically impossible. The first line of defense is the perimeter provided by Camp Williams. Just to get near the general vicinity, a visitor has to be associated with the National Guard or military. If a criminal somehow managed to get onto the army post, he would encounter a completely different set of security controls around the NSA building: guards with guns, razor wire on top of a twenty-foot fence, and motion sensors hidden around the facility to prevent even the most determined intruder from unauthorized access.

The interior of the building is further secured with state-of-the-art controls like dual-factor authentication, biometric scanners, and high-definition cameras that cover every square inch of the premises. Despite the elaborate cost, the security controls were absolutely necessary. The NSA had to protect their prized asset for eavesdropping in the digital age: the quantum computer operated by Tanner and his team of systems analysts.

Melvin Otterson stood at the quantum computer's console, looking over the shoulders of two of his peers. The NSA analysts were in the Chamber—a cave-like room that was separated from rows of computer equipment by a thick glass partition. On one side of the glass wall was the operations desk, complete with multiple monitors and keyboards. On the other side of the partition was QC, the NSA's massive quantum computer that officially didn't exist.

"This is driving me crazy," Rachel York said. The forty-year-old mathematician worked on Tanner's team, creating the complex mathematical algorithms that QC used to decrypt messages on the Internet. Code breaking and mathematics went hand in hand, and Rachel's brilliance was absolutely critical to the team's operation. "We've cracked every code out there, even that new one the Russians started using last year. How come we can't figure this one out?"

"It must be a completely new cipher," Kevin Granger said, seated next to Rachel. Kevin was the new analyst hired by Tanner over the summer. Dressed in business casual clothes, the friendly fifty-year-old looked like a typical office employee.

"I'd expect something like this to come out of China, not Panama," Mel said in a perturbed voice. Mel was in charge of the QC team while Tanner was on vacation. A former chain smoker with a crotchety attitude, Mel had made as many enemies as friends over the years. He was a grumpy man in every sense of the word, but his peers didn't take his abrasiveness to heart. He was the most tenured member of the QC team, and he knew more about the internal workings of the NSA than anyone in the group.

"Maybe we're looking at this wrong. Even QC can't figure it out," Kevin said. After thirty hours trying to decipher the message that was found on the dead terrorist, the supercomputer hadn't made one step of forward progress. "I mean, it's a code on a piece of paper. It might not even be computer language to begin with."

A female voice rang out from behind the other analysts. "You're probably right." It was Sydney Littlefield, the youngest member of the QC team. Sydney's background was in computer programming, not mathematics or cryptanalysis. She was the main computer programmer who input the complex mathematical equations for QC to run.

"Whoa, when did you get in here?" Mel asked. He hadn't heard Sydney come into the super-secure operations room.

"I came to get you guys. Tanner is on the phone in the conference room. He wants us all in there," she said excitedly. The twenty-eight-year-old always had an upbeat personality, but after she had gotten married over the summer, her bubbly demeanor was at an all-time high.

"I guess it's time for a break," Mel said to the rest of the group. They all got up and walked out of the Chamber together. For security reasons, nobody was ever allowed to be alone in the operations room.

A few moments later, the systems analysts were gathered in a high-tech and completely eavesdrop-proof conference room. Several large HDTVs hung on the wall, and a secure fax machine stood off in the corner. At the center of the room was a large table with ten high-back chairs. The QC team spent countless hours brainstorming and discussing classified information in this room.

Mel brought the meeting to attention. "I think everyone is here now," he said.

"Thanks, Mel," Tanner replied over the secure speakerphone.

"Are you in Albuquerque?" Rachel asked.

"Yep. I'm at the exact same place I was five years ago when this all started," Tanner said, referring to the beginning of his unanticipated career at the NSA. "The irony is so thick I can see it in front of me."

When Tanner was hired on at the NSA over three years ago, only Helen knew about his mysterious background. But the details of Tanner's past, including his former life as a computer hacker, all came to light during the incident with the Chinese computer virus. It was during that same time when the QC team learned something else about Tanner's secret history. He had thwarted an earlier attempt by cyberterrorists to steal the plans for QC while it was being designed at Los Alamos National Labs in New Mexico. Since Tanner had inadvertently learned about the details of the hush-hush computer before it even became operational, the NSA decided to give him a job to prevent him from leaking his knowledge to anyone else. Even now, Tanner's teammates marveled at the intricate, intertwined history of how he came to work for the NSA.

"Have you guys been playing nice since I left?" Tanner asked with a laugh.

"Yeah, but we've been too busy to enjoy your absence," Mel said with a plastic golf tee in his mouth. Even though he had given up smoking three years ago, his body still craved to have something in his mouth. Gnawing on a plastic golf tee was his unusual approach to calming his nerves in times of stress.

"I'm sorry you didn't get to finish your vacation," Sydney said.

"Well, there might be more of that to come," Tanner said. He jumped right to the point of the conversation. "I think the reason why you haven't been able to crack that message is because it's not even encrypted computer code. I think it might be a rare native dialect from Central America."

"What are you talking about?" Rachel asked over the speakerphone.

Tanner took the next ten minutes to explain his theory before Rachel answered. "Well, that's a relief. I'm glad to learn that it wasn't our fault we couldn't decode it."

"So you think someone in Guatemala can decode that message? That sounds like a long shot," Kevin chimed in.

"It is a long shot, but it's not completely unreasonable," Tanner said.

"Who do we know that can understand any of those old dialects?" Mel asked.

"My father-in-law met an old man down there once. His name is Miguel, and he knows dozens of those rare dialects. Unfortunately, Miguel moves around a lot, so someone needs to go Guatemala and track him down," Tanner said.

"Really?" Rachel asked. "And who do we know that would be willing to go down there and find Miguel?" Her sarcasm came through loud and clear over the speakerphone.

Tanner chuckled before delivering his final point. "Helen is working on my travel approval right now with the higher-ups in DC. If she gets the green light, I'll head out tomorrow with my in-laws and wife."

"It looks like your vacation will be extended to Guatemala," Sydney said. "I wish I could go too."

"Unfortunately, I'm not going down there to see the sights. I have to find Miguel and see if he can decode the message," Tanner said.

"What do you want us to do in the meantime?" Rachel asked.

"Trying to crack that code is a waste of time, but that doesn't mean we shouldn't be looking to see if anyone else is using it. I want you guys to turn QC loose on the Internet. Have her scan emails, chat rooms, and blogs to see if anyone else might be communicating using the same encryption," Tanner said.

"We can break down the original message into smaller character strings and do a search for pattern matches," Sydney said. "We might have more luck that way."

"If you find anything, call Helen directly. It might be hard to get in touch with me while I'm in Guatemala," Tanner said. Then, before ending the call, he offered some encouragement for the team. "Keep up the good work. There's got to be something on the Internet that can help us out. Think outside the box. Be resourceful."

"Yeah, that's easy for you to say. You're the guy who received the Presidential Medal of Freedom," Mel said.

"I know," Tanner reluctantly said. There wasn't anything he could do to defend his award, but he didn't mind the banter. He would have said the same about Helen when she had been the boss.

OCTOBER 23
WHITE HOUSE, WASHINGTON, DC

H ELEN WALKED ALONG the luxuriously hallway in reverence. Although she had worked here for more than a year, she still felt like she was on holy ground. She considered it a privilege and honor to work at the White House. Just standing in the foyer of the alabaster mansion was overwhelming. The national land- mark symbolized many of the great principles of the Founding Fathers, but she knew that not everyone shared her views. Just as the White House stirred positive feelings for Helen, she knew that it did the opposite for other people in the world.

Few individuals had access to the raw intelligence that Helen did as the National Security advisor. She had seen the ugly truth, and it was absolutely convincing. There were rotten people in the world who wanted to destroy the United States. They desired noth- ing more than to watch the White House burn to its foundation in a fiery catastrophe. Helen knew such terrorists wouldn't be satisfied until they killed every single American.

The hours Helen put in were long and hard. It was already 8:00 p.m., yet she wasn't anywhere near ready to clock out for the day.

As she had learned when she managed the NSA analysts back in Utah, bad guys didn't keep normal business hours. However, that didn't mean that she had to look haggard after a long day. She had been at work for nearly fifteen hours, yet she still made an effort to appear immaculate. Her hair and makeup were impeccably done, and her dress somehow managed to remain wrinkle-free.

Helen's last task of the day was to attend a special meeting of the National Security Council. Unfortunately, the president and the attorney general had another important engagement, so she had invited only those leaders who oversaw the nation's intelligence agencies to attend. Approaching the conference room, Helen turned the corner and nearly knocked over a sharp-dressed man in a dark suit. He was hastily walking the opposite direction.

"Oh, I'm sorry about that," Tony Criddle said.

"No. It was my fault," Helen replied. "I was rushing off to a meeting."

Tony was a duty officer for the Situation Room. In his late fifties with a bald-shaved head and a grayish-black moustache, he looked like he should have been a drill sergeant in the military. Despite his powerful and intimidating appearance, Tony was very gentle and kind. He was a favorite among the White House staff. He was also a respected duty officer, having faithfully and impartially served three different presidents.

"How are you doing?" Tony asked. Helen appreciated that he knew she was carrying a lot of the burden for overseeing the investigation into the vice president's assassination.

Helen let out a long sigh. "I'm trying to keep afloat, but I definitely feel overwhelmed."

"This reminds me of the days immediately after 9/11," Tony said. He had been on duty the day the planes crashed into the Twin Towers. He had successfully managed the Situation Room during that awful crisis, working almost thirty-four hours straight. "Let me know if there's anything I can do to help you out."

Helen nodded her head in understanding. "Thanks for your support. I appreciate it, Tony."

"You better get in there. They're all waiting for you," he said, pointing his thumb over his shoulder toward the conference room.

"Thanks. I'll talk to you later." Helen walked a few more steps and arrived at her destination. She briefly waved to the uniformed division officer guarding the entrance to the conference room in the West Wing of the White House. She let herself in before he even had the chance to open the door for her.

Several members of the National Security Council were already present, waiting for the meeting to start. Usually the president conducted, but Helen was fully qualified to handle the agenda in his absence. With her trademark grace and confidence, she took her seat at the large oak table.

To her immediate left was Howard Wiseman. Howie, as his close friends called him, was the secretary of defense. He wasn't a military man by trade, even though he did serve four years in the Air Force to earn money for college. He had spent his career in the wireless communications industry where he pioneered a novel way to compress data transmitted over cellular networks. He had also developed several discreet patents used exclusively by the NSA to communicate securely over satellite. A maverick in thought and action, the secretary of defense brought a world-class business mentality to the military. He had cut the defense budget while making the organization run more efficiently.

"Howie, how are you doing?" Helen asked.

"Doing well, considering the events," he replied. At fifty-five, he was relatively young for his position. But his youth was often misleading, and Helen was still surprised by Howie's success. He had sold his communications company for millions of dollars before moving from Austin, Texas, to the nation's capital.

Helen turned her head toward the other side of the table and spoke to the secretary of state. "Thanks for coming, Elizabeth."

"I'm glad to help out in any way that I can," the secretary of state said. Elizabeth Godfrey was a well-respected diplomat. She had many friends "Inside the Beltway"—an idiom used to describe government officials who worked inside the loop formed by Interstate-495. Elizabeth's demeanor was calm and poised, but she wasn't afraid to dish out a verbal tongue-lashing if needed. As the only two females on the National Security Council, Helen and Elizabeth naturally formed a close connection with each other.

But Helen wasn't necessarily friends with all the members of the Council. She flat out despised Rodney Groth, the attorney general. Fortunately, the pompous head of the Department of Justice wasn't at the meeting tonight. Helen breathed a sigh of relief that she would avoid the man who had made a name for himself as a flamboyant trial lawyer. In his place, the attorney general had asked the director of the FBI to attend, someone whom Helen found both more reasonable and more agreeable.

The remaining leaders seated around the table included the secretary of Homeland Security, the director of the CIA, and the director of National Intelligence. As the leader of the "Sweet Sixteen," or the sixteen separate agencies that formed the US intelligence community, the director of National Intelligence was the nation's head spy as mandated by law. To some, the director of National Intelligence would have been a natural choice to lead the Security Council in the president's absence. But the director of National Intelligence post was created after the attacks of September 11, 2001, and the role was considered a new position compared to the National Security advisor, who had first served during the Eisenhower Administration.

Every president used his National Security advisor differently, but there was a specific reason why the current president put his full trust in Helen. The National Security advisor was appointed by the president without confirmation by the Senate. As a result, Helen answered to the president, not Congress. Authorizing Helen to act in his behalf gave the president powerful control over the nation's security agenda in a world of constant congressional bickering.

"Thank you for coming," Helen began in general. "I'm sorry about the late meeting, but I hope to keep it brief." The others in the room slowly nodded their heads in understanding. The chair normally occupied by the vice president was clearly vacant. "After we met together last time, I took the liberty of sending off the message we found on the dead terrorist to my former team at the NSA. They have been looking at it for almost two days now, and they've come to the conclusion that the message is probably not encrypted at all."

"What?" the head of the CIA interrupted. "If it's not encrypted, what is it?"

"They think it's a dialect used by native Guatemalans," Helen said. The unexpected announcement caught most of the council off guard.

After a brief pause, the director of National Intelligence spoke. He was the most logical and pensive member of the group. "Well, that would make sense." As the head of the entire intelligence community, the director of National Intelligence had tasked people from the DIA, NRO, FTI, INR, and a half dozen other three-letter-acronym government agencies to analyze the strange note. Apparently none of them had made any progress in deciphering the memo's contents.

"Doesn't the CIA have someone who would have recognized that it was a native dialect?" Elizabeth Godfrey asked. Her question immediately put the director of the CIA in the hot seat. The fact that the secretary of state and the head of the CIA didn't care for each other was widely known inside the White House.

"We have some of the best linguists in the government," the CIA boss said, defending his organization. "But there are strange languages spoken all around the world. Unfortunately, we don't have the resources to be experts in all of them."

Helen recognized the classic political countermove used by the CIA boss—always equate failure to a lack of funding. She spoke up, steering the conversation away from an impending argument. "The native dialect is just a theory. Nevertheless, we need someone to track it down, and I know who can do just that." She spent the next ten minutes outlining Tanner's proposal to go to Guatemala to find the mysterious Miguel. She told the group about Tanner's father-in-law, and his unique experience while living in Guatemala.

Helen finished by illustrating how Tanner, traveling as a tourist with his family, would make a good cover without creating any suspicion. She had barely completed her proposal when the director of the CIA injected vehemently.

"That's insane. This Tanner guy isn't a trained spy. He's a computer nerd. Let me have one of my men down there find Miguel. We'll get the answers," he said overconfidently.

Helen was about to reply when the head of the FBI spoke. Up until this point, he had remained quiet. "I agree with Helen. Tanner Stone is more than just a computer analyst. If this Miguel guy does exist, I think that Tanner could track him down."

"You act like Tanner is a modern-day James Bond," the CIA chief retorted.

"That's kind of what I thought after reading his bio," the director of the FBI said. "Obviously, he's not a shoot'em-up spy. That's not his style. Tanner is more analytical. He's loaded with street smarts."

"Is this the same guy that stopped the Chinese virus a couple of years ago?" asked the secretary of Homeland Security.

Although the members of the National Security Council were never fully briefed on Tanner's heroics dealing with the Chinese cyberattack, they knew the political firestorm created by the event. The US government now mandated that all computer equipment made in China had to undergo rigorous testing for hidden malware before being sold in the United States.

Helen answered the question posed by the secretary of Homeland Security. "Yes, and Tanner's found a way to meld facts out of nothing on more than one occasion."

"I don't like it. Let the professionals handle it," the CIA director said.

Howie entered the rapidly changing conversation. "Let's have Tanner meet up with someone from the CIA in Guatemala," he said. "Working together, they'll have a better chance of success."

The simplest plans were often the best, and the proposal from the secretary of defense was right on the mark. Silence fell around the table as everyone considered the proposal. It seemed to satisfy all parties.

"I guess that's okay," the CIA chief said. "As long as Tanner follows my guy's lead and doesn't get in trouble."

"That won't be a problem. Tanner isn't interested in being a hero. He just wants to figure out what the secret message means," Helen said. Her resolute voice reassured the leaders seated around the table that sending Tanner to Guatemala was the right decision.

ALBUQUERQUE, NEW MEXICO

A secure speakerphone at the FBI field office in Albuquerque rang out, interrupting a conversation between Agent Green and Tanner.

"This is Nicole," answered the Special Agent in Charge.

"This is Helen. Is Tanner with you?"

"Yes, we've been talking about this trip to Guatemala," Nicole said.

"Good, because we need to get Tanner and his family down there as soon as possible," Helen said. "His trip has been approved."

Tanner felt his smile break across his face as he heard the announcement. "That's it? I thought the decision would take longer," he said into the speakerphone.

"The president gives me a lot of discretion," Helen said, but she continued with a word of warning, "Remember, this isn't an official trip endorsed by the US government. You're going down as a tourist, and you'll be meeting up with someone from the CIA once you get down there."

"Okay, who's paying for it?" Tanner asked.

"We've got people who handle those arrangements," Helen said. "When can you leave?"

Nicole spoke up. "We've been talking about that. If we can somehow get Tanner and his family to Las Vegas, his parents can come down from St. George, Utah, and pick up his kids."

"That's a great idea. I'll have my people work on it. Let's plan on Tanner and his family leaving for Vegas first thing tomorrow. His parents will pick up the kids there, and then everyone else will head out to Guatemala," Helen said authoritatively.

Tanner was thrilled about the spontaneous trip. Before he left, however, Tanner had a couple of items to clear up. "Uh, I don't have a passport," he said sheepishly.

Helen laughed in response to her former employee's statement. "We already know that. Someone is fast-tracking your passport as we speak. We're also making a new one for your wife since hers expired two years ago," she said. "But your in-laws' passports are still valid, right?"

"I'm sure they are, but their passports are at their house. We'll have to pick them up when we go there tonight," Tanner said.

"I'm not sure if that's such a good idea," Nicole countered. "The last time you were in Albuquerque, things got a little messy. I think it would be best if we kept you and your family out of sight. We'll put you up in a hotel somewhere."

It seemed like the plan was coming together, yet Tanner still had one issue that needed to be resolved. "What about our car back at Mesa Verde?"

"I'll let the FBI handle that," Helen said.

Nicole looked at Tanner. "We'll see what we can do," she said. "Maybe we'll have someone pick it up and drive it back to Utah for you."

Before ending the conversation, Helen added a couple of words of caution. "Enjoy your trip, Tanner, but make sure to find Miguel. That's what this is all about."

"I will," Tanner said.

"Follow your instincts. I trust you," Helen added. She had said the same thing just before Tanner discovered the pending cyberattack two years ago. That didn't bode well with Tanner, but it was time to go.

OCTOBER 24
LAS VEGAS, NEVADA

A WOMAN'S VOICE CALLED out over the public speaker system. "Ladies and gentlemen, we've started our descent into the Las Vegas area. Please make sure your seat backs and tray tables are in their full upright position. Make sure your seat belt is securely fastened and that all carry-on items are stowed underneath the seat in front of you or in the overhead bins."

Tanner felt someone nudging him, waking him out of a quiet sleep. "We're getting ready to land," Megan said. Tanner opened his eyes and saw his wife carefully shift in her seat, making sure not to wake their six-month-old baby, who was still asleep in her arms.

In the next seat to Tanner, little Sara Nicole was also asleep. It was Sara's first time on a plane, and Tanner had thought that his two-year-old would be too thrilled to sleep. But after being up most of the night from the excitement of the previous day, Sara had passed out just after the early morning flight left Albuquerque.

Tanner had actually woken up a few minutes before his wife prodded him, but he kept his eyes closed as he replayed the crazy events of the past twelve hours in his mind. After getting off the phone with Helen, the FBI took Tanner and his family to a hotel near the Albuquerque airport. The two-bedroom suite had a full kitchen and provided ample space for everyone. Nicole then ordered room service for the family and joined them for dinner while another set of FBI agents went to retrieve Glen and Julie's passports and extra clothes from their home.

After dinner last night, Tanner called his parents in Utah and gave them a non-classified explanation about what was happening. His parents readily agreed to drive down to Las Vegas to pick up their grandkids, excited to spend some extra time with them. Overall, the entire evening seemed to flow well, but it was well past midnight when everyone finally went to bed. Five hours later, they woke up to catch the 7:00 a.m. flight to Las Vegas.

Tanner put his seat back in the upright position and glanced across the aisle at his in-laws. Glen gave his son-in-law a "thumbs-up" sign, reinforcing his excitement in their upcoming adventure. Although Glen and Julie didn't know all the reasons for the trip, they had seen a snippet of the encoded message. They knew that Miguel was probably the best person to decipher the secret letter and that Tanner needed their help in tracking him down. Beyond those few facts, Glen and Julie were left to their imaginations for the time being to determine any deeper motives for their unantici-pated journey.

Tanner's thoughts came back to the moment as the plane taxied along the runway. His kids were still sleeping, completely oblivious to their surroundings. Tanner looked at his wife and noticed concern in her eyes.

"Are you going to be okay?" he asked. He knew Megan was worried about leaving the kids for a week, but she was most anxious about her six-month-old infant.

"She's so little," Megan said, stroking her sleeping daughter's hair.

"You could stay with my parents," Tanner offered.

"And miss a trip to Guatemala?" Megan asked rhetorically. "No way. This is the chance of a lifetime."

Tanner took his wife's hand. "The kids will be okay. Amber does well with a bottle, and she's already eating cereal."

"It's never easy, Sweetie," Julie said from the seat across the aisle. "I had a hard time letting you go when you moved to Utah, and you were almost thirty years old."

Tanner saw his wife's eyes moisten up. He leaned over and gave her a delicate kiss on the cheek. "It will be okay. I promise," he said.

The plane soon arrived at the gate, and everyone prepared to leave. Tanner and his family waited to be the last passengers off, just as they had been instructed by Nicole before leaving Albuquerque. She said the FBI would have someone waiting at the gate to meet the family in Las Vegas.

Tanner woke up his daughter and helped her walk up the aisle of the empty aircraft. "Where are we, Daddy?" Sara asked, holding her pink teddy bear.

"Grandma Carla and Grandpa Gordon are going to take care of you for a little bit, remember?" Tanner said.

"Do I get to take Pink Bear?" Sara asked. It was her stuffed animal's basic, yet sensible name.

"Of course, and Grandma and Grandpa will take you swimming in their pool," Tanner said. He hoped to distract his daughter's uneasiness of being alone with the idea of going swimming. He held Sara's hand as they walked up the last part of the ramp. Stepping out into the concourse, he was surprised to see his parents.

"Grandma!" Sara shouted. She dropped Tanner's hand and ran to hug her other grandmother. Standing next to Tanner's mom was his father and another man dressed in business casual clothes. Tanner quickly assumed the other person was the escort from the FBI, who had gotten his parents through the security checkpoint and to the gate.

Tanner gave his dad a hug. "It's good to see you again, Dad," he said.

"I tried asking this fellow what this was all about, but he said that we knew more about it than he did," Gordon said, pointing to the FBI agent.

Unlike his in-laws, Tanner's own parents knew that their son did covert work for the government. Gordon and Carla had been directly involved in Tanner's kidnapping five years ago, and they understood everything that happened back then. They even knew that he was given a job at the NSA and relocated to Utah. Shortly after their son's move, Gordon and Carla relocated from Arizona to the desert community of St. George. They had wanted to be closer to their only child.

Tanner turned from his dad and gave his mother a solid hug. Just then, the rest of the family came out the door to the ramp, and everyone quickly greeted each other in a friendly manner. Among the commotion, Tanner took the opportunity to have a side conversation with the FBI agent.

"It's nice to meet you. I'm Agent Ron Yarbrough," the man in his mid-fifties said. He extended his arm and shook Tanner's hand. "Your flight leaves in an hour. We have you going through Houston, then down to Guatemala City," he said. He handed Tanner the newly made passports for him and his wife.

Tanner took the blue booklets. "Thanks."

The FBI agent then handed Tanner a cell phone. "You're supposed to have this with you at all times. It's programmed for international calling, but it auto-switches to a satellite if there aren't any cell towers around."

Tanner took the device. It was bulkier and heavier than a normal cell phone, but it still had all the similar features of calling and texting.

"You know, I've worked for the FBI for twenty years now, and I've never seen something this unusual. But then I looked up your name in the government's classified employee database and saw who you worked for," Agent Yarbrough said.

"Don't tell anybody," Tanner said with a smile.

The FBI agent gave Tanner the six-digit PIN number to the phone. Tanner unlocked the device and saw that he already had a text message.

"That's from us," the FBI agent said, seeing the confused look on Tanner's face. He opened the message and saw a picture of a man. "That's your contact when you get to Guatemala. He'll meet you at the airport. His name is Robert Garcia, and he's part of the CIA team stationed down there."

"I hope he knows where to find us," Tanner said, studying the photo.

"I'll walk you guys over to the gate, and then I'll make sure your parents and kids get out of here okay."

"I appreciate that," Tanner said. He put the phone in his carry-on backpack, next to a printout of the encoded message.

The FBI agent slowly and nonchalantly directed the group down the concourse to another part of the airport. Ten minutes later, they arrived at Gate D59. Tanner knew the good-byes were going to be hard, and he prepared himself for his daughter's outburst of sadness. Fortunately, Tanner's dad unexpectedly saved the day as he reached into his pocket and pulled out a charm bracelet at the right moment.

"You see this?" he said as he took his granddaughter's little wrist. "It's a magic bracelet, and it will help you not be scared when your parents are gone." He gently put the silver chain on Sara's wrist.

"Mommy, Mommy, look what Grandpa gave me!" she shouted. She held up her wrist for everyone to see. "He said I don't need to be scared!"

With tears in her eyes, Megan bent down and gave her precious daughter a long hug. "I'm going to miss you so much."

"Maybe Grandpa can get you a bracelet too," Sara said.

"That's a great idea," Gordon said. "You can help me make one for your mommy and daddy while they're gone."

The group took their time saying good-bye. Megan gave her mother-in-law a sheet of paper, detailing the children's exact schedule. She then spent several minutes explaining how and when to feed the baby. Carla smiled at the exceedingly detailed memo, silently communicating that she perfectly understood her daughter-in-law's anxiety. Watching his wife and mother talk, Tanner acknowledged the influential society of motherhood. It didn't matter how old a woman was or where she came from, mothers all over the world shared a common bond.

The time eventually came to board the plane. Waving and blowing kisses at their daughters, Tanner and Megan walked down the ramp toward the aircraft, followed by Glen and Julie. They soon found their seats.

"Are you okay?" Tanner asked his wife.

Megan dried her tears with her hand. "I'll be all right." She looked out the window at the airport terminal and stared a moment, as if she was telepathically saying good-bye to her small children.

"They'll be okay," Tanner said.

"I know they will," Megan said. She dried her eyes once more and turned toward her husband. A small smile formed across her face. "This trip is like a second honeymoon."

"Or a five-year anniversary celebration," Tanner said. He gave his wife a quick kiss on the lips. Megan held the kiss a littler longer than he had expected. When she ended the intimate embrace, she whispered in her husband's ear.

"It's an anniversary with an element of danger," she said.

Tanner drew back his head and laughed. "Does that mean you're my femme fatale?"

Megan flirtingly batted her eyes at Tanner. The couple laughed out loud and then sat back in their seats. Their adventure together had begun.

DALLAS, TEXAS

"What does it do?" asked El Flaco. In his hand he held a small laptop loaded with Kali Linux, a custom operating system used by hackers and network penetration testers all over the world.

"It will cause an overdose of insulin, killing him in a way that can't be traced back to you," Travis said.

The meeting between the former Army acquaintances was

straightforward. In a steak house on the edge of Dallas, they anonymously discussed their plans among the ruckus of the lunch crowd. The restaurant was packed with guests, causing a commotion that obscured the treasonous conversation on how to kill the speaker of the House of Representatives.

"How do I know it will work?" El Flaco asked.

"Trust me, it will work," Travis assured his contact.

The speaker of the House had been all over the press during this midterm election season. Recently diagnosed with diabetes, he placed a strong emphasis on diabetes research. In fact, health care was a major tenant of his reelection campaign. The politician had appeared on all the major news channels, showing off his state-of-the-art insulin pump. He had even posted a picture of it on his Facebook account—with the model number completely legible.

"I contacted one of my Anonymous buddies with ties in the medical device community. He told me that that specific insulin pump has a built-in wireless component that allows the user to wirelessly monitor his blood sugar on a cell phone app. Few people know, however, that the Wi-Fi also has an unknown security flaw that allows unauthorized access to the chip controlling the insulin settings.

"Why would anyone use an insulin pump if it could be hacked?" El Flaco asked his lunch companion. The mercenary was captivated by the ability to kill someone without pulling a trigger.

"I call it the Bacon Principle," Travis said, taking a bite of his rib-eye steak.

"What?" the skinny man asked.

"The Bacon Principle—everything is cooler with bacon," Travis repeated. He pointed to the steak in front of him that came garnished with bits of bacon. "And everything is cooler with Wi-Fi access. The web is everywhere now. We're creating a massive Internet of things, but most of these things have no reason to be on the web. I read the other day that someone actually created a Wi-Fi enabled toilet. Can you believe that? Why in the world would anyone trust a plumber to connect a toilet to their home wireless network?" Travis shook his head in disbelief. "Manufacturers are adding the web to everything because it makes it cool and trendy, but nobody is securing this stuff. A lot of the Wi-Fi that's imbedded in medical devices uses weak encryption. It only took me a couple of weeks to figure out how to bypass the security controls of the insulin pump. Just get that laptop within three hundred feet of the speaker of the House, and it will automatically upload a program that will give him a fatal dose of insulin."

"Unbelievable," El Flaco said. He started up the laptop, but it asked for a password.

"You'll get the password once I get the rest of my money," Travis stated matter-of-factly. He patted a red backpack on the bench next him. It contained the fifty-thousand-dollar down payment that El Flaco had brought to the meeting.

"Welcome to the future of warfare," Travis said. He cut off a piece of his steak and shoved it in his mouth. "People will attack from thousands of miles away, using computers instead of guns. And that's not just the military. Technology will become terrorists' favorite tool," he said, stepping up onto his virtual Anonymous soapbox. "People are so stupid. The more technology they use, the more vulnerable they become. Everyone just assumes that all these things on the Internet are secure, but a lot of them still have default passwords or weak encryption. Technology is advancing so fast that nobody can keep pace on the security side." He paused for effect and to take another bite of his steak. "I'm not talking about trivial stuff like stealing credit card numbers. Serious hackers don't care about that anymore. Home automation systems are especially vulnerable. Hackers can remotely open the front door and then steal whatever they want." Travis took a quick sip of his drink, clearing his throat. "Modern cars aren't any better. All the hi-tech gadgets and GPS navigation systems give hackers the ability to take control away from the driver. And don't even get me started on the power grid. That sucker is a complete mess. You'll see a cyberattack on the power grid soon. I guarantee it," Travis said. He pointed his fork at El Flaco for emphasis.

The lieutenant in the Chiapas cartel listened to Travis as he continued his hacktivist monologue. El Flaco had considered eliminating Travis to protect his identity, but now he realized that would be a colossal mistake. The disenfranchised computer hacker was extremely valuable.

"I might have some more work if you're interested," El Flaco said.

"Why not?" Travis asked. He again patted the backpack full of money. "I've even got a few friends who might want to get in on the action."

Travis continued his monologue, describing some of the unique computer hacks his associates in Anonymous had recently accomplished. El Flaco listened intently, realizing that Travis was absolutely right about technology.

It was the new weapon of terror.

OCTOBER 24
GUATEMALA CITY, GUATEMALA

IT WAS AROUND dinnertime when the plane arrived in Guatemala City. Tanner watched out the window during the entire approach, fascinated with the landscape surrounding the capital. His father-in-law pointed out four distinct volcanoes that circled the city of nearly three million people.

"Are they active?" Tanner asked with concern.

"Just two of them, Pacaya and Fuego," Glen said. He sat in the row directly behind his son-in-law. "If you look closely, you can see smoke coming out of Fuego."

Straining to see out the window, Tanner noticed faint wisps of smoke rising out of a mountain that ascended into a sharp point. "Aren't they worried the volcano will erupt?"

"Ironically, it's not the volcanoes that they worry about. It's the earthquakes," Glen said. His statement caused some trepidation for Tanner.

"This sounds like a dangerous place to live," Tanner said.

Glen let out a chuckle. "Yeah, but you can't beat the climate. The temperature averages seventy-five degrees year-round. That's why they call it the Land of the Eternal Spring."

51

"I like the sound of that," Megan said, entering the conversation.

Tanner noticed a dozen skyscrapers on the horizon. For some reason, he had imagined Guatemala City to be more underdeveloped. "It seems modern for a third world country," he said.

"The capital is very modern," Glen replied. "You can get anything here that you can get in the United States. But if you travel to the outskirts of town or to the smaller villages in the mountains, that's where you'll see a lot of poverty."

The plane landed and rolled to a stop at the gate. Tanner and his family remained in their seats while the other passengers slowly got off the plane. Then, grabbing their carry-on items, the small group of four travelers stood up and disembarked.

"What now?" Glen asked as they stepped out into the concourse.

"We're supposed to get our luggage first and then go through customs. We'll meet a guy from the embassy just after we clear customs," Tanner said. He omitted the fact that the man rendezvousing with them was a CIA employee.

"How will we recognize him?" Julie asked.

"I've got a picture of him on my phone. His name is Robert Garcia."

The group of Americans slowly made their way toward the baggage claim area. After getting their luggage, they went through customs where they had their passports stamped with a tourist visa. They had barely cleared customs when a middle-aged gentleman appeared out of nowhere. Dressed in jeans and a button-up shirt, the man had dark hair and brown skin. He blended in perfectly with the other native Guatemalans.

"Helen said you'd be coming." The mysterious man spoke in perfect English. His impromptu greeting startled the Americans.

Tanner glanced at the stranger. He recognized the man's clean-shaven face from the photo, but he wasn't sure how to introduce himself. "Hi," Tanner simply said.

The shorter man reached out his hand in a friendly manner. "I'm Robert Garcia. Welcome to Guatemala."

Tanner shook the extended hand. "It's nice to meet you. I'm

Tanner," he said before introducing the other members of his family.

"Looks like I get to be your tour guide for the next couple of days," Robert said to the group. He had a warm and easygoing smile. "But I understand that two of you have already spent quite a bit of time in Guatemala." He gestured to Glen and Julie Holland.

"Yes, we lived here for almost two years as missionaries for our church," Julie said.

"Mormons, right?" Robert asked in a sociable tone.

Julie was surprised. "How did you know that?" she asked.

"You just look like Mormons," Robert said. His comment wasn't unfriendly. It was just a statement of observation. "Well, that and the fact that some folks back in the US gave me an update on who was coming down."

"Are you from here?" Megan asked.

"Nope. I'm from LA, but I've been stationed here at the embassy for almost four years now," Robert said. "Let's grab your stuff and get something to eat. I've got a great place in mind."

Tanner immediately liked Robert. He seemed down-to-earth and comfortable in any situation. He had a confident swagger, but it didn't come across as boastful. It was more of an outward expression that he knew exactly what he was doing. Robert helped the women with their luggage, and then he led everyone out the airport exit toward a Chevy Tahoe.

On the opposite side of the customs area, an airport janitor noticed the group of American tourists as they left the airport. He usually wouldn't have paid any attention to the travelers dressed in jeans and casual shirts. After all, tourism was one of Guatemala's biggest industries. However, the manner in which the Americans were instantly approached by a strange man seemed too obvious. Something wasn't right, and since the janitor was paid to be on the lookout for suspicious Americans coming into the country, he decided that he should notify his contact in the Chiapas drug cartel.

The restaurant was unlike anything that Tanner had imagined he would find in Guatemala—it was clean and fancy. The tiled floor and white-plastered walls provided a warm and friendly ambiance. Colorful murals covered various sections of the interior, while tropical plants accented the open spaces of the dining room. Again, Tanner recognized that his preconceived notions of Guatemala were wrong.

Megan sat next to Tanner. On the other side of the table, Glen and Julie scoured over their menus. At the head of the table, Robert was speaking to their waiter.

"What should I get?" Tanner asked. The menu was entirely in Spanish, and he quickly realized that his few years of high school Spanish were woefully inadequate.

"Go with the *plato típico*," Glen said from over the top of his menu. "You can't beat that."

"What?" Tanner asked.

Megan pointed out the entry on the menu for her husband. "It's right here. It's the traditional meal of Guatemala," she said as she translated the menu. "It's a steak with rice and black beans."

"Don't forget the fried bananas. Those are the best part," Julie said.

Tanner looked up at his in-laws. They were so excited to be back in Guatemala that even a belt sander wouldn't have removed their enormous smiles.

"Let's go ahead and order," Robert said to the group.

Megan and her parents each ordered their meals in Spanish. When the waiter came around to ask Tanner what he wanted, he felt pressured to do the same. "*Playa tipo*," he said. The others at the table chuckled at his innocent mistake.

"I think you just ordered something from the beach," Megan laughed. She leaned over and gave her husband a loving hug.

Tanner was embarrassed at his gaffe, but his father-in-law quickly corrected the mistake for the confused waiter.

"Now don't go off and try saying that you're embarrassed in Spanish," Glen said after the waiter disappeared. "If you say *embarazada*, you'll be telling the waiter that you're pregnant."

The group at the table erupted in laughter. The other patrons in the restaurant looked at the *Norteamericanos* and wondered what was so funny. After a few moments, Tanner and the others regained their composure.

"It will take a while to get our food, so let's talk about how this is going to happen," Robert said. He lowered his voice to be audible only to the people at his table. "I'll be with you the entire time," he said. "We'll tell everyone that I'm your private tour guide, and that I'm taking you around to see the sites." Tanner and his family nodded their heads. Robert's idea was both obvious and practical. "We'll start our search for Miguel in Antigua since that's the last place you said you saw him."

"What's Antigua?" Tanner asked.

"It's the old capital from the colonial times," Julie replied. "It's beautiful. You'll feel like you've walked back into eighteenth-century Spain."

"It's the main tourist attraction in Guatemala," Glen added, before turning his attention back to Robert. "How long will we be in Antigua?"

"That depends on you. We're clueless about Miguel at the embassy. We're hoping that you can track him down."

"We saw him in Antigua back in May, so hopefully he'll still be there," Glen said.

"Tell me more about this guy," Robert probed.

"We met him six months ago and taught him about our church. He wasn't interested in religion, but he really knew his history of Guatemala. He's literally a hundred years old and very frail. He hitchhikes around to different areas, taking odd jobs or begging for money," Glen said.

"Nobody has a picture of Miguel?" Robert asked.

Glen shook his head. "Not that I know of."

Robert leaned back and folded his arms. "Well, Guatemala is a diverse place. I'm not sure we can find this guy."

"We know that he tends to stick to places filled with tourists," Julie said. "He likes to ask foreigners for money."

The waiter and another server approached the table with trays of food. The conversation paused as the meals were set in front of the guests. After the servers left, Robert resumed the private conversation. "Even if we find this guy, I doubt he can translate that note. The folks at the embassy say its gibberish. We haven't seen anything like it down here."

"I'm not so sure about that," Glen countered in a friendly tone. "Miguel knew a dozen dialects that I had never heard of."

Robert took a bite of food before responding. "I hope you're right. I was one of the few people at the embassy who didn't think this was a complete waste of time. I guess that's why I was assigned to work with you." He chuckled softly before taking another bite of his dinner.

"What do you do at the embassy?" Megan asked.

Tanner noticed that Robert didn't flinch or hesitate at the question. He just went right into the speech he had likely memorized long ago. "I do analysis of news events and information coming out of Guatemala. I organize everything into a daily report that goes back to the folks at the State Department. It's mostly a desk job, so it will be nice to get out of the office for a week."

Tanner knew that Robert wasn't lying about his job. It probably did involve a lot of data collection and analysis, but Robert had intentionally left out the fact that he was a full-fledged CIA spy. Over the years, Tanner had rubbed shoulders with several CIA folks like Robert. Most of them had been trained at "The Farm" near Williamsburg, Virginia. Even though Robert mostly had a desk job now, Tanner had no doubt that the CIA agent kept his skills sharp. When they sat down to dinner, Tanner even thought he saw the outline of a gun tucked under Robert's shirt.

"When we finish dinner, we'll head straight to Antigua," Robert said.

"How long will it take to get there?" Megan asked.

Robert looked at his wristwatch. "Just over an hour. I've already got reservations at a hotel. You're going to love staying there."

Dinner soon ended and the waiter brought the check. Robert paid for the meal with a common credit card. Before the waiter took the payment to run through the register, Tanner casually glanced at the name on the card. It was Pedro Morales. Tanner figured the CIA folks had all sorts of different aliases, but it did make him wonder what Robert's real name was.

Thirty minutes later, the group was traveling on Highway CA-1 to Antigua. Riding in the passenger seat of the tan Chevy Tahoe, Tanner marveled at the modern road that cut through the lush green hills. If he hadn't taken the time to consciously think about his surroundings, he would have thought he was somewhere in Northern California.

Megan and her parents sat in the rear seat of the SUV and chatted about the children back in Utah. Tanner took the opportunity to strike up a different conversation with their driver. "You mentioned that you spoke to Helen. What did she say?"

Robert smiled as he carefully chose his words. "She said that you're sharp, and that you've gotten yourself out of a mess more than once." Tanner didn't ask Robert to elaborate. He could tell that the CIA agent knew more about Tanner's clandestine background. "She also said that you came up with the idea about this message being a Guatemalan dialect. She was impressed."

"What do you think?" Tanner asked.

Robert shrugged his shoulders. "I'm still up in the air on that. It sounds reasonable because there are more native dialects down here than wannabe movie stars back in LA. But the real problem will be finding Miguel in the first place."

"Yeah. He's definitely a cipher, with a capital 'C,'" Tanner said.

"What?"

"It's a play on words," Tanner said. "He's a cipher, meaning that he can crack the code, but cipher also means someone who is poor or unwanted."

The definition seemed to fit Miguel well. "I like it," Robert said with a smile. "We'll call him the Cipher from now on."

Driving the Chevy Tahoe over the top of a gentle hill, Robert announced that they had arrived at their destination. Looking out the front windshield, Tanner saw a small town nestled in the Panchoy Valley. The fading sunlight illuminated the colonial city in various shades of yellow and orange, yet it still provided enough light for Tanner to recognize the red tile roofs that covered the landscape.

"Wow," Megan said from the backseat. "Even from this distance, I can see some of the features of the colonial Spanish architecture."

"What mountain is that?" Tanner asked. He pointed to a classic-shaped volcano on the other side of the city. The lone mountain dominated the landscape.

"That is Agua," Robert said. "It's the most famous volcano around."

"I can see why," Megan said. "It looks like a picture out of a textbook."

"Is it active?" Tanner asked. He had never lived anywhere near volcanoes, and while he wouldn't admit it, being so close to one made him nervous.

"Nah," Robert said. "It just sits there and provides a spectacular backdrop for pictures from the city."

The Chevy Tahoe slowed down as it came off the highway. Robert took a right turn on to a side road, and immediately the SUV started bouncing around.

"Are these cobblestones?" Megan asked.

"Yes. Aren't they wonderful?" Julie said with a nostalgic laugh. "Just like the old parts of Europe."

The SUV took another corner and turned down a small street. The buildings on either side of the cobblestone road were painted in bright colors.

"The roads are super narrow because nobody had cars back then," Glen said, pointing to the tight quarters.

"When was the city built?" Tanner asked.

"Back in the 1500s," Glen said. "A lot of this architecture is from the Baroque period."

Tanner gazed out the window in amazement. They drove past a magnificent cathedral that must have been five hundred years old. The ornately carved pillars on the front of the building were spectacular.

"It's called Antigua because it was the old capital of Guatemala. They moved the capital to its current location after a massive earthquake in 1773," Robert said. As he maneuvered down the road, he pointed to the rubble of an old church. "They intentionally left some of the ruins to show the damage." Tanner nodded in fascination, realizing the history of the event. The earthquake happened three years before the signing of the Declaration of Independence.

Robert drove the SUV around for twenty minutes, pointing out a few of the interesting sites. The group passed by a dozen magnificent cathedrals and several colorful marketplaces. Everywhere they went, tourists covered the narrow cobblestone streets. Tanner wondered if someone was going to get hit, but Robert expertly navigated the tight roads, constantly beeping his horn to warn of the approaching danger.

Eventually, Robert brought the Chevy Tahoe to a stop in front of a white adobe wall. "Welcome to the Casa Santo Domingo," he declared.

From the backseat, Julie clapped her hands with excitement. "I was hoping we'd stay here," she said. "It's one of the most famous hotels in Antigua."

Tanner didn't see anything sensational about their accommodations. He only saw a white stucco wall with a set of large wooden doors.

"Doesn't look like much to me," Megan said.

"Just wait, you'll see," Glen reassured his daughter.

The group got out of the SUV and walked toward the entrance of the hotel. Up close, the large and richly stained doors looked like they had come off an old church. The hotel attendant opened the entrance, and Tanner and his wife stepped into another world.

The plain and unassuming exterior of the hotel completely obscured the breathtaking interior. Tanner and Megan walked to the edge of a meticulously groomed courtyard with lush vegetation and colorful flowers. Decorative stone paths crisscrossed the grassy patio. An ornamental water fountain stood out in the center of the lawn, anchoring the picturesque scene.

"Whoa," Tanner said at the impressive view. The hotel was nothing like he had seen before. The guest rooms weren't bunched together in a single structure, but they were lined up around the perimeter of the complex.

"It's beautiful," Megan said, after a moment of silence.

"It was originally a monastery from the seventeenth century, but it was destroyed in the big earthquake," Julie said.

"Now it's a five-star hotel," Robert said with a smile. He took the group on a quick tour of the hotel grounds.

The sun had mostly set now, and hundreds of candles lit the walkways of the courtyard. Robert led the guests past some of the restored structures. "Most of the woodwork and stone are from the original monastery." He pointed to a magnificent brick arch that was surrounded by dark-brown wood. "They tried to keep the grounds as authentic as possible."

Robert directed the group around another corner and abruptly stopped at a small reflecting pond. Rose petals of different colors floated in the water. Around the edge of the pool, dozens of white candles twinkled in the night.

"How romantic," Megan said. She grabbed her husband's hand and squeezed, but Tanner momentarily ignored his wife's loving gesture. He had shifted his gaze from the sparkling water to something on a ledge overlooking the pool.

"Is that real?" he asked, pointing at a red bird with colorful wings.

"Certainly," Robert said. "It's a macaw."

"Look, there's another one," Megan said. She gestured to a yellow-and-blue bird on a different ledge.

Tanner had always envisioned paradise as a small island somewhere in the Pacific, but he concluded that he was wrong. He had found paradise in the central highlands of Guatemala. The hotel was absolutely amazing. With thousands of candles accenting the unique architecture of the restored monastery, he conceded it was indeed romantic.

"Do we get to stay here long?" Megan asked.

Robert laughed at Megan's question "It all depends on how long it takes to find the Cipher," he said.

"Who?" Julie asked.

"It's our code name for Miguel," he said, pointing toward Tanner.

"When do we start?" Glen asked.

Robert looked at his watch. "Let's call it a day," he said. "You've been traveling since 6:00 a.m., and I'm sure you're tired. Enjoy the night here at the hotel, and we'll meet for breakfast at 7:00 a.m. sharp." He reached into his pocket and took out a room key for each couple. "I'll show you to your rooms."

"You don't need to do that," Tanner said. "We can get our stuff."

"Don't worry about it. It's no problem," Robert countered. He led the group toward the first hotel room.

A few moments later, Robert unlocked the door to Tanner and Megan's room. "Here you go," he said. He held the door open for the couple.

The hotel room was clean and modern, but Tanner was a little disappointed. He had hoped the room would be more authentic, matching the restored features of the magnificent courtyard. A king bed and TV occupied the center of the area, and a fireplace was tucked into the corner. Off to the side, a door opened into a comfortable bathroom.

"I love it," Megan said. A knock on the open door startled the group. They turned in time to see a hotel valet bringing the couple's belongings.

"Your parents are staying next door, and I'll be in a room across the hall," Robert said. "If you need anything, call me on your cell phone. I'm speed dial number one."

"What are you going to do the rest of the night?" Megan asked.

"Don't worry about me. I've got a bunch of busy work to take care of," Robert said. "Enjoy the hotel. They have a fabulous pool, so you might want to check it out. But stay on site and don't wander off. We don't want you to get lost."

Tanner watched as Megan waved good-bye to her parents. Then she quickly closed and locked the door. With a flirtatious smile, she turned around and moved toward him. Tanner recognized that look, knowing that his wife had no intention of leaving the room for the night.

OCTOBER 24
NSA DATA CENTER, UTAH

AT 10:00 P.M. back in Utah, two members of the QC team were busy working at the Bumblehive. After years on the job with the NSA, the analysts had learned that an eight-to-five shift wasn't part of their world. In fact, they had become so used to working off-hours that they had perfected a rotating schedule. Right now, Sydney Littlefield and Rachel York were on duty. At some point in the early morning hours, Mel Otterson and Kevin Granger would come back to work to relieve their peers. Although the hours were long, the rotating shift allowed the NSA analysts to monitor the quantum computer continuously for an extended period of time.

Gazing at the computer monitor, Sydney and Rachel weren't happy with the results. Their program had been running all day on QC with no output.

"There's nothing out there," Rachel said. Their script had been searching the Internet for any emails, chats, or websites that used the same special characters found on the encrypted note.

"You're right," Sydney said. "If there was something, we would have found it by now."

"I guess we could keep the job running all night and see if we have any results tomorrow," Rachel said. She stood up and stretched, running her hand through her disheveled black hair.

"Maybe we should kick off an archive search. It might be worth a try," Sydney said.

Their current program routine only looked for similar strings of encrypted text in active emails or chats flowing across the Internet. To search messages that had been sent in the past, they had to scour zettabytes of data stored at the top-secret data center. The NSA had a record of practically everything sent across the Internet over the past three years, but the archived data was compressed to conserve space. Searching through that information would be extremely time-consuming.

"Yeah, we could do that," Rachel said passively. "It would take a lot of horsepower. I'm not sure if QC has enough bandwidth to keep the active search going while looking though the archives." Even though the quantum computer was exceptionally fast, it was optimized for code breaking, not necessarily mining through random amounts of stored data.

"I think we should do it anyway," Sydney said. "It's not like we're finding anything useful on the Internet right now."

Rachel let out a big sigh. She knew her teammate was correct. They might have better luck finding the strings of encrypted text in the archives, but it was going to be a long night.

DALLAS, TEXAS

El Flaco had hardly slept the past week. He was exhausted, but he reminded himself that he could sleep once the Chiapas cartel became the major supplier of illegal drugs into the United States. The cartel's grand plan, the accumulation of two years of work, was on the cusp of realization. But El Flaco still had some last minute business to take care of, and he wished that he had more time to prepare for the final arrangements.

The meeting with the computer hacker had gone exceptionally well. So well, in fact, that El Flaco had told Travis Boston to reach out and enlist some members of Anonymous to research a few more hacking jobs. El Flaco was flabbergasted by what he had learned. Apparently, Anonymous already had access into many of the computer systems that controlled the critical infrastructure of the United States. He wondered why the hackers hadn't already launched a cyberattack against the power grid or the air traffic control system. In the end, he decided that Anonymous was probably waiting for a more appropriate time to attack. Timing was everything, and nobody understood that better than the skinny mercenary.

El Flaco got back to work. He was sitting at a desk in his hotel room on the outskirts of Dallas. He had just reviewed the phone call from his informant at the Guatemala airport. The janitor had been on the cartel's payroll for years, and his access to the restricted areas of the airport had proven instrumental to the drug cartel's success.

Guatemala was a key country in the cartel's overall drug operation. Strategically located next to Mexico, Guatemala was the staging area for illegal drugs as they made their final journey into the United States. Drug producers throughout South America flew their shipments to Guatemala in small aircraft. Landing on makeshift runways cut out of the vast jungle, the planes delivered contraband that was unloaded and put onto trucks. The drugs were then driven through Mexico to the United States. All the Mexican drug cartels used Guatemala as a preparation area, and it was estimated that 70 percent of the illegal narcotics that entered the United States came through the Petén region of Guatemala.

When the janitor called El Flaco to say a group of strange Americans had arrived at the airport, the lieutenant took the information seriously. But it wasn't because the two men and two women appeared to be DEA agents. On the contrary, they seemed to be tourists in every sense of the word. Nevertheless, a man the cartel believed to be a CIA agent had greeted the Americans at the airport, and that raised all sorts of concerns. El Flaco wasn't sure what to make of the meeting between the tourists and the suspected CIA spy, so he decided to email his source inside of the United States government for help.

Double-checking his electronic message, El Flaco saved it as a draft before exiting the shared email account. Tomorrow morning, his contact inside the government would log into the same shared email account and read the unsent message before posting a response. The communication process was tedious and time consuming, but absolutely necessary. Using unsent email drafts to communicate, the group of conspirators kept their messages off the Internet and out of the hands of notorious government agencies like the NSA or FBI.

WASHINGTON, DC

It was well after midnight when Helen Ripplinger ended her long day in Washington, DC. Crawling into bed, she took great care not to disturb her loving husband of thirty-eight years. Ed Ripplinger had never understood his wife's passion for government service. Content with being an insurance agent for the greater portion of his adult life, Ed decided long ago that he wasn't going to keep the insane hours his wife did. Nevertheless, he was a loyal supporter of Helen's career, and he willingly moved with her around the country as she took on greater responsibilities at work.

Helen snuggled next to her snoring husband and let her thoughts drift off. She was exhausted, but she couldn't just turn off her mind like it was a TV. She recounted the events of the day as she tried to relax. She heard that Tanner and his family had arrived safely in Guatemala, and that the CIA operative escorting them was first-rate. He was well trained and well informed. If Miguel was still alive, Helen had full confidence that Tanner and the CIA agent would eventually track down the mysterious hermit.

But there was another issue that concerned Helen, and it didn't have anything to do with Tanner or Guatemala. It had to do with the vice president's assassination. Howie Wiseman also had similar feelings. Helen recalled the exact conversation she had earlier in the day with secretary of defense as she drifted off to sleep.

"Something doesn't add up," Helen said.

Howie took a bite of his pancakes. "You don't like how the investigation is going?" he asked.

For the past six months, Helen and Howie had a standing weekly appointment for breakfast. The private meeting was an informal outlet for two of the top officials in the government to discuss national security matters without any bureaucratic baloney. Helen frequently learned more in her one-hour breakfast chat with Howie than after hours looking over classified material.

"No. I think the investigation is going okay. The Panamanians are cooperating with us, and it seems like everyone is on the same page about one of the drug cartels being responsible for the attack," Helen said.

"Is there something else?"

"Yes," Helen said with frustration. "I can't put my finger on it, but I still feel unsettled. I thought it was just frazzled nerves from the assassination, but the attack was three days ago and I'm still on edge."

Howie put down his utensils and wiped his mouth with a cloth napkin. "I kind of feel the same way. It's like we've hit a lull in the storm."

"What's your take?" She completely trusted Howie's view-point, but it was more than just the fact that he was the secretary of defense. He was an analytical genius. His intelligence was clearly highlighted by thirty-four different patents he held for his work in the field of satellite communications. Howie was smart, but Helen was no idiot herself. She could hold her own in any conversation.

Together, she felt the two of them formed the intellectual crème de la crème of the National Security Council.

Howie responded to Helen's question with another question. "Okay, why the vice president?" he asked. "I know he was a fierce anti-drug proponent, but was he really that big of an influence that some drug cartel decided to take him out?"

"You don't think they did it?" Helen asked.

"I admit, all the facts right now point to a drug cartel, but I have a hard time with that. Killing the vice president seems too much, like it ups the ante to a completely different level."

Helen thought of a different angle. "Maybe it's something more. Maybe the cartels in general are worried about their future," she said. "The VP is a shoo-in to be the next president. It might make sense for some drug lord to take him out before he has a chance to push his agenda as a newly elected president."

"That sounds reasonable. Killing him now would guarantee that the war on drugs won't escalate in the near future."

"Should we tell the boss?" Helen asked.

"Not just yet," Howie said. "We've got to keep digging. Our gut instincts won't hold up under the scrutiny of a congressional hearing."

"I agree," Helen said. "Whichever way this ends up going, we'll need solid facts to back us up."

OCTOBER 25

ANTIGUA, GUATEMALA

TANNER REMINDED HIMSELF again that he wasn't on vacation. With the sound of tropical birds filling the open-air patio, he found it difficult to focus on the upcoming business of the day. Adding to his distraction was the scrumptious breakfast buffet that he was currently surveying. If he didn't have kids and a job back home, Tanner figured he might stay another month at the luxurious hotel with his wife.

Megan and her parents were seated back at the breakfast table with Robert. He was dressed in casual pants, a Polo shirt, and a jean jacket. His appearance was much less of a tourist than the others in the group. "Did you hear Fuego this morning?" he asked.

"Was that what the faint 'pa-pa' sound was this morning?" Megan asked. "I thought it was someone lighting off firecrackers in the distance."

"Nope. That was the volcano, releasing tiny clouds of ash. But you can only hear it in the quiet of the early morning," Robert said.

"I think I'm addicted to these fried bananas," Tanner joked as he sat back down at the table with a plate of food. The rest of the group laughed at his admission of weakness.

"Did you get a chance to see the rest of the hotel?" Robert asked the group.

"We got up before breakfast and took a walk around," Megan said. "The hotel is lovely."

"I can't believe how big it is," Tanner added. "There's even an old church on the other side of the property."

"They do a candle-making demonstration there. It's quite interesting," Robert pointed out. He finished his breakfast and stood up. "If you'll excuse me, I'll go get the car and meet you in the lobby." He left the group and walked toward the lobby.

Ten minutes later, Tanner and his family loaded into the tan Chevy Tahoe and headed off down a cobblestone road.

"Okay, where are we going first?" Robert asked. Glen was sitting in the passenger seat, while Tanner and Megan rode in back with Julie.

"What?" Glen asked the driver.

"You know the Cipher better than anyone else. Where do we find him?"

"I guess we go back to where we saw him last," Glen said. He directed Robert toward a tiny home on the edge of town. After fifteen minutes and a few course corrections, Robert stopped the car in front of a humble home.

Tanner looked out the window at the simple structure. From the street, it didn't seem like much of a place to live. The walls of the tiny shelter were made of gray cinder blocks. The roof was formed by sheets of corrugated metal overlapping each other in a haphazard method. Even the yard, which was nothing more than a small patch of brown dirt with weeds, seemed untidy.

"The Cipher lives here?" Tanner asked in disbelief. He couldn't believe how quickly his surroundings had changed. Just twenty minutes ago he had been enjoying breakfast at a five-star hotel.

"He doesn't really live anywhere," Glen answered. "He moves around from area to area until he finds someone to take him in."

"So who lives here?" Megan asked.

"The Relief Society president," Julie answered. She was referring to the common assignment in the Mormon Church. Each congregational unit, or ward, in the Mormon Church had a women's group called the Relief Society. The leader of that organization coordinated the social activities and service events among the women in the congregation. In most areas of the world, the Relief Society president was keenly aware of the happenings among her fellow churchgoers.

"Wait, we're not going in there, are we?" Tanner asked as the others got out of the SUV.

"You'll be just fine," Julie said. She grabbed her son-in-law's arm and pulled him out of the car. "Besides, it will give you the chance to see how other people in the world live."

Tanner cautiously followed the group as they walked up to the metal door of the simple home. Julie knocked three times before a short Latino woman answered. The woman was momentarily startled, but then she flashed an enormous smile and hugged Julie. Phrases of Spanish were quickly exchanged between Julie, Glen, and the woman.

"What are they saying?" Tanner quietly asked Robert.

"Apparently they know each other," the CIA agent said jokingly. The group followed the woman into her home.

The interior of the single-room home was very modest. A bare cement floor stretched to the corners of the living area. Along the far wall of the home, a primitive cast-iron stove dominated the rudimentary kitchen containing a simple wooden table and four stools. On the opposite side of the kitchen area, a small bed rested against the wall. Two little children sat on the bed, their brown eyes opened wide with anticipation at the group of *gringos* who had just entered their home. There was no couch, but the woman in her early twenties eagerly grabbed the wooden stools from the table and offered them to her visitors.

Robert declined to sit, but stood in back behind Tanner and the others.

After they sat down, Julie spoke to Tanner. "This is Hermana Sanchez. She's been the Relief Society president for two years. Her husband shines shoes for a living."

Tanner looked toward the woman and gave her a friendly wave while saying "*hola*." She returned his greeting with a laugh and a smile of crooked teeth before vigorously shaking his hand. Megan then introduced herself, using quite a bit more Spanish than Tanner's simple phrase. After she was done, Robert cordially introduced himself to the woman.

With the greetings finished, Hermana Sanchez spoke animatedly to Glen and Julie for several minutes. Tanner managed to catch a simple word of Spanish every now and then, but the conversation was moving so fast that he soon gave up trying to be involved. To pass the time, he looked around at his surroundings. The poverty of the home was unnerving, and he decided to find something to distract him. He glanced at the two small children sitting on the edge of the bed. They hadn't moved an inch since his arrival. He figured they were probably around six and eight years old. He smiled and gave them an innocent wave.

"They haven't said anything about the Cipher yet. It's mostly just small talk," Robert whispered from behind the group. Tanner turned his focus back to the conversation, but it seemed to be moving even faster now.

"Can you understand what they are saying?" Tanner quietly asked Megan. She was sitting on a stool next to him.

"Most of it, but I'm rusty for how quick it's going."

Unable to comprehend what was being said, Tanner again lost interest and looked back at the children. They were still in the same position, frozen like little statues. He reached into his pocket and took out a couple of breath mints that he had gotten from the breakfast buffet. He cautiously extended his hand toward the two siblings. The oldest child, a girl, slowly walked up to Tanner and examined the contents.

"Say *dulce*," Megan coached into her husband's ear, witnessing his gesture.

With his hand still extended, Tanner repeated the Spanish word for candy to the young child. Her eyes lit up with excitement as she gingerly took the sweets out of his hand. In the innocent way that children often do, the older sister lovingly offered the second breath mint to her younger brother. He took the candy from his sister and grinned happily as he ate the simple treat.

Tanner waved again to the children before focusing back on the conversation. His in-laws and the woman were still visiting, completely unaware of what he had been doing on the side.

Robert brought Tanner up to speed. "They just asked about the Cipher. He had been living in a shed out back, but she said he moved out two months ago."

"Does she know where he went?" Tanner asked.

"It doesn't seem like it. She's telling us to check with someone named Hermano Carrillo, but I don't know what all this hermano and hermana stuff is about. I guess everyone is related," Robert said.

"It's how we address people in our church, by calling them 'brother' or 'sister,'" Tanner replied.

The conversation went on for a few more minutes before Glen and Julie stood up. Tanner took it as a sign that the meeting was coming to an end. He shook Hermana Sanchez's hand once more before saying "*adios.*" As he stepped out of the door, the little boy who hadn't spoken a single word the entire time ran up to Tanner and gave his leg a strong hug. The group laughed at the innocent gesture, and Tanner rubbed the little boy's black hair before leaving with the others.

Back in the Chevy Tahoe, Glen explained what he had learned. "Miguel moved out two months ago. She doesn't know where he went. She said to check with Hermano Carrillo. He's a bishop on the other side of town."

"Like a Catholic bishop?" Robert asked. He slowly pulled the Chevy Tahoe away from the curb.

"Not that high-ranking. A bishop in our church is more like a pastor or minister," Glen clarified as the Tahoe headed off down the road.

OCTOBER 25
NSA DATA CENTER, UTAH

I THINK I MAY have found something," Kevin said to Mel. The NSA analysts were huddled around the console to the quantum supercomputer deep inside the Utah Data Center. Even though the normal business hours had just begun, the two had been at work since 2:00 a.m.

"Bring it up on the wall," Mel said. He pointed up to a large 55-inch monitor mounted over the operations desk. The big screen was easier on the eyes than staring at a small console. Kevin typed in a couple of commands, and soon the image on the console was duplicated up on the larger monitor.

"Look at this," Kevin said. He stood up and pointed to an open email message on the monitor. "QC found it two years ago and archived it without doing any analysis."

Kevin's observation wasn't critical of the supercomputer's abilities. With so many communications happening simultaneously on the Internet, it was impossible for QC to examine every single one. Only the emails that corresponded to the most important priorities of the NSA were flagged for further analysis by the employees at the top-secret complex.

Mel studied the email. With strings of gibberish, it appeared similar to the paper note found on the dead terrorist. "Did you check it against our codes? We need to make sure it's actually that strange dialect and not just regular encrypted text."

"I did. It didn't match any of our known ciphers. It's not AES, RC5, TDEA, or Serpent," Kevin said, listing off some of the more common block ciphers for encrypting computer data.

"What about the stream ciphers?" Mel asked.

Kevin sat back down in his chair and ran a few commands to verify. "Nope. It's none of those."

"Let's do a visual check," Mel said. "Put our copy of the original message with the strange dialect next to this email. I've been burned more than once by failing to do a thorough investigation."

Kevin opened a scanned copy of the note found on the dead terrorist and displayed it on the monitor next to the email that he had just discovered. At that point, the similarities between the two messages became exceedingly obvious. Mel took the plastic golf tee out of his shirt pocket and put it in his mouth. "I believe you may have just found something," he said. "What's the background on this email?"

Kevin studied the metadata that was associated with the email. "QC found it twenty-eight months ago. It originated on an email system in Mexico," he said.

"Mexico? What's Mexico got to do with this?" Mel asked in bewilderment.

ANTIGUA, GUATEMALA

The tan Chevy Tahoe bounced over the cobblestones lining a street named Calle de Rubia. Tanner and his family were heading back into the more tourist-filled parts of Antigua. Looking out the windows, he stared at the massive volcano that was just a mere five miles away. It was both impressive and intimidating at the same time.

"I hope the kids are okay," Megan said to Tanner.

"Let's call them," he said. Tanner reached into the pocket of his jeans and pulled out the cell phone that had been given to him before he left the United States. He unlocked the device and got ready to dial, but then realized he didn't know how to make an international phone call.

"How do I call back to the US on this thing?" he asked.

"Just dial 001 first, and then the normal phone number with the area code," Robert said from the driver's seat. The CIA agent paused a second before following up with another question. "Who are you calling?"

"We just want to check in on the kids," Tanner said. His response was simple yet informative. The casual reply let the CIA official know that Tanner wasn't preparing to discuss classified information in the presence of others.

Tanner dialed the number and briefly spoke to his mother before handing the phone to Megan. He figured she would want to talk mother-to-mother to get the information firsthand. While Megan talked on the phone, Tanner listened to the conversation between Robert and Glen in the front seat of the SUV.

"Do you think that Hermano Carrillo knows where the Cipher is?" Robert asked.

"I don't know. I'm just going on what Hermana Sanchez told us," Glen said.

Robert nodded his head. "You have some good contacts in your church group. It sounds like they keep in touch with each other."

"I just hope Hermano Carrillo will talk to us. Since I don't know him personally, we'll have to be more casual in our questioning," Glen said. The SUV turned a corner and stopped at a small store.

Megan finished up her conversation. "Okay, that's good to hear. Call me back on this number if you have any problems." She turned toward Tanner, and he saw a look of relief on her face. "The kids are doing well. Sara just wants to stay in the pool all day."

"How's the baby?" Tanner asked.

"She's eating and sleeping well. I was worried that she might be up a lot at night, but your mom said she's doing fine."

"Let's go in," Glen said, eager to get going.

"Something smells good," Tanner said as he stepped out of the car with the others.

"You're going to love this," Julie said. "They don't have many places like this in the United States anymore."

Tanner looked at the sign over the door. He tried pronouncing it in his best Spanish accent, "Pan-a-der-ia."

"It's a bakery. Most of Latin America still has these mom-and-pop shops on every corner," Glen said. He opened the door to the small establishment, and a wave of fresh-baked goodness flooded out into the street.

Tanner followed the delicious aroma into the store. The inside of the establishment was simple but well maintained. White shelves were lined up along the shop's walls. Wooden bins on each shelf contained breads of various shapes and sizes. Along one particular edge of the store were cookies and other sweets that looked delicious. Behind the counter, Tanner noticed several balls of dough on a tray, ready for the baking process.

"*Buenos días*," the portly proprietor said to the *Norteamericanos*. Wearing a white apron and having his sleeves rolled up, the owner looked like a baker from the early 1900s.

Tanner watched as Robert took the lead in this interaction. He started out by ordering several items of baked goods, showing that he was willing to patronize the owner before asking questions. The proprietor placed various rolls and pastries in brown paper bags and handed them to Robert. The CIA agent paid in cash, gesturing for the owner to keep the change as a tip.

Tanner witnessed the smooth exchange in silence. Although he couldn't understand what Robert was saying, it was obvious that the CIA agent was using social engineering to prep the owner for disclosing important information. It was a process that Tanner had employed on many occasions as a former hacker.

Robert took the paper bags and passed them around to the group, letting everyone sample the delicious bread. After a few moments of small talk, Robert motioned for Glen to join him at the counter. Tanner noticed the owner was taken aback when the *gringo* entered the conversation, speaking Spanish fluently.

While Robert and Glen talked to the owner, the others walked around the shop, admiring all the different baked goods. "This is really more of a bread store than a bakery," Tanner said.

"That's right," Julie agreed. "Even though they have some cookies, you're not going to find a bunch of donuts or éclairs here. In Latin America, most of the pastries are called sweet-bread. It's more bread and less sugar than what you find in American pastries, but I think they are just as good."

Megan and her mother continued browsing the store while Tanner found a small wooden bench to sit on. As he sampled a few more of the delicious items in his paper sack, he watched Robert and Glen talk to the owner. The conversation seemed friendly and cordial. After several minutes, Tanner sensed the dialogue was coming to an end. Robert ordered another round of bread to take on the road. It was too much food for five people to eat, but Tanner understood that the extra purchase was Robert's final act of social engineering. He reciprocated goodwill back to the owner, who had told Robert all he knew about the Cipher.

The group piled back into the SUV and buckled up for another trip. As they pulled away from the bakery, Robert summarized the conversation. "The owner was very nice and willing to help. He said the Cipher would come into his store looking for something to eat. Unfortunately, he said the Cipher hasn't come around for about three weeks. That was the last time he saw him."

The Chevy Tahoe started its journey down the narrow cobblestone street. "Did he give us an idea of where to go next?" Tanner asked.

"Yep. He gave us the name of another person to visit, but don't get discouraged," Robert said. "This is a normal process for tracking someone down in Latin America."

As the Chevy Tahoe disappeared out of sight, another car pulled up to the bakery. Two men exited the black sedan and headed into the store. They, too, had some questions for the owner of the shop, but they weren't as well versed in the subtle tactics that Robert had just used. These henchmen worked for the Chiapas drug cartel, and they wanted to know who the *Norteamericanos* were and why they were driving all over Antigua with a suspected CIA official.

OCTOBER 25
NSA DATA CENTER, UTAH

IT WAS ALMOST lunchtime at the Bumblehive spy complex in Utah. All the analysts on the QC team were gathered together for a few short hours before the night shift went home to get some much-needed sleep.

"This is the only email we've found so far," Kevin said, updating his fellow employees who were coming on duty.

"How much of the archives have we searched?" Sydney asked.

"We're about two-thirds of the way through, right?" Kevin asked, looking at Mel. He nodded his head.

"So you know the email came from a server somewhere in Mexico. And you know the account is still active because an anonymous email you sent to that address didn't bounce back," Rachel summarized. "But you said that nobody is using the account. That doesn't make sense."

Mel rubbed his tired eyes before taking the plastic golf tee out of his mouth. "No. That's wrong." His response was terse, but not unusual for the irritable analyst who needed some sleep. "According to the data in our archives, we haven't seen anything sent from

81

that email account in almost two years. We never said that it wasn't being used."

"So this must be a dead-drop account," Sydney said. "Just like those terrorists used to communicate with each other when planning the Madrid train bombings back in 2004."

"That would explain why we haven't seen a new message," Kevin said.

"Wait, this still doesn't make sense," Rachel interrupted. "If they aren't sending the emails, then why bother encrypting the message with this funky dialect? They'd only need to do that if they were worried about us eavesdropping on the email as it traveled across the Internet."

Compliments of a whistle-blower named Edward Snowden, most of the civilized world now understood that the NSA had its fingers in the digital pie of global communications. The NSA's special abilities made sense, given the fact that the United States had created the framework for the modern-day Internet. As a result, 90 percent of all global Internet traffic flowed through network wires and switches physically located inside the United States. If an email was sent from Europe to Africa, there was an extremely high probability that the message would, at some point in its journey, traverse the geographic boundaries of the United States.

It was this remarkable phenomenon that allowed the NSA to be so effective and ruthless in its eavesdropping abilities. Leveraging the NSA's privileged access to dozens of Internet junction points in the United States, Tanner and his team of analysts were able to copy and archive practically every electronic message sent in the world.

"Maybe they're just ultra-paranoid, and they want to encrypt the emails for added protection," Kevin said.

"Or maybe they started out with the intention of sending and receiving emails, but stopped when they got worried that someone might read their messages in transit," Sydney added.

"Those are all possible ideas, but we need to finish our search of the archives first," Mel said. He stood up and spoke to Sydney and

Rachel. "You ladies are in charge now. Keep the searches running. In the meantime, dig around and see if you can find anything else about this email address or the server that's hosting it. I'm not sure what the Mexico connection is, but we need to track that down."

"Maybe we should get someone to hack into the server?" Rachel said. "If they're using unsent emails to communicate, I bet there are a bunch of them stored on the system."

Although the NSA had all sorts of unique capabilities when it came to cyber-spying, the government agency was exceedingly compartmentalized. Every group was assigned a limited and specific task. For example, the QC team only focused on reading encrypted emails and messages as the information moved across the Internet. Responsibility for hacking into a computer system or eavesdropping on a cell phone conversation happened back at Fort Meade. By spreading out the covert tasks, the NSA prevented any single analyst or team from controlling or tampering with the full set of raw data as it was processed.

"That's a good idea. Contact our folks back at Meade and see how they can help." He paused for a second before continuing. "But let's call Tanner first and see if he needs anything."

ANTIGUA, GUATEMALA

Thousands of miles away in Guatemala, a cell phone chirped in a tan Chevy Tahoe. The incoming call startled Tanner, who was busy talking with everyone in the SUV. He pulled the phone out of his pocket and checked the caller ID. Unsurprisingly, it said it was coming from an unlisted number. "Oh, this might be work," Tanner said. Erring on the side of caution, he decided he'd keep the conversation brief and vague. "Hello," he answered.

"Tanner, this is Kevin. How's it going?"

With an SUV full of individuals not cleared for classified communication, Tanner had to choose his response carefully. "We haven't found anything yet, but we're making some progress."

"Where are you at?"

"In a small city just outside the capital. It's amazing down here," Tanner said.

"We've found a couple of amazing things up here also," Kevin said. He quickly highlighted the discovery of the single email in the NSA's digital archives. "Do you need anything from us?"

"No. I think we're doing okay down here," Tanner said. "But will you call Helen and let her know what you found?"

"Will do. Be safe," Kevin said.

"We will. Take care," Tanner replied before ending the conversation.

It was dusk when Tanner and the others called it a day. Even though they hadn't located the Cipher, their search wasn't a complete failure. They had talked to six different people around Antigua. Each contact had shed a little more light on the where-abouts of the Cipher. As with most investigations, good detective work combined bits of deductive reasoning with ample amounts of patience. The payoff for the group's endurance came just after 5:00 p.m. when they tracked down a particular bus driver.

The middle-aged driver drove the daily route between Antigua and another popular tourist destination called Lake Atitlán. Located thirty miles to the northwest of Antigua, the picturesque lake was often considered one of the most beautiful in the world. The bus driver's clientele normally consisted of tourists from Europe, which was why the Cipher seemed so out of place when he had made the journey five days ago.

With the solid lead that the Cipher was likely now in the Lake Atitlán region, Tanner and the others headed back to their hotel room to freshen up for dinner. Tomorrow they planned to relocate their search to the scenic lake surrounded by three volcanoes. Once again, Glen and Julie were ecstatic about their future plans. They fully agreed with Robert that Lake Atitlán was one of the most beautiful spots on earth.

Returning to their hotel room, Megan headed off to the bathroom while Tanner went to retrieve something from his suitcase. Despite the fact that he had spent most of the day sitting in a car, he felt worn out. He looked forward to a relaxing dinner before taking a refreshing swim in the hotel's pool.

Unfortunately, he wouldn't get the chance.

As Tanner approached his suitcase, he noticed something strange. His luggage was about a foot closer to the fireplace than where he had left it that morning. He found it odd, but dismissed the adjustment as the possibility that the housekeeping unit had moved it when cleaning. But when Tanner opened his suitcase, he noticed something else awry. His clothes had been disturbed. The change was so slight that most people wouldn't have noticed, but Tanner was far more observant than most people. As he studied his luggage, he saw the discrepancies. An orange T-shirt, on the bottom of the stack of clothes that morning, was now on top. Also, his folded jeans had flipped direction and were now pointed the opposite way.

With several distinct changes to his personal belongings, Tanner grew very suspicious. He went into the bathroom to tell his wife. "Put your stuff down and don't touch anything else."

Megan turned from the mirror and looked at her husband with a puzzled expression. "What?"

"I think someone was snooping around while we were gone. We need to tell Robert."

Megan set her hairbrush down next to her makeup bag. "He's not just a tour guide, is he?"

"No. He's not," Tanner said.

"I didn't think he really worked for the State Department," Megan said to her husband. Tanner's perplexed expression prompted her for more details "Hey, you aren't the only one around here who can figure stuff out," she said. "Robert told us he's from LA, but did you see how he's completely at ease among the locals? He knows his way around the country far too well for someone who just sits behind a desk at the embassy. Given how much I've interacted with you and some of your coworkers over the years, I'm getting pretty good at spotting government spy folks."

Tanner nodded his head and smiled. His wife was dead on in her observations. "Let's go get Robert," he said as he led his wife across the hall.

They knocked on Robert's door, but nobody answered. After knocking a second time, Tanner pulled out his cell phone. He was just about to press the speed dial for the CIA agent when he heard someone call out from down the hall.

"Are you guys ready to eat?" Robert shouted as he walked toward the couple.

"Where did you go?" Tanner asked. His question had a slight hint of suspicion.

"I checked us in at the restaurant. Why, what's up?"

"Someone's been looking through our stuff," Tanner said. He led Robert into their room and pointed out the discrepancies in his clothes.

As Robert listened to the explanation, his countenance changed. Instead of being the jovial and easygoing tour guide, he was now as serious as a judge during sentencing. "Don't touch anything. Just leave everything where it is," he said. "Let's get your parents and head out to Lake Atitlán tonight."

"What about our stuff?" she asked.

"I've got a couple of guys who'll sweep the rooms. They'll bring our stuff to us once they say it's clean."

"Do you think someone is following us?" Tanner asked.

"With all the corruption from drugs and crime down here, anything's possible. But it could just be a group of thieves targeting tourists."

Robert's explanation seemed a little too weak. "We're not just a group of average tourists, remember?" Tanner asked.

"Correct. That's why our best move right now is to get out of town. If it's some local punks causing trouble, they won't follow us to Atitlán," Robert said.

"What if it's someone else?" Megan asked with a bit of fear in her voice.

"I'm prepared for such a situation," he said. His voice revealed absolute confidence in his abilities.

Robert led Megan and Tanner out of their room and knocked on the next door. After a quick explanation to the Hollands, Glen and Julie abandoned their room and hastily followed the others down the hall. Less than sixty seconds later, they pulled out of the parking garage at the Casa Santo Domingo Hotel. Instead of riding in a tan Chevy Tahoe, however, the group was now in a white Toyota Sequoia.

"Whose car is this?" Julie asked.

"It belongs to some friends of mine who are helping me out. Like I told your daughter earlier, I'm prepared for any contingency," Robert said. He quickly checked the rearview mirror to make sure they weren't being followed.

The passengers rode in silence as the white SUV accelerated down the road. The seriousness of the situation was manifested in Robert's thoughtful, yet fully-competent demeanor. Working his way toward the edge of town, he took several unnecessary turns and detours, clearly making sure they weren't being followed. Finally, after twenty long minutes, he visually relaxed as the SUV started down the highway toward Lake Atitlán. He took out his cell phone and dialed a number. The conversation was short and simple.

"We might be compromised. We're heading out tonight. Implement our contingency plan," he said before disconnecting his call. Robert then cleared his voice and spoke to the anxious passengers in the SUV. "Sorry about the abrupt exit." He was back to his pleasant and easygoing manner. "Things can get a little intense from time to time down here in Guate."

"Who are you?" Glen asked from the rear passenger seat. Because of the recent events, it was now obvious to everyone that Robert was more than just some desk jockey at the embassy.

"I work for the CIA," he said bluntly. "I just called a couple helpers who are providing backup and administrative support. We're supposed to make sure you stay safe while you're down here." Robert's forthright admission of who he worked for caught Tanner's family off guard.

"Are you a spy?" Julie asked.

"Not anymore. I'm more of an administrator now," he said.

"Should you be telling us this?" Glen asked.

"It's okay, just as long as you don't go out and post it on Facebook or Twitter," he said. "Besides, I'm not an active spy. It's the deep-cover folks that we don't talk about."

Tanner decided he wanted to change the topic of conversation. As a fellow member of the intelligence community, he wasn't comfortable with Glen and Julie's newfound interest in Robert's employment. "Who do you think was following us?"

"First of all, we aren't even sure that we were being followed. It could be nothing," Robert said. "But it's always best to be cautious, so we'll just head to Lake Atitlán a day early. If anyone has been snooping around, this will throw them off our trail."

"What about our clothes back at the hotel?" It was Julie asking the same question that her daughter had mentioned earlier.

"Remember those two helpers I just called? " Robert asked rhetorically. "They're highly skilled folks. They'll check out the rooms and make sure nothing is out of the ordinary. Then they'll bring our stuff to us, but we probably won't get it until later tonight. Sorry about that."

LAKE ATITLÁN, GUATEMALA

A short time later, the white Toyota Sequoia arrived at the beautiful Lake Atitlán. Unfortunately, it was nighttime and the breathtaking view of the lake would have to wait until tomorrow. Robert avoided the main portion of the city, driving to a nice hotel on the edge of the lake instead. He pulled the SUV to a stop in front of a modern-looking building.

"A lot of foreigners stay here. We'll blend in and be safe. You guys stay in the car while I go get some rooms for us," Robert said. He stepped out of the vehicle and walked off into the night.

Ten minutes later, he returned and got back in the driver's seat. "We're all set." He passed out standard looking hotel room keys for everyone. "Here are your keys, but you'll have to remain in your room the rest of the night. We want to keep a low profile until I hear back from my helpers back in Antigua."

"What about dinner?" Tanner asked. It was almost 8:00 p.m., and he was hungry.

"The hotel has excellent room service. Order what you want, and it will all be charged back to me," Robert said. He directed the couples out of the car and to their rooms. "As soon as I find out about our luggage, I'll let you know."

The arrangements were similar to the night before. Tanner and Megan had a room next to Glen and Julie while Robert stayed across the hall. Tanner opened the door for his wife, allowing her to enter first. Although this hotel was clean and contemporary, it didn't have the ambiance or history of the Casa Santo Domingo. "It's not like the one back in Antigua," he said.

"It's still nice and comfortable," Megan replied. Tanner could tell she was determined to make the best of an unplanned situation. "Find something for us to watch on TV while I order our food."

It was past midnight when the deep-cover CIA agents arrived from Antigua. Meeting with Robert in the parking lot of the hotel, the men delivered their update with the anticipated luggage. The secret rendezvous was partially concealed by a fog coming off Lake Atitlán, creating a scene reminiscent of many cloak-and-dagger spy novels.

"We swept the rooms for bugs and trackers, but we didn't find anything. Everything checked out okay," the taller of the two CIA agents said.

"Any idea who it was?" Robert asked.

"We're still working on it. But that's an upscale hotel, so I doubt it's just some street thugs. It's probably someone else," the agent said.

"*Mafiosos*?" Robert asked, referring to organized crime gangs that operated throughout different parts of Guatemala.

"Possibly," the shorter and stockier CIA agent answered. "But it could also be one of the drug cartels."

"What would a cartel want with them?" Robert asked. He knew the drug cartels usually left the tourists to themselves.

"That's a good question," the taller CIA agent said. "Unfortunately, their passports were hidden in their luggage. So it's safe to assume that whoever broke into the room knows their identities now."

Robert's thoughts drifted off for a moment. The realization that Tanner and his family's identification were compromised wasn't too much of a worry. They were, after all, acting as tourists. Someone would have to link Tanner back to his top-secret employment at the NSA to realize that he wasn't just a normal American. Robert pondered the situation for a few seconds before charting a new course.

"Well, someone doesn't like us snooping around, and they might not give up so easily. I want you guys to step up your recon. Shadow us around town and keep a lookout for trouble," Robert said. The two deep-cover CIA agents nodded their heads. Both of them had firsthand experience in these tricky situations.

OCTOBER 26
STATE OF TABASCO, MEXICO

Javier Soto woke up at his normal time of 6:00 a.m. The forty-six-year-old leader of the Chiapas drug cartel had always been an early riser. For some biological reason, he didn't need a lot of sleep. It was a trait that he had since his childhood in Acapulco, Mexico.

Javier was the oldest of six children. His family didn't have much in the way of material possessions, so Javier spent most of his youth working odd jobs to help care for the family. During his teenage years, a man approached Javier and asked him if he wanted to sell drugs to the tourists on the Acapulco beach. Javier readily accepted the lucrative offer and the chance to perfect his English while interacting with Americans.

Javier's employment was valuable, but he had bigger plans beyond the Acapulco beach. Working as a grunt selling drugs, he recognized that the local crime operation was poorly organized. It functioned like a single man's hobby, not an efficient business. Javier knew that if he ever had the chance, he could create his own drug operation with ten thousand times the profit.

Driven to succeed, Javier saved up enough money from his illegal employment to enroll in the University of Mexico after graduating from high school. He studied both business and English, and received good enough grades to qualify for a study abroad program in the United States. During his junior year, Javier moved to Massachusetts to study at Harvard for a semester. Leveraging his good looks and easy smile, he soon became close friends with the elite of the student body.

It was then that Javier fully understood the enormous effects of having powerful and influential friends. Doors seemed to magically open as new opportunities presented themselves for the Mexican national. First, he was given the chance to finish his last year of school at Harvard. Then, astonishingly, he was awarded a financial scholarship to pay for the entire year of schooling. Javier eagerly embraced his newfound fortune, seizing the chance to rub shoulders with future leaders of the American government.

Upon graduating from Harvard, Javier turned down several business opportunities and decided to move back to Mexico. He still embraced his original dream of running his own drug cartel. Leveraging his business knowledge and associations with friends back in the United States, Javier created the Chiapas cartel from scratch. Almost overnight, he became one of the youngest and most respected drug lords in Mexico. For the past twenty years, he had been running his organized crime syndicate with astonishing success.

Javier stumbled out of bed and put on a pair of silk pajama bottoms. The bachelor quietly navigated his way down the dark staircase of his spacious villa. He went straight toward the kitchen where the coffee maker had just finished its morning brew. The drug boss didn't expect his staff to be up at the early hour. In fact, he preferred to have the quiet mornings all to himself. Pausing to take a couple of sips of his drink, Javier quietly grabbed his laptop from the office and headed outside.

The leader of the Chiapas cartel had perfected his morning

wake-up ritual over the years. Heading past the pool and down toward his private beach, he stopped at a chair and table perched under a small cabana. He set his laptop on the table before relaxing in the beach chair. On the eastern horizon, he could see a pink splinter of light as it crested over the ocean. Sitting in solitude, Javier enjoyed the sunrise while listening to the waves crashing on the beach. This was the best time of day for him to clear his mind and meditate.

Thirty minutes later, the pink spec of light had morphed into a bright yellow ball. Javier remained at the same location on the isolated beach, but he was now working on his laptop. Running his bare toes through the sand, he started up a custom application to decode the new message he had received from his lieutenant.

El Flaco reported that he had identified the four North Americans who were snooping around Antigua. Unfortunately, he didn't see anything unusual about the US citizens because they appeared to be typical tourists. The most puzzling part of the situation, however, was the man who had greeted them at the airport. Did the Americans have some special connection to the CIA? El Flaco wasn't sure, but he reiterated his determination to use whatever means necessary to get the answers for his boss.

Javier smiled as he crafted his email response to his lieutenant. El Flaco felt justified in his duties, but the ex-Army Ranger was also a bit overzealous. His harsh tactics might frighten off the American tourists before discerning their true motives. Javier instructed El Flaco to tread lightly, and to let the situation in Guatemala develop naturally. Before ending his email, he emphasized how close the cartel was to its ultimate goal. It was not the time for rash behavior. In just a few days, the United States government would change forever.

Javier was a member of a secret society called the Order of 28. The group was created by a mysterious Washington bureaucrat known to the other members as Votan. While he didn't necessarily agree with Votan's politics, Javier was supportive of the Order's goal from a business perspective. The Order of 28 was created solely for the purpose of overthrowing the United States government and establishing a monarchy.

The drug lord finished his message and ran it through a custom encryption program that altered it from plain English into a rare Guatemalan dialect. For the past two years, all the emails drafted among the Order of 28 had used this exact encoding routine. The program was originally created by the cartel to obscure its clandestine operations, but it was so effective that Javier later convinced members of the Order of 28 to adopt the encryption practice.

Javier saved his message as a draft copy, making sure not to accidently send it out over the Internet like he had done when he first used the encryption routine with the Order of 28 nearly two years ago. The message remained in the specific folder that he shared only with his lieutenant. That email folder was different than the other folders Javier used to communicate with his fellow conspirators. There were twenty-eight members of the secret society, and Javier shared a separate, password-protected folder with each one of them. He often thought about the implication of having hundreds of draft messages stored by the members of the Order of 28 on the same server, but he wasn't too worried. The email server was located in a private data center in Mexico City, and it was completely secure from both physical and legal attacks.

LAKE ATITLÁN, GUATEMALA

Approximately five hundred miles southwest of the drug lord's location, Tanner and Megan also enjoyed the magnificent sunrise. Eating a delicious breakfast on the patio overlooking beautiful Lake Atitlán, the couple was awestruck by the view. The lake was a massive crater lake, formed by the collapse of an ancient volcano. Over a thousand feet deep in spots, the lagoon with no outlet to the sea was a brilliant color of blue.

"I can't believe this view," Megan said to the others seated at the table. The small hotel restaurant was filled with a mix of both foreign and local tourists, each enjoying the spectacular lake surrounded by several mountain peaks.

Robert nodded his head. "I've been here dozens of times, and I'm still impressed by it. Are you guys ready to head out?"

"I think we're finished," Julie said. She wiped her mouth with a napkin and placed it on the table. Robert left a generous tip for the waiter, and everybody headed back toward their rooms.

"Let's stick close together," Robert said. He led the tourists down the hall of the hotel. "We're still not sure what happened back in Antigua, so it's best if we don't go wandering off. Go grab what you'll need for the day and meet me back in the lobby," he said.

As Robert took a seat in the lobby, he caught a brief glimpse of a man out of the corner of his eye. Turning around in a quick motion, he relaxed when he recognized the stranger as one of the deep-cover CIA agents. His right hand was obscured in his coat pocket, having just sent a text message. Suddenly, Robert felt his cell phone vibrate. He opened up the text message and quickly read the contents. The message was brief and unnerving:

Two men in Antigua asking about American tourists. Likely Chiapas cartel. Keep watch for a black sedan.

OCTOBER 26
NSA DATA CENTER, UTAH

AT THE BUMBLEHIVE in Utah, the members of the QC team were brainstorming their next move. Their counterparts back at NSA headquarters had positively located the server that sent the lone email discovered in the archives. The computer in question was hosted in a private data center on the outskirts of Mexico City. The business that owned the data center leased email accounts and web servers to exclusive clientele who had lots of money and lots of reasons for privacy. With segmented networks and bombproof access control systems, the data center was state-of-the-art. Getting in would be difficult.

"I guess that's smart in a way," Kevin said. "By keeping the server off American soil, they can avoid all our laws for subpoenaing email records."

"And since they don't ever send their messages, we can't intercept them while they travel over the Internet," Sydney added from across the table.

"That's why hacking into the primary server is our best option. If we can get in at the operating system level, we can find out where the emails are stored and read them," Rachel pointed out.

"I wish Tanner were here. He'd know what to do," Sydney said with a sigh. Although Mel was trying his best to lead the team in Tanner's absence, Sydney had a point. Tanner had a creative way of solving problems.

"Well, it's not like he's dead. Let's give him a call," Kevin said enthusiastically. He grabbed the conference room phone at the center of the table and dialed a number. A few moments later, they had Tanner on a secure call from his hotel room in Guatemala. After briefly explaining the situation to their boss, Tanner responded with a novel idea.

"Don't go after the primary data center. See if there's a backup site and hit it instead," Tanner said.

"What do you mean?" Sydney asked.

"Obviously this email server is in a high-availability data center. So the owners must have redundant controls to make sure everything is up and running one hundred percent of the time," Tanner said.

"Yeah, so?" Rachel said.

"So Mexico City is prone to earthquakes. They gotta have a failover site somewhere in case of a natural disaster," Tanner said. "Those failover sites usually run on a shoestring budget to minimize cost. See if there's a duplicate email system at the failover site that is easier to hack into." The silence over the phone line emphasized Tanner's brilliant suggestion.

"It won't be easy to find the backup site," Mel said.

"Sure it will. We just need to ask them," Tanner said.

"What?" Rachel asked.

"These folks that run the data center in Mexico City are just a normal business, right?" Tanner asked rhetorically. "So find someone to pose as a potential client. Tell the company that you're interested in using their data center to host a server, but that you need to have a good understanding of their backup strategy."

"You think we'll be able to con them into telling us where the backup data center is?" Mel asked.

"Sure, especially if you are talking to a sales guy. He'll tell you almost anything if you can guarantee a sale," Tanner said, laughing.

"But none of us speak Spanish," Mel said. "This data center is in Mexico, remember?"

Tanner was silent for a moment. "I've got an idea. Send me a text with the name of the hosting company and the phone number from their website. I'll get you that information."

LAKE ATITLÁN, GUATEMALA

"I can't do that. I'm not a spy!" Megan exclaimed. Tanner had just asked for her help in getting the information about the backup data center. They were still in their hotel room on the shores of Lake Atitlán, getting ready to head out to search for Miguel.

Tanner put his arms gently on his wife's shoulders. "It will be easier than you think. I'll coach you on what to say."

"My dad or Robert can do it. They speak Spanish better than I do," Megan said.

"It's has be you," Tanner countered, patiently. "We can't get your parents involved in this. They won't like the deception aspect of it, and they'll probably balk at the pressure. But more importantly, I need a woman to make the call. Women are inherently more trustworthy."

Megan shook her head in disagreement. "I'm not supposed to be involved in this stuff, remember?" she said as a last defense. "I can get in trouble."

"You can't get in trouble. There's nothing illegal about it," Tanner said. "You're just making a phone call to a business and asking them about using their services. It's the same type of call that any potential customer would do. Besides, you don't even know the exact reason why I need you to do this. If anyone asks, you can just tell them that I needed your help to ask about the company's services."

Megan considered all the other excuses for why she should avoid making the call, but she realized that her husband would countermove any defense she offered. In the end, her curiosity got the better of her. She knew her husband had done stuff like this in his former life as a computer hacker, and she often wondered how it worked.

"Okay, I'll try it, but don't make fun of me if I do it wrong," she said.

Tanner leaned in and gave his wife a peck on the cheek. "You're awesome. I'll go tell Robert that we need some extra time before we head out to look for the Cipher."

A few minutes later, Megan and Tanner were hunched over the small desk in their hotel room. On a notepad, Tanner wrote a brief list of things for his wife to remember when she made the phone call. Megan was nervous with anticipation, but she was ready to begin. Tanner put his cell phone on speaker and dialed the number to the data center company located on the east side of Mexico City. A polite operator answered the phone, and Megan cautiously proceeded in Spanish. She asked to speak with someone in the sales group. The call was placed on hold.

"You're doing great. Remember, you're just a normal person, asking for information about their company. Be friendly and encourage the salesman to talk. The more he talks, the better," Tanner said while soft music played, indicating that the call was still on hold.

Megan nodded her head as she took a few deep breaths. Even though she had repeatedly told herself that she wasn't doing anything illegal, the secretive nature of the call made her feel like she was breaking the law. Her time to worry, however, was short-lived because the phone call was soon answered by a man.

Megan spoke to the salesman in Spanish, translating the rough script that Tanner had hastily prepared for her. She told the sales agent that she was an American, working in Mexico City for an American company. Her business hoped to establish a relationship with Pemex, the state-owned petroleum company. Megan informed the salesman that her company was new in the area, and that they needed temporary computer services until they found a more permanent solution.

Megan looked up from translating the short message. Tanner smiled and gave her two thumbs-up for encouragement. Even though she had stumbled over some of the Spanish words, Megan figured it probably didn't matter. It added credibility to the fact that she was posing as an American businesswoman who didn't speak Spanish as her first language.

Finished with her brief introduction, Megan and Tanner quietly waited for a reply. But the response wasn't anything that Megan had anticipated. "Your Spanish is good, but would it be more comfortable for you if we spoke in English?" asked the salesman.

"Yes, it would be. Thank you very much," Megan said. She relaxed, relieved that she could now communicate in her native tongue.

"Where did you learn your Spanish?" the man asked, clearly trying to make a connection with his potential client.

"I learned it in college, but I haven't used it much since then," Megan said.

"Maybe you'll use it more, now that you're in our beautiful country," the salesman said. "You mentioned that you're working with Pemex?"

"Yes. We're setting up our business in Mexico. We hope to lease some of your computer equipment until we get our own data center established," Megan repeated. She was gaining more confidence in her façade.

"I'd be glad to help," the salesman offered. He took a breath to continue, but Megan interrupted him.

"Would it be okay if I had my employee join the call? He handles all of our computer needs," Megan said, watching her husband as she caught him off guard. She had found a way to gracefully bow out of the conversation while putting Tanner on the spot. She flashed a patronizing smile at her spouse, emphasizing the brilliant countermove.

Tanner quickly shook off his stunned expression and jumped right into the conference call. When he started speaking, Megan was shocked at what he did. In just a few milliseconds, Tanner transformed himself. Using a convincing Southern accent, Tanner introduced himself as David Martinez.

"Martinez? That's a common Hispanic last name. Where are you from?" the salesman asked in a friendly tone.

"Born and raised in Texas," Tanner said.

"Are you a Rangers fan?" the salesman asked.

"You bet," Tanner replied. "I love their pitching, especially the younger talent they have coming up next year."

Tanner and the salesman spent the next two minutes talking about baseball. Megan had no idea that her husband even followed baseball. She couldn't even remember a time that he had watched a game on TV. But it was more than his knowledge of trivial baseball facts that amazed Megan. It was how he was communicating with the sales agent that blew her away. Tanner's actions were completely captivating and absolutely convincing. He spoke to the salesman like he was talking with a close neighbor over the backyard fence. Using humor, flattery, and keen observation, Megan listened as Tanner quickly broke down the invisible barrier that was naturally present in first interactions.

After a few minutes of casual talk, Megan watched as Tanner skillfully shifted the conversation from baseball to computers. Suddenly, they were talking about network throughput and memory capacity in much the same way they had been discussing baseball statistics. The conversation was mesmerizing to Megan. Before long, Tanner had the salesman chatting about his company's backup and data recovery options, elaborating how they were better than any of their competitors. Sensing that he was close to sealing a deal, the salesperson didn't flinch at all when Tanner skillfully asked about the failover facility. Eighteen minutes into the conversation, the salesman willingly divulged the physical address of the failover site. It was located in Hermosillo, in the northwestern Mexican state of Senora.

With the information that he wanted, Tanner didn't abruptly end the conversation. Instead he shifted the topic of discussion back to the salesman and his personal life. Tanner asked him about his family. The sales agent gloated about his children, especially his fourteen-year-old son who was quite good at soccer. Tanner admitted that he didn't know much about the sport, but he eagerly indulged the salesman's passion for the game. After a few more minutes of spontaneous talk, Tanner thanked the sales agent for his help. Before ending the call, the two men agreed to meet for drinks the next time Tanner was in Mexico City.

Megan looked at her husband in bewildered amazement as he finished the call. *Who had he become?* Unfortunately, she didn't get any time to explore Tanner's new identity. Just as fast as he had changed personas, he was back to his normal self.

"I'm not sure if I should be impressed or scared," Megan said. "Is that what you did when you were a hacker?"

"Yes. It's called social engineering, but it's really just elaborate manipulation," he said. "Years ago, I loved the thrill of working someone like that. But I felt slimy doing that today."

"I'm surprised that you can still manipulate someone so well," Megan said. The tone of her voice emphasized that she didn't approve of Tanner's skills.

"It's all just a lie," Tanner said. "I don't care about that guy, and we're never meeting for drinks. I just needed his information."

"How often have you done that to me?" Megan asked.

"What? Social engineering?" Tanner asked.

"Yes, that," Megan said. She was dead serious.

"I've never done that to you. I promise. I care about you too much to do that," Tanner said. "And now that you've seen me do it, you can tell it's a lot different from how I normally act. That's how you know that I'm being honest." His sincere statement faded into the quiet of the room.

Megan's thoughtful pause faded into a warm smile. She didn't like what she had just witnessed, but she decided that her husband's answer was genuine. She felt there wasn't any point in further accusations. "Okay, you got the information. Now what?"

"I've got to call my team and let them know. They'll take care of it while we go look for the Cipher," Tanner said.

NSA DATA CENTER, UTAH

When the speakerphone rang in the Bumblehive conference room, the members of the QC team were surprised to hear Tanner's voice. They imagined that it would take a day or two for Tanner to get back to them. But when he told them that he knew the location of the failover site for the data center in Mexico City, they were absolutely astonished. Tanner took a couple of minutes to quickly review how he had discovered the information. Despite his success, it was Mel, with his ever-present skepticism, that quickly pointed out the additional issues still facing the team.

"Okay, we have the address for the failover data center, but that doesn't really help us much," he said.

"It's the first step. Remember, hacking is a process," Tanner said.

"Yeah, but we haven't learned anything. We don't even know if the backup system has the encrypted emails or not," Mel said.

There was only one way to find out if they were on the right track. They had to break into the failover data center, but that required a hacking skill set that the analysts in Utah didn't have. Fortunately, there was a group at NSA headquarters that specialized in all the nefarious aspects of computer hacking.

"See if you can get ahold of someone on the Red Team. If anyone can hack into that backup email server, it's them," Tanner told his peers.

OCTOBER 26
WHITE HOUSE, WASHINGTON, DC

IT WAS AT times like today when Helen questioned why she had accepted her position. Returning from her meeting with the president, she shut the door to her office and threw herself down on the chair behind her desk. Uncharacteristic of her ladylike demeanor, she kicked off her heels and put her feet up on the mahogany desk. She closed her eyes, tilted her chair back, and massaged the sides of her forehead.

The president could be a jerk when he wanted to be, and today was one of those occasions when he acted more like a two-year-old than of the Commander in Chief. The midterm elections were just a week away, and the president was completely engrossed in assisting his party's campaign. Everything else was pushed off his plate, including the fact that his vice president had been recently murdered. To make matters worse, the attorney general had convinced the president to uceremoniously postpone the vice president's funeral until after the midterms were done. In some ways, Helen felt that the attorney general had elevated himself to become the de facto vice president.

Helen took a deep breath, recognizing that she could never be a politician. Her life revolved around solid facts, not poll numbers. The president's approval rating had dropped since the assassination, and now he was more concerned about looking good for the camera instead of looking for the vice president's killers. In the end, Helen just couldn't reason with politicians. They would say two completely contradictory things in the same breath, expecting everyone to believe them both.

For the general public, ignorance was bliss. Fortunately, Helen wasn't wired that way. She lived on facts like a college freshman lived on pizza. The more she knew the better, and right now, she didn't know enough about the assassination of the vice president to conclude whether or not it was just an isolated event.

The desk phone blared out, startling Helen into an upright position. She grabbed the receiver, but she didn't feel like speaking to anyone. Fortunately, the friendly voice on the other end of the line was a welcomed surprised.

"This is your favorite former employee calling from Guatemala," Tanner said.

"Tanner, it's so good to hear your voice," Helen answered wearily. It was clear that her frustration was evident a thousand miles away.

"Tough day in DC?" he asked.

Helen sighed in exasperation. "Take my word for it. You want to stay far away from DC. People can't think straight out here. It's just one big popularity contest."

"What's going on?" Tanner asked.

"I can't get anyone to consider the VP's murder was more than just an anomaly. Even the attorney general is telling me to drop it," Helen said.

"Yeah, but you don't work for him. You work for the president," Tanner said.

"We're in the middle of election season, and the AG has the president's undivided attention. They're trying to decide when to select a new vice president. The pollsters say if the president nominates someone right now, it could help his party get control of both houses of Congress during this election."

"That's interesting. I guess I hadn't really considered the vice president's assassination in a political aspect," Tanner said.

"Sometimes I wish I could go back and just be an analyst," Helen said.

Tanner laughed. "You could always come back out to Utah and work for me."

"Don't tempt me," Helen said. "I just might do it." She decided to get away from politics and into a topic that she found much more appealing. "What's going on down there?"

Tanner quickly summarized the group's efforts to locate Miguel. He told Helen that they had moved their search from Antigua to Lake Atitlán upon evidence from a bus driver that the Cipher had recently relocated there. Tanner also spoke about the single email uncovered by the QC team back in Utah. The message was sent almost two years ago, but it contained cipher-text similar to the original note found on the dead terrorist.

Helen listened to the update, digesting the information slowly. When Tanner finished, she added some thoughts of her own. "It sounds like you're on the right track to find Miguel, but it might not matter anymore. The president is growing weary of what you're doing down there."

"Does he think we're wasting our time?" Tanner asked.

"He's not ready to pull the plug just yet, but he's not interested in prolonging the search either. If you don't find Miguel in the next day or two, I bet he'll decide to have you come home," Helen said.

"Don't give up on us yet. We still might find him," Tanner said optimistically.

"Honestly, I'm beginning to have my own doubts," Helen said. "If we lose the president's support, this manhunt will fall apart quickly."

"Okay, we'll double our efforts," Tanner said.

Helen paused a second before changing the direction of the

conversation. "The connection between us sounds great. Are you using that phone with the EDES chip?"

She was referring to the new, ultra-fast encryption chip embedded in Tanner's cell phone. The ultra-secure phone had several classified patents for global satellite communication, but the device came with a hefty price tag. At $7,500 each, the device hadn't gained much adoption by other government agencies.

"How do I know if this has the chip?" Tanner asked.

"I guess you probably can't tell by just looking at it. But if that's the phone the FBI gave you before you left, it has the chip. I specifically requested it," Helen said.

"Well, you know me. I don't believe anything is completely secure," Tanner said. Helen laughed out loud at the comment. After working at the NSA, she completely understood Tanner's sentiment.

PANAJACHEL, GUATEMALA

The white Toyota Sequoia slowly drove down the streets of Panajachel. Located on the northeast shore of Lake Atitlán, Panajachel was more along the lines of what Tanner had expected to see in Guatemala. The small city didn't have any of the colonial grandeur of Antigua. Most of the buildings were constructed of gray cinder blocks, accenting the third world feel of the town. Although some foreigners visited this urban area, most of the tourists decided to remain at the upscale hotels directly overlooking the beautiful lake.

It was just about lunchtime, and Tanner and the others were following up on their second lead of the day. A street vendor, who set up her stand next to the bus terminal, said she remembered a person fitting the description of Miguel. The man had arrived in Panajachel several days ago. He bought a bottle of water from the vendor before slowly heading down the road toward a cathedral. With the information from the street merchant, Tanner and the others headed off toward the church.

Robert parked the Toyota Sequoia in front of the cathedral, but he left the engine running. "Wait here while I go inside," he said.

"Shouldn't we come in with you?" Glen asked.

"I think that might be too intrusive. I'm not sure how the priest would react to a bunch of North Americans looking for a Guatemalan. It would be best if I handled it," Robert said. He stepped out of the SUV and strode into the church. Out of the corner of his eye, he recognized the two deep-cover CIA agents waiting across the street in the tan Chevy Tahoe.

"How long do you think he'll be in there?" Megan asked. She was seated in the back of the SUV with her mom and Tanner, while Glen was in the front passenger seat.

"I'm not sure. I guess it all depends on if they are having any kind of service right now," Glen said.

"Do you think the Cipher is here?" Tanner asked.

"I hope so. He likes to follow the tourists so he can ask them for money."

"We better find him soon; the folks in DC are growing weary of our search. They think it's a waste of time and money," Tanner said. His statement hung in the open air. Everyone recognized that they needed a lucky break in their search or they would never find the Cipher.

Ten minutes later, their prayers were answered. Robert strode out of the church, almost skipping in a euphoric movement. He jumped in the car and exclaimed, "He's here. The Cipher is in Panajachel!"

"Where is he?" Glen asked.

"The priest spoke to him just the other day. The Cipher is living in an abandoned shack down by the river," Robert said. He pointed toward the medium-sized river that flowed into the lake on the edge of town.

"Let's go find him," Tanner said. The SUV flipped a U-turn in the road and headed toward the river just as the bell in the small cathedral started to chime.

APPROXIMATELY HALFWAY BETWEEN the cities of Baltimore, Maryland, and Washington, DC, is an Army installation called Fort Meade. Recognized as one of the most secretive military complexes in the world, Fort Meade is home to surreptitious organizations like the Defensive Information Systems Agency and the United States Cyber Command. The most clandestine group on the military base, however, is the National Security Agency. As part of the United States Department of Defense, the NSA is responsible for the collection and analysis of all foreign communication and signals intelligence. For better or for worse, the NSA is regarded as the premiere electronic intelligence gathering organization in the world.

The NSA tries to maintain a low profile, but many secret details of the agency were leaked by Edward Snowden in the summer of 2013. Billions of radio signals, Internet messages, phone calls, and other electronic communications are captured every day by the NSA. The most pertinent messages are recorded in hundreds of databases for further analysis. In addition to electronic eavesdropping, the NSA also works to protect critical government communications and information systems. Engineers and analysts at the NSA are also heavily involved in research and development on new software programs and hardware devices related to secure communications. In almost every way, the NSA is the Cyber-cop for the entire United States government.

Like many covert government agencies, the NSA has projects and teams that do not "officially" exist. One such classified operation is the quantum computer operated by Tanner and his peers in Utah. Another top-secret project is a highly sophisticated computer hacking team located in an inconspicuous building at Fort Meade. Created to mimic cyberattacks from foreign countries like China and Iran, the NSA's cyber-ops group is simply called the Red Team.

Lieutenant America Sakamoto was one such person who was fortunate enough to be a member of the elite Red Team. The thirty-eight-year-old Navy officer was a whiz when it came to website vulnerabilities. Her specialty was assessing and hacking web servers that ran everything from basic email services to highly sophisticated military tracking software. Over the past two years, America's penetration testing skills had earned her a unique reputation that was almost as unique as her name.

America Sakamoto was a third generation Japanese-American. After graduating from a Seattle high school, she moved across the country to study at the US Naval Academy in Annapolis, Maryland. Finishing in the top ten percent of her class, she caught the attention of a special recruiter associated with the NSA. After hearing the recruiter's pitch about some of the innovative computer work going on at the NSA, America accepted a commission to the super-secret government agency.

A staff sergeant stepped into Lieutenant Sakamoto's office and came to attention before speaking. "Lieutenant, you have a call from the admiral," he said.

America was reviewing the reports of her team's hacking exercise last week against a computer network managed by the State Department. The results clearly showed the Red Team had dominated the cyber-war simulation. She looked up from her desk with a confused expression.

"*The* admiral?" America asked, referring to the head over the entire NSA.

"Yes, ma'am," the enlisted man said. He left the office and closed the door.

Although it wasn't unheard of to have the director of the NSA call upon a member of the Red Team, it wasn't a normal occurrence either. America sat upright in her chair and prepared herself to take the waiting call. She had seen Admiral Lewis on several occasions, but she had never spoken with him directly.

"This is Lieutenant Sakamoto, sir," America said.

"Lieutenant, it's a pleasure to speak to you," the director of the NSA said. "Your name came with a high recommendation by someone on my staff."

"Thank you for the compliment, sir," America said. She was eager to understand the reason for the unexpected phone call. "What can I do for you, sir?"

"I've got a special project for you. It involves our group out in Utah," Admiral Lewis said.

While America had never directly interacted with her peers in Utah, she knew about the state-of-the-art data center and its ability to eavesdrop on Internet traffic. "I'd be glad to help out. What can you tell me about it, sir?" she asked.

"The folks in Utah are working on a special project for the National Security advisor. They found a suspicious email that came from a server somewhere in Mexico. They need your skills to help them hack into that computer," the admiral said.

"Why do they need access to the server?" America sincerely asked.

"They think it has a lot of other emails stored on it. They can't capture the messages on the Internet, so they need someone to get into the computer to look around."

"How soon do they need the information?" America asked.

"Yesterday," the admiral said. He lowered his voice. "This

is off the record, so you can't mention it to anyone, but they think the email server has information about the vice president's assassination."

The revelation was a big surprise to America, but she took her orders in stride. "I'll start on it right away," she said.

"Great. I want you to give me daily updates, but don't involve anyone else, got it?"

"Yes, sir," America said.

When the call ended, America leaned back in her office chair and thought about the short, but fascinating conversation she just had. Although the Red Team had implemented their skills against foreign nations like Syria and North Korea, hacking a computer system in Mexico was extremely unusual. Nevertheless, she didn't question her orders. They came directly from the top, and that was all the explanation she needed.

OCTOBER 26
PANAJACHEL, GUATEMALA

WHEN THE WHITE Toyota Sequoia pulled up to the dilapidated shack just outside the town of Panajachel, the attitude of the occupants seemed to change. An optimistic wave of energy filled the vehicle, causing Tanner and the others to speculate that their search for the Cipher was drawing to a close.

"This just might be it," Glen said. He looked out the window from the front passenger seat. "It fits the type of place where the Cipher would live."

The one-room shack stood among a small grove of trees next to a river. Examining the exterior of the hut, Tanner easily concluded this was the home of a pauper. It was meager in every sense of the word. Rotted-out wood framed the sides and top of the dwelling. Scraps of tar paper overlaid the roof in a feeble attempt to weatherproof the structure. There were no windows, just a couple of open holes in the wall for ventilation and light. A tattered piece of cloth hung over the entrance, providing a makeshift door for the house.

"Buenos días," Robert shouted, leading the group from the car. He stopped their procession about twenty feet away from the home. He wanted to make sure they didn't startle the owner.

A faint male voice rose out of the shack, quietly answering in Spanish. A few seconds later, a frail old man looked past the cloth that draped over the entrance. With a perplexed expression on his face, he stepped out into the noonday sun.

It had to be the Cipher.

Tanner gazed in awkward silence as he got his first good look at the mysterious man. When his father-in-law had said the Cipher was a hundred years old, Tanner thought Glen had been exaggerating. However, the man who had just come out of the shack looked like he might have witnessed the great Guatemala earthquake of 1773.

The Cipher's dark skin was wrinkled and worn. He was practically bald, but he still had a few strands of hair on the top and sides of his head. Shorter than most Guatemalans, the Cipher accentuated his small stature by hunching over. His clothes were ill fitted and worn, yet he didn't look malnourished. Overall he appeared in every way to be the simple hermit that Tanner had envisioned.

"That's him," Glen whispered in Tanner's ear.

"He's really old," Tanner whispered back, unsure of what else to say.

Robert cautiously moved ahead of the group and spoke to the Cipher. The old man paused and then said something in return. Robert replied, and the Cipher shook his head in disagreement. The old man appeared reluctant to help out.

"He doesn't want to talk," Glen said. "He thinks Robert is a cop or something."

Julie, hearing the exchange between Robert and the Cipher, slowly stepped forward and took the CIA agent by the arm. "Let me talk to him," she said. Robert stood back, making room for Julie to try her approach.

Julie gently shook the old man's hand and asked if he remembered her. Suddenly, the Cipher's eyes opened wide as he became more alert. A smile, which was missing most of its teeth, broke out across his face. He grabbed Julie's arm with both of his hands and replied that he did recognize her.

"He always liked her," Glen said to nobody in particular.

Tanner and the others waited patiently while Julie interacted with the lonely man. His countenance softened as he let down his guard. The Cipher motioned for Julie and the others to follow him inside.

"He's inviting us in," Julie said to the others.

When Tanner entered the hut, he found it mostly bare. The floor was dirt. A small bed with a tattered blanket lay against one side of the room. Next to the bed was a wooden nightstand with a small pitcher of water and a bowl. A few open boxes of food were stored under the bed. Looking around, Tanner didn't see any sign of electricity or running water.

The Cipher walked over and sat down on his shabby mattress. Julie took a seat next to the old man, while the others in the group stood back about ten feet. It was obvious the Cipher trusted Julie, and everyone seemed content to let her handle the delicate situation.

"We should have brought him something to eat," Tanner said.

"I have a granola bar from yesterday," Megan said. She reached into the side pocket on her cargo pants. She quietly leaned forward and offered the food to her mother. In turn, Julie offered the snack to the Cipher. The old man smiled and accepted the gift.

Tanner wondered how the Cipher would be able to eat since he was missing most of his teeth. But he eagerly grabbed the granola bar, opened the wrapper, and started gnawing on the food. It was then that Tanner realized the Cipher wasn't as fragile as he had first appeared. Even though he permanently bent forward and moved slower than normal, he still opened the granola bar with a fair amount of dexterity.

The visitors waited in silence as the Cipher enjoyed his snack. Then, without warning, he spewed out several sentences in Spanish. His rapid and concise speech caught everyone off guard.

"I guess he can still communicate well," Megan whispered to the others.

Julie, who was sitting on the bed next to the Cipher, spoke a few sentences in response to the old man's sudden outpouring. Then she looked toward Tanner.

"He wants to know why we are here. Do you have that piece of paper with the message on it?" Julie asked.

Reaching into the backpack that he had carried with him ever since he arrived in Guatemala, Tanner took out a copy of the encrypted note. He handed the message to Julie. She then gave the note to the Cipher and asked if he could determine what language it was.

"I guess we're about to find out whether or not our search was justified," Robert said to Tanner.

The room was silent for nearly a minute. Holding the sheet of paper close to his aged eyes, the Cipher studied the message. He shook his head several times, as if he was confused and needed to clear his mind. Finally, after great anticipation, the Cipher spewed out an answer in rapid Spanish.

"Whoa, have him say that again," Robert told Julie. She politely asked the Cipher to repeat his message, and this time the other Spanish speakers understood what the old man had said.

"Impossible," Robert exclaimed. He turned to Tanner and gave him a fascinating translation. "He says it's Itza."

"What's Itza?" Tanner asked.

Glen looked toward his son-in-law. "It's an ancient Guatemalan dialect that was spoken in the Petén region, next to the border of Mexico." A big smile formed on his face. "You were right," he said, giving Tanner a celebratory slap on his back.

"But it's a dead language. Nobody out there speaks it anymore," Robert said.

"There might be a handful of elders in some of the Mayan tribes who still understand it," Glen said.

"That wouldn't matter. Itza was never written. It was only a spoken language," Robert said. He turned his focus back to Julie. He instructed her to ask the Cipher how he could read Itza.

Julie asked the simple question, but she got a long explanation in return. The old man spoke for several minutes, probably relating part of his history in the process. When the Cipher ended his last sentence, his words hung in the air. For a moment, everyone was quiet. Nobody wanted to disturb the astonishing claim the Cipher had just made. But Tanner was dying to know what had shocked everyone, and he broke the silence by asking Robert for a translation.

When Robert turned around to face Tanner, he only muttered one word, "Incredible." He shook his head in disbelief.

"Wait. What's incredible?" Tanner asked.

Glen answered, giving his son-in-law a better summary. "The Cipher says his great-grandfather taught him how to speak Itza when he was a boy. Apparently, his great-grandfather had learned Itza from a Catholic priest when he lived in Flores over 200 years ago. Flores is the capital of the Petén region," he clarified.

Robert added to Glen's explanation of the fascinating story. "The Cipher's great-grandfather was the favorite altar boy of the Catholic priest. The priest taught him how to speak Itza so that he could help out with the Mayans when they came to church."

"You said that Itza was never written. How does the Cipher know it's Itza if nobody wrote it down?" Megan asked. Robert motioned for Julie to ask the Cipher for an explanation, but what happened next completely shocked the group.

The Cipher didn't verbally respond to Julie's inquiry. Instead, he reached under his bed and pulled out a frayed burlap sack. He carefully opened the bag and removed a rolled up towel. Slowly unfolding the frayed cloth, the Cipher uncovered a worn but beautiful book. He handed the fragile artifact to Julie. Larger and thicker than a normal book, the object appeared to be a journal or ledger. Julie gingerly opened it and glanced at the contents.

"It's a Bible," she said to the rest of the group.

"A Bible?" Glen asked. He seemed confused.

Julie carefully stood up and stepped over to show her husband the book. Robert also leaned in to see what she was holding.

Unfortunately, Tanner and Megan were standing behind the others, and they couldn't see what was so fascinating.

"It's not just a Bible. It's a handwritten copy with translations between Spanish and Itza!" Robert said, almost shouting out in surprise. The CIA agent quickly stepped back to let Tanner and his wife have a look.

The custom-made Bible was extremely old but lovingly kept. Bound in rich leather, the yellow-faded, oversized pages contained two columns of handwritten text. On the left side was the original Spanish. On the right was a translation of the words into Itza. Although many of the words were faded, the document was still legible.

Sensing the group's fascination with his most prized possession, the Cipher quietly spoke from his bed. After a moment, Julie translated the conversation for Tanner. "The book belonged to his great-grandfather. He manually copied the important stories of the New Testament in Spanish, and then wrote a corresponding translation into Itza."

Robert added more details. "But it's just a rough translation into Itza. The Cipher said his grandfather guessed at some of the Itza phrases, using bits and pieces from other native dialects."

"Still, this is the closest thing to what the Itza language might have looked like. Do you know what kind of archeological find this is?" Glen asked. He carefully turned a few of the pages. "This could be the discovery of the century."

Tanner's focus shifted from the antique Bible back to the old man sitting on the bed. The Cipher was studying the sheet of paper with the encrypted text that Julie had given him. Tanner motioned for the others to pay attention to the old man. He was getting ready to translate the contents. Carefully and slowly, the Cipher read parts of the letter aloud in Spanish.

"It sounds like a list of times and locations," Robert said. "Maybe it's an agenda of some sort."

"No, it's not an agenda. It's a detailed itinerary," Glen said. "It's for something in Panama."

The hair on the back of Tanner's neck stood up at the mention of Panama.

"Whose itinerary is it?" Megan asked. Quickly, Julie translated her daughter's question for the Cipher.

The old man skipped to the last part of the message. It took him some time to answer the question, but Tanner didn't need to wait for the translation. He had already figured out that the encrypted message contained the confidential travel arrangements for the former vice president of the United States.

Plichwaajpds
hu'ltaqwr
xir'kun
rosadh
ihvaral-
dikdakils
achik'axtxAji

OCTOBER 26
FORT MEADE, MARYLAND

LIEUTENANT AMERICA SAKAMOTO listened to the explanation from a civilian employee named Mel Otterson. While she didn't know specifically what Mel did for the NSA, she quickly recognized that he needed the skills of a professional computer hacker.

"You said that you don't know the IP address for this backup computer?" America asked.

"That's right," Mel said.

"If I don't have an IP address, I can't identify which computer you want access to," she said.

Lieutenant Sakamoto was referring to the IP or Internet Protocol address. Every computer on the Internet had an IP address. It was a unique number that identified a specific computer. In many ways, the IP address acted like a computer's individual phone number. It allowed the computer to connect and talk to other systems across the world.

"All we have is the physical address of the backup facility. Sorry, I know it's not much to go on," Mel said.

America thought of a different option. "Where's the primary data center again?" she asked.

"Mexico City."

"Chances are they have some kind of routine to sync up the computers between the two facilities. Otherwise, the failover site would have outdated information if the primary site went down," America said. "I might be able to sniff the network traffic during the sync process and isolate the backup server that way."

"That might work," Mel said.

"This computer is an email server, right?" America asked.

"That's correct."

"Good. My specialty is getting into systems like that."

"Okay, what do you need from me?" asked Mel.

"Send me a copy of the original email you found. I'll take a look at it and see what I can determine," America said.

"When will you know if you can get any information from that backup server?" Mel asked.

"That's difficult to tell. First of all, I have to isolate the server. Then I have to check and see how vulnerable it is. If the server hasn't been patched for common weaknesses, it will be pretty quick for me to hack into it. But if it's maintained, I'll have to do some more creative stuff. Depending on how deep I have to go, it could take a week or more," America said.

PANAJACHEL, GUATEMALA

"Why does that message mention the vice president?" Julie innocently asked.

Tanner couldn't blame his mother-in-law for posing the question. It was a natural and obvious query. Even though he wasn't authorized to do so, Tanner decided it was time to let his family know the full purpose behind their trip.

"That note was found on one of the people who assassinated the vice president, but nobody could crack the code. I had a hunch that the message might be a rare dialect, and that's why we needed to track him down," Tanner said, gesturing toward the Cipher.

"That's right," Robert added.

Tanner pressed forward. He needed his mother-in-law's help to determine if there was anything else hidden in the message. "Does the note mention who ordered the attack?" Tanner asked.

Julie again translated the question, and the Cipher examined the contents of the letter. After a few moments, he answered. Julie nodded her head and spoke to the group. "He's having problems understanding some of the words, but it sounds like the letter spells out someone named Votan."

"Who's Votan?" Glen asked.

"It might be somebody's last name," Megan speculated.

"It's not that," Robert said. "Votan is the Mayan god of death and war. There's a lot of mythology down here regarding Votan coming to earth to start a new society or kingdom."

An intense silence fell over the room.

Tanner went back to the encrypted message, ignoring the implications of Robert's uncomfortable revelation. "That's it? There's nothing else?" he asked.

Julie poised the question to the Cipher. "He says the letter has several words he doesn't understand, but that's the bulk of the message."

Nobody spoke as the group processed the meaning of the letter. The most obvious fact was that someone named Votan had sold out the vice president of the United States.

"I wonder how the bad guys were able to encode that message into Itza," Tanner asked. "Does he know if anyone else can write Itza like that?"

Julie turned to the Cipher and asked the question. The Cipher nodded his head and gave a response. The answer startled both Glen and Robert, but Tanner had to wait for a translation to understand the significance.

"He says his great-grandfather made two copies of the book, one for himself and one for the priest. This copy was his great-grandfather's," Julie said, lifting up the copy of the book in her hands. "But the priest's copy was lost and never found."

"Do you think the terrorists found the other copy and used it to encrypt their messages?" Megan asked.

"That would be my guess," Tanner said.

Robert turned toward the group and spoke with excitement. "Remember how the Cipher said his great-grandfather learned Itza when he lived out in Flores?"

"Yeah," Tanner said.

"Flores is the center of the Petén district. Petén is like a state, but it's not very developed. It kind of reminds me of the Alaskan frontier, only with jungles and much hotter."

"Okay," Tanner said. He wondered where the conversation was going.

Robert continued explaining his idea. "The drug lords use Petén as the staging ground for their drug shipments to the US. The jungles out there are infested with drug runners. I'm betting you one of the drug cartels stumbled upon the second copy of that Bible, and they figured it was the perfect way to conceal their conversations."

"That might explain why the bad guys went after the vice president. He was strongly opposed to drugs," Megan said.

Tanner added to his wife's observation. "The current president's second term ends in two years. He can't run again, so the vice president would likely have been the next candidate for president. If I was a drug lord, I'd take out the vice president before he ever got to the White House."

Just like that, the small group found their answers. They understood the contents of the encrypted message and who the likely suspects were. However, Tanner knew they weren't completely done with their investigation. "We've got to get the Cipher and his book back to the embassy," he stated.

"Why? He already told us what the message means," Glen said.

"There are likely other messages out there besides this one," Tanner said.

Glen looked confused. "Really? Where are the other ones?"

"Out on the Internet somewhere," Tanner said. "We need to create a key so we can decrypt any other emails we might find. We'll need the Cipher and his book to do that."

"Should I see if he wants to come back with us?" Julie asked. She was still seated on the bed next to the old man.

"Yes, and tell him that we'll take him where he can get some food and a lot more of this," Robert said. He took a small wad of money out of his pocket and handed it to the old man.

The bribe seemed to work. The Cipher nodded his head and answered that he would go back to Guatemala City with the unusual tourists.

OCTOBER 26
PANAJACHEL, GUATEMALA

AFTER RETURNING TO the hotel and packing their belongings, Robert took the Cipher and the others out for a quick lunch. It was a mini-celebration for their success in cracking the encoded message, but the meal was ill-timed. As the white Toyota Sequoia navigated the steep road from the edge of the lake up to the highlands above, Tanner's stomach rebelled with an acid-filled burp. "Maybe we should have waited to eat until after we got off this crazy road," he said.

The highway out of Panajachel had many tight turns, accented by sharp drop-offs to the basin below. The fact that the road was just one lane in each direction made the journey even more precarious.

"It wasn't this scary on the way down," Megan said. She turned her gaze away from the unprotected drop-off. "But I guess it was nighttime when we got here."

Despite the dangerous driving conditions, Robert handled the curvy road like a pro. Glen rode in the passenger seat next to the CIA agent. In the middle seat, Megan and Julie sat next to the Cipher, who had hardly said a word since he left his home. In his lap, the Cipher held the burlap sack containing his rare copy of the translated Bible. In the very back of the SUV, Tanner sat next to a pile of luggage in the tiny and cramped third-row seat.

"Can you take it a little slower, please? I'm getting car sick back here," Tanner said. He wasn't sure how long his stomach would handle the road that twisted like a coiled snake.

"Sure," Robert said. He slowed down the vehicle to a crawl.

"I wonder who Votan is," Megan said out loud.

"I've been thinking about that," Robert said. "It's obviously a code name for someone who's familiar with Mayan mythology, but I don't have any clue who it is." He braked hard, practically stopping the SUV to navigate around a tight turn.

"Tanner, what will it take to create a key so you can crack other messages?" Glen asked.

"First, we'll have to make copies of the Cipher's Bible. Then someone will have to input each Itza word and its English equivalent into a computer database. Once all the information is in there, the computer will be able to quickly decode any new messages. The most time consuming process will be inputting every word into the computer," Tanner said. "But if we can have a bunch of people working on different pages as the same time, it will go much faster."

"You forgot a step," Julie said from the middle seat. "You'll need to find people who can speak both Spanish and English. All the Itza translations are in Spanish, and you'll have to convert them into English to do you any good because the Cipher doesn't know any English." She glanced over at the old man. Unable to understand the conversation, he appeared to have drifted off to sleep.

Megan noticed her mother's longer than usual gaze. "I wonder if he has anyone around to care for him," she said.

"He never married, and all his family is now dead," Julie said.

"Maybe we could convince him to come back with us," Glen said. "He has nothing here. You saw the horrible conditions he was living in."

"I could talk with some folks at the State Department and see what they think. Maybe they can do something to . . . ," Robert said as his voice trailed off.

A black sedan zipped by on the opposite lane of the highway. Suddenly, a cloud of smoke appeared as the car locked its tires and screeched to a halt. Flipping a dangerous U-turn on a narrow section of the highway, the sedan accelerated back up the road toward the white Toyota Sequoia.

"Hold on, everyone! We've got trouble!" Robert shouted. He smashed down the accelerator, causing the SUV to lurch forward.

Tanner looked out the rear window at the fast approaching car. Just like he had seen in the movies a hundred times, a man leaned out the passenger window and pointed something at the fleeing SUV.

"I think he's got a gun," Tanner said. Suddenly, two loud "pops" rang out, causing him to duck for cover.

"Everyone get down!" Robert screamed. He tried to outrun the pursuing car, but he had to slam on the brakes to make a hairpin turn. The black sedan smashed hard into the rear bumper of the Toyota Sequoia, pushing everyone forward in their seats. Again, two more shots rang out, and the rear window of the SUV shattered. One of the bullets narrowly missed Tanner's head and exploded in a puff of foam in the ceiling.

Robert fishtailed around the corner and stomped on the gas. The risky maneuver caused everyone in the SUV to shout out in panic, except for the Cipher, who was inexplicably still asleep.

"Who's shooting at us?" Megan screamed.

Tanner quickly glanced over the shattered glass and out the rear window. The black sedan had slowed down to make the same tight corner, giving him the chance to get a good look at the suspects. "It's two men with dark hair. They look like Guatemalans," he said.

"Tanner, here!" Robert yelled from the driver's seat. He passed something back with his free hand.

It was a gun.

"Shoot back at them!" Robert shouted, shaking the gun's handle.

Tanner had never fired a gun in his life. He wasn't really fond of firearms, but it wasn't because he was anti-gun. He just never had a reason to own one.

"Take it!" Robert shouted with increasing urgency. Another curve was fast approaching, and he needed both hands on the steering wheel to navigate the tight turn.

Tanner's senses slowed down as he reached over the middle seat and grabbed the pistol. In a calm yet disjointed way, he turned and pointed the weapon out the opening where the rear window had been. He pulled the trigger. The 9mm Beretta fired surprisingly easy, but it kicked a lot more than Tanner had expected. His shot at the pursuing vehicle missed wildly.

Robert slammed on the brakes and threw the SUV around another corner. The sudden change of momentum caused everyone to smash up against the left side of the car. The black sedan, anticipating that the Toyota Sequoia would have to slow down to make the tight turn, took the opportunity to land a glancing blow against the corner of the SUV. The Toyota fishtailed, but Robert expertly turned the vehicle into the spin and brought the SUV safely out of the turn. Again, two more shots were fired from the pursuing black car. One hit the tailgate of the SUV and the other one destroyed the passenger's side mirror.

"Shoot again! Shoot again!" Robert ordered.

Tanner sat up, shielding himself against a suitcase that realistically didn't provide any protection. Pointing the gun at the pursuing black car, he prepared to pull the trigger. He stopped short of squeezing his finger when he noticed another vehicle fast approaching in the distance.

It was the tan Chevy Tahoe they had traveled in the previous day. Cruising up the hill at an insane pace, Tanner wondered who was driving that SUV. The occupants of the black sedan were so focused on their pursuit that they failed to notice the Chevy Tahoe barreling up the road behind them. Just as the sedan slowed down to make a turn, the Tahoe smashed full-speed into the side of the black car. The momentum of the larger SUV completely overpowered the small sedan. In serene slow motion, Tanner watched the black car go into a sideway skid and plunge over the edge of the cliff.

Unfortunately, the Chevy Tahoe was still moving at an incredible speed. The driver had to do everything in his power to keep his vehicle on the road. He flipped the SUV around at the last second, smashing the rear bumper into a road sign. The metal pole held just long enough for the driver to stomp on the gas. A large cloud of dust formed, obscuring the vehicle. Suddenly, the tan Tahoe shot out of the haze, accelerating away from the cliff's dangerous edge.

"Is everyone okay?" Robert shouted.

The passengers in the car were still in shock at the quick turn of events.

"Tanner, talk to me!" Robert yelled. The wind rushing through the broken window was making it hard to communicate.

"I'm fine," Tanner said. He still had the handgun pointed out the back of the SUV. Off in the distance, he could see the Chevy Tahoe approaching quickly.

"I think we're okay," Julie answered for the passengers in the middle seat. She leaned over and checked on the Cipher. The old man was awake now, wondering what he had just missed.

"I smashed my head on the dash," Glen said. He pulled his hand away from his forehead. It was covered in blood.

"Dad, you're bleeding!" Megan shouted. Red liquid oozed down her father's face.

"I don't think it's very deep. Just give me something to put over it," Glen said.

Tanner quickly reached into his suitcase and pulled out one of his T-shirts. "Here," he said. He passed the makeshift bandage up to his father-in-law. Glen took the gray shirt and pressed it against his injury.

"There's a field kit under your seat. It has bandages and everything you'll need," Robert said.

Tanner observed that the CIA agent's eyes remained in a hawk-like focus as he continued surveying the situation. A few moments later, the Toyota finally crested over the top of the hill and leveled out on the flat road. The sudden and unexpected flash of danger had passed.

Robert's cell phone rang out. He pulled the device out of his shirt pocket and answered without much of a greeting. "We're okay. How about you?"

Looking out the broken window in the back of the SUV, Tanner saw the passenger in the Chevy Tahoe on the phone. He figured Robert was talking with that man.

"Did you ID them?" Robert asked. The rest of the car rode in silence as they listened to one side of the conversation.

"Agreed, it's too risky. We go straight to the airport," Robert said. He disconnected the brief call and then spoke to the passengers in his SUV. "Those were my helpers. They're in the Chevy behind us. It looks like we just had a run in with the Chiapas cartel. Those were probably the same guys who were after us in Antigua."

"Where did they go?" Megan asked.

"Over the edge," Robert said callously.

"Do they know we have the Cipher?" Tanner shouted from the rear seat.

"I'm not sure, but they clearly didn't like what we're doing. That's why I'm taking you straight to the airport. We'll have a private jet ready to take you home when we get there."

"What about him?" Glen asked. He pointed with his thumb toward the confused Cipher in the middle seat.

"Looks like he's getting a first-class trip to the United States," Robert said.

GUATEMALA CITY, GUATEMALA

Tanner stood on the tarmac at a secure and private section of the Guatemala City International Airport. A Gulfstream jet was fueled up and ready for the flight back to the United States. Megan, her parents, and the Cipher were already on board. The old man grinned like a little child when he found out that he was going to the United States. He had never been on a plane, and it was something that he had always wanted to do.

Tanner firmly shook Robert's hand. "Thanks for everything."

"It was good working with you. I'm glad that I got you back here in one piece," Robert shouted as the plane's jet engines started up.

"We couldn't have done it without you," Tanner said.

"Likewise," Robert replied. "You're one heck of an analyst."

Tanner gave Robert a final handshake and turned to board the plane. He stopped just as he got to the bottom of the staircase. "Hey, what's your real name?"

Robert let out a laugh. "You wouldn't believe me if I told you."

Tanner smiled back. "Try me!" he yelled. The jet engines were getting so loud that it was almost too noisy to hear.

"It's also Miguel!" the CIA agent shouted. With a wave of his hand, Robert turned and walked off toward his banged-up SUV.

OCTOBER 26
GEORGETOWN, WASHINGTON, DC

H IS ALIAS WAS Votan. Wickedly smart and devilishly handsome, the sixty-two-year-old was a power broker among the Washington elite. His permanent tan and his silver-gray hair added to the allure of his captivating personality. Ever since he could remember, Votan had craved attention. He constantly searched for ways to feed his ego, just like a hungry tiger that stalked the jungle.

Votan was gifted in many aspects, but his oratory skills were exceptionally polished. He had the unique ability to read and inspire people, but he didn't use his talents to make the world a better place. Instead, he leveraged his charisma to usurp power and control. He was smarter than most people, and he viewed his intelligence as justification for his supremacy. Completely blinded by his arrogance, Votan had an ambitious goal—he desperately wanted to overthrow the government and become the sole leader of the United States.

Unfortunately for Votan, the pathway to permanent leadership in the United States had no precedent. To become a president for life, he had to disregard a menacing document called the

Constitution of the United States. While he truly believed the Constitution to be obsolete, Votan knew that he couldn't become a king until he convinced approximately 315 million of his fellow citizens to also abandon the Constitution.

To fulfill his misdirected vision, he created a secret society called the Order of 28. Each handpicked member of the order had sworn allegiance to Votan, sustaining him as their new king. In exchange for their loyalty, the members of the Order of 28 were promised positions of leadership and authority in his new regime. With his devoted accomplices fully supporting him, Votan was prepared to make his sweeping change.

The venomous traitor logged into his computer and checked an email from one of his coconspirators. Votan had only met Javier Soto once. It was during the drug lord's initiation into the Order of 28. As the last member to join the secret society, Javier was the force of violence, planning and executing the vice president's assassination in Panama. In his email to Votan, Javier reiterated his cartel's goal to carry out the murders of several additional high-profile politicians in the coming days.

Finished reading the email, Votan crafted his email response and ran it through the encryption process. Like his fellow collaborators in the Order of 28, Votan didn't understand how the encoding routine worked. Nevertheless, he completely trusted Javier because the drug lord had used the same encryption process for years in his cartel. Confident that his response was sufficiently scrambled, Votan saved the message as a draft copy and logged off the shared email account.

FORT MEADE, MARYLAND

Lieutenant America Sakamoto was looking through the enormous list of saved emails when a new message suddenly appeared. Similar to the thousands of other encrypted letters on the email server, this one also contained gibberish. Nevertheless, the fact that someone had just posted a draft email verified that at least one person was actively using the server.

Hacking the computer system didn't take nearly as long as Lieutenant Sakamoto had anticipated. But she was always conservative in her approach, and she had intentionally padded her estimate with extra time to account for any unseen problems that she might encounter. Using the NSA's clandestine access points on the backbone of the Internet, she eavesdropped on all the network traffic going between Mexico City and Hermosillo. Sniffing the data as it flowed across the wire, she isolated the specific communication between the two data centers described by the analysts in Utah. She tapped into that data pipeline and pilfered the IP address to the email server at the backup facility. The email system wasn't well maintained, and it was vulnerable to an unpublicized web server bug. Ironically, it was the exact same exploit that America had used the previous week during her team's penetration test against the State Department's email servers.

Once Lieutenant Sakamoto got shell access to the base operating system of the computer, she initiated a buffer overflow routine to grant herself administrator privileges. She then created a hidden account, allowing herself to log back into the computer as a valid user. Before signing off as the root user, she covered her footsteps by deleting the last section in all the log files. Only an extremely astute and very lucky computer operator would ever know that the email server had been compromised.

Despite her initial success in hacking the computer, America's work was far from done. For the past three hours she had been snooping around on the server using the backdoor account she had created for herself. She had determined several things from her examination so far. First, the base computer system was a virtual machine running a standard Linux operating system. It was similar to millions of web servers found in data centers all over the world. Second, the server had only one shared user account. Multiple IP addresses were listed in the host access log, signifying that users from all over the world had logged into this same account.

And third, after looking through the records, it was obvious that the emails exchanged between the users never left the system. The people who accessed this server never wanted their messages sent out over the Internet.

The most unusual thing about the computer system was, by far, the unsent emails. Every single email contained strings of random nonsense, and America had yet to find a message that she could read. Nevertheless, she knew this was precisely what the folks in Utah were looking for, so she started downloading copies of the messages for further analysis.

While she transferred megabytes of unsent emails, America uploaded some of her own special binaries on the server. These stealthy scripts, or mini-programs, would notify her whenever someone logged into the system. A detailed copy of every transaction the computer made would then be emailed back to Lieutenant Sakamoto in an untraceable fashion. This way, she would keep constant watch on the server without having to remain logged in all the time.

The download of the email files completed, and America logged out of the system, confident that she would get a copy of any future messages as soon as they were saved. She quickly crafted a private email for the director of the NSA, updating him on her special assignment. She then zipped up all the downloaded messages and sent them off to Mel Otterson in Utah. Finished with her task, America checked her watch. There was a twenty-four hour café down the road that had the best pie in the world. Even though it was well past midnight, she decided it was time for a celebration.

SALT LAKE CITY, UTAH

Just as Lieutenant America Sakamoto finished her work at NSA headquarters, a private, black-and-white Gulfstream jet landed at Salt Lake International Airport. The small airplane, however, didn't taxi toward the main concourse like all the other passenger jets. Instead, the jet headed straight for a secure section of the airport that belonged to the Utah Air National Guard. The Gulfstream didn't come to a complete stop until it was safely concealed inside a large hanger, hidden from the eyes of curious travelers at the late hour.

The stairs of the Gulfstream jet had barely been lowered when Tanner came down the steps. He was met by a small cadre of FBI agents, who had been assigned to protect Tanner and the mysterious Cipher known only as Miguel.

"Welcome back," the senior FBI agent said. He extended his hand toward Tanner.

Tanner shook the agent's hand. "Thanks."

"Where's Miguel?" the FBI agent asked.

"He's coming, but he moves slowly," Tanner said. "When do they head out?" he asked, gesturing his thumb back toward the jet.

Tanner and the Cipher were the only ones getting off in Salt Lake. Megan and her parents still had another leg of their journey to complete. They were flying back to Albuquerque to drop off Glen and Julie. Then Megan would fly to southern Utah to rendezvous with the kids. She planned on staying the night in St. George before getting a ride back to Salt Lake City with Tanner's parents.

"They'll head out as soon as the aircraft is refueled," the FBI agent said.

Tanner nodded his head. "Excellent." He looked up at the top of the stairs. Megan was helping the Cipher get off the plane. It took a couple of minutes for him to descend the steps, but soon the Cipher was on the ground. A female FBI agent, who was fluent in Spanish, approached the old man and carefully took him by the hand. She greeted her guest and then guided him to a waiting Suburban.

Tanner turned toward his wife. "I love you," he said, pulling her in for a kiss and prolonged hug.

"I love you too. Be safe," Megan replied.

"I will."

"I know you're going to be busy, but give me a call when you have a chance," Megan said.

"Will do." Tanner gave his wife another hug and then jumped into the waiting Suburban. It was fortunate that he had managed to catch several hours of sleep on the way home from Guatemala. He knew he wouldn't be sleeping anytime soon.

OCTOBER 27
NSA DATA CENTER, UTAH

I T WAS GOOD to be back. Although Tanner was weary from his long flight, he felt at ease inside the secure walls of the Bumblehive. The isolated NSA building, with armed sentries and a twenty-foot fence, was the perfect spot for his upcoming task. With his wife safely in route to pick up the children, Tanner was now free to dedicate his time to creating the Itza-to-English decryption algorithm.

It was just after 1:00 a.m., and Tanner was in a large meeting room on the first floor of the data center. Two members of his team were present, including a dozen other NSA employees. The additional staff members had been hastily called in to help with the translation of the Cipher's Bible. These NSA employees were fluent in both English and Spanish, many of them having learned Spanish while serving missions for the Mormon Church. Two additional employees were also present to help take care of the Cipher. While the old man was out of his element, he seemed to be taking the uncertainty of the past twelve hours in stride. He was tucked away in the corner of the large room, sleeping on a couch that had been commandeered from the lobby.

Kevin Granger located a photocopier that could handle the larger pages of the Cipher's Bible. He had it wheeled down into the conference room, and he was now making the copies of the first pages of the Bible. Seated at their makeshift workstations around the room, the bored analysts waited patiently to get their copies and start the translation process.

"I wonder if there's something we should be doing to take care of that Bible," Sydney Littlefield asked Tanner. The book was, after all, a rare antiquity.

The thought had crossed Tanner's mind also, and he instructed Kevin to be extra careful while making his copies. But Tanner wasn't a trained archivist, and he wasn't sure how else to protect the two-hundred-year-old book. "If we were back in DC, we could probably find someone at the National Archives who would know how to take care of a book like that."

"But does an archivist have a security clearance?" Sydney asked.

"Probably, but maybe not a top secret one," Tanner said.

Just then, Mel Otterson and Rachel York came into the conference room. They were each carrying a large bag of food and drinks purchased from a local twenty-four-hour supermarket. The snacks weren't anything special, but it was the least that Tanner could do after summoning some of his peers back to work in the middle of the night.

As Mel and Rachel handed out the food to the bilingual analysts, Tanner decided to get things going. Technically, there were several managers in the room who outranked Tanner, but their presence was mostly to keep the all-night cram session running smoothly. In the end, this was Tanner's party, and he moved toward the front of the room to address the group.

"Thanks everyone for coming back to work. I know this isn't what you normally do," he said. "But we have something going on tonight that you won't regret being part of. In fact, I think we're witnessing a little bit of history in the making."

Tanner briefly related the background of the Cipher's Bible, and the importance of creating an algorithm to decipher the strange Itza dialect. He explained that each bilingual analyst would simultaneously work on a different section of the Bible. Using their laptops, they would input their best-guest English translation for the Itza words found in the Bible. All the information would be correlated into a shared database to create a master decryption key. "It's important to make sure that you focus on translating the individual words and not worry about the complete sentence," Tanner said. "If you see a word that you can't figure out, write it down and we'll ask the Cipher to translate it for us."

"How long do we have to get this done?" a female analyst asked.

"It will take several days to do it all, but we don't need to be completely finished to be successful," Tanner said. "Many words in the Bible are repeated, so we only need to figure out the translation once. As you go along, the program on your laptops will alert you if someone else has already finished translating the word you are working on."

"This looks like a lot of work. Why don't we just scan the Bible into the computer and use some optical character recognition tools to figure it out?" another analyst asked.

"Unfortunately, this strange Itza language doesn't lend itself well to digital scanning. And, as you'll soon see, some of the handwritten ink is already fading. We're just going to have to do the translation the old-fashioned way," Tanner said.

"Is anyone else going to help?" someone else asked.

"We're organizing a second shift to come in and take over around noon," Tanner said. "But remember, we don't need every word translated to figure out the general context of an encrypted message."

Kevin finished copying the first dozen or so pages of the Bible, and he was now passing out the copies to the analysts. The quiet group looked at their handouts, getting their first glimpse of the bizarre Itza language.

"Are there any questions?" Tanner asked. The analysts remained silent, and he took that as a sign they were ready to get to work.

"Good luck," he said. The linguists turned toward their laptops and started their ominous task.

Mel walked over to Tanner and handed him a cold Mountain Dew. "Maybe we should have the old man go through some of those encrypted emails we pulled off the server. He could possibly translate them on the fly," he said.

Tanner thought about Mel's suggestion. "That's a good idea. Print off a dozen or so emails for him to look at once he wakes up. Maybe he can determine something by directly translating them."

The bilingual analysts quietly worked on their translation. The process was slow as they familiarized themselves with the Bible's unique layout. An hour later, they were up to speed and working diligently. Tanner and Mel excused themselves to call Helen, leaving the remaining members of the QC team behind to monitor the translation.

Walking toward the team's private conference room, Tanner opened the door for Mel before closing it behind them. He then grabbed the secure speakerphone in the center of the table and dialed the extension to Washington, DC. After two rings, a chipper female voice answered.

"Good morning," Helen said.

Tanner checked his watch and realized that it was 4:40 a.m. Eastern Time. "Oh yeah, it's already morning out there," he said with a yawn. For Tanner and the others in Utah, it still felt like midnight.

"I normally get into work at five, but it wasn't much of a hassle to come in sooner," Helen said. "I arrived early to get an update on what was happening out there."

"We've got a dozen different people working on the translation right now," Tanner told Helen. "We didn't have much time to prepare, but I think our makeshift translation center will work."

"We have some other good news," Mel said, entering the conversation. "The folks back at NSA headquarters were able to hack into that backup email server in Mexico. They downloaded thousands of unsent messages for us to look at."

"Are they all written in Itza?" Helen asked.

"Yes, but that confirms that we have multiple people all using Itza to conceal their communications," Mel answered.

"What about the Cipher? Where is he?" Helen asked.

"He's sleeping on a couch downstairs," Tanner said. "I think he's a little overwhelmed with everything that's going on, but he still seems willing to help."

"Yeah, he sleeps more than a lazy house cat," Mel added sarcastically.

"Let's get him involved in the work as soon as possible. Maybe we'll get lucky and find an important message like the one that the terrorists had," Helen said.

"We will," Tanner replied. "What did you find out about the attackers in Guatemala?"

"I just read through a briefing from the CIA. The local cops identified the people in the car who tried to run you off the road. They were definitely members of the Chiapas drug cartel," Helen said.

Tanner nodded his head. "That's what we had suspected."

"Who's the Chiapas cartel?" Mel asked.

Helen briefly explained what she had learned from the CIA memo. "The Chiapas cartel is a medium-sized drug organization that bases its operations in southern Mexico. The boss is a man named Javier Soto. He's trying to become a big-time player in drug trafficking to the United States. The CIA says the cartel cuts makeshift runways out of the Guatemalan jungle to land their drug planes."

Tanner added his own comments. "We think the cartel must have stumbled upon the second copy of the Spanish-to-Itza Bible somewhere. When they realized that nobody could understand Itza, they started using it to scramble their secret communications."

"That makes sense. If they had learned that you were down in Guatemala, trying to find someone who could read Itza, they'd consider that a serious threat to their drug operation," Helen said.

"But we won't know for sure until we can get some of those emails decoded," Tanner said. "Until then, I guess it's a waiting game."

"I have my morning briefing with the president in an hour. I'm going to update him on what we have learned," Helen said. "Keep up the good work on your end. We're making progress, but we've still got a lot of questions to answer."

WASHINGTON, DC

On the other side of Washington, DC, a man also woke up early. Despite his lack of sleep, Votan made sure to maximize his last day of preparation. Tomorrow was October 28. It was the day that the Order of 28 had designated to begin their villainous rebellion. The Constitution was hanging by a thread, and nobody could stop the landslide of revolution bearing down on the nation's capital.

NSA DATA CENTER, UTAH

Tanner couldn't force himself to stay awake any longer. At 6:00 p.m., he called the end of a very long day. He was grateful that his wife had decided to spend some extra time in southern Utah before coming back with the kids. He was in desperate need of sleep, and he greatly anticipated going home to a quiet house.

He estimated that about 15 percent of the Itza Bible had been translated into English. While there still weren't enough words to make sense of any of the encrypted emails, Tanner felt confident enough in the overall progress that he decided he could go home for some rest. As he got ready to leave, however, Tanner realized that he didn't have a way to get home. When he had returned from Guatemala, he went directly to work. Fortunately, Kevin volunteered to give him a ride.

"How far along do you think they'll be when we get back?" Kevin asked as he drove Tanner to his home in Draper.

"I think they'll be around thirty percent," Tanner said. He forced his eyes to remain open, fearing that he would pass out in the car. "They might even be closer to forty percent depending on how many words are already entered in the database. At some point we'll hit critical mass where the last part of the translation will go extremely fast."

Kevin nodded his head in agreement. "I saw that a lot when I worked cryptology back at Meade. Breaking a code always takes more time at the beginning. But as the corresponding matches between letters and words are identified, the decoding process increases exponentially."

"Yeah, it's like a jigsaw puzzle. The pieces seem to come together faster at the end," Tanner said with a yawn.

"Maybe forty percent will be enough to start figuring out the meaning to some of those encrypted emails," Kevin said. He pulled his car into Tanner's driveway to let him out.

"We've uploaded all the encrypted emails into QC, and I told Mel to try cracking some of those messages with updates from translation. Hopefully, that will give us a head start," Tanner said. He slowly got out of the car. "See you tomorrow morning, bright and early." As he walked up toward the door of his quiet house, it took all of Tanner's willpower to keep from just lying down on the cement porch and going to sleep.

NEAR THE BORDER of Wyoming and Utah sits Flaming Gorge Dam. At five hundred feet, the massive concrete structure is one of the tallest dams in the United States. The dam blocks the Green River, forming a reservoir that extends ninety miles back into southwest Wyoming. Built in 1964 as a key component of the Colorado River Storage Project, the dam's hydroelectric plant is capable of producing over 150 megawatts of power.

Many aspects of the dam's operation have been upgraded since 1964. The original switches and levers that manually controlled the facility had been replaced by modern computers. As a result, the staffing needs of the dam had also decreased. Configured to run at optimum efficiency, a single person could manage the entire power plant during the night shift.

Earl Farnsworth was the graveyard worker on duty the early morning of October 28. Earl didn't mind working the night shift alone. In fact, he enjoyed the quiet solitude of the dam's operation center. With his feet propped up on his desk, he sipped his coffee while browsing through the current edition of his favorite hunting magazine.

In the background, Earl heard the constant hum of a generator in the powerhouse. The generator was connected to a propeller-like turbine that rotated as water passed through the dam and into the riverbed below. If more power was needed, the computer system would automatically open up additional gates, allowing more water to enter a ten-foot pipe called a penstock. The increased water flow would turn additional turbines and, in conjunction, spin more generators to create more electricity.

As Earl read about a championship elk recently bagged in the mountains of northern Idaho, he noticed a slight change in the hum coming from the powerhouse. The higher pitch meant that additional water was now flowing across another turbine, but the change wasn't abnormal. It was exactly how the automated system was designed to operate. But the rise in pitch didn't stop. It kept increasing, signifying that more and more water was now rushing through the penstocks.

Earl looked up at the control monitor mounted on the wall. The lights were all green, suggesting normal power operation. But more generators continued to spin up, causing a slight vibration in the operation center. That was odd. Earl set down his magazine and logged into the computer console to verify the system's status. His login attempt failed. Three more times he tried to get into the control system, but he had no luck. It appeared that his account was locked out.

While he was concerned at the sudden surge of power production, Earl was not overly panicked. The turbines and generators were designed to handle the full flow of water through the ten-foot penstocks. The increased power supply might be a waste of water, but it was nothing dangerous.

Then Earl heard another faint noise. As the sound grew louder, he realized this noise was completely abnormal. The dam's floodgates were opening, allowing water down the 675-foot spillway. He quickly ran to a window on the other side of the operation center. In the glow from the industrial lights at the dam's base, Earl saw a massive fountain of water coming out of the spillway opening.

He had a serious problem.

In a desperate attempt to close the floodgates, Earl again tried to access the automated controls on the computer terminal. His account was still locked out. Suddenly, he had a sickening thought. *Someone else is controlling the dam's functions!* The only way to stop the massive and unexpected release of water was to engage the manual override. Unfortunately, the fail-safe to close the floodgates was at the top of the fifty-story dam.

Earl ran out of the control room and sprinted down the hall. The roar from the rushing water coming off the spillway was nerve-racking. He jumped into the waiting elevator to quickly ascend to the top of the dam, but the elevator didn't budge. Despite pressing numerous buttons, nothing happened. Earl knew that he didn't have time to waste trying to figure out why the elevator was suddenly broken. Instead, he ran down the hall and started ascending hundreds of stairs that would get him to the top of the dam. Ten minutes later, out of breath and dripping sweat, Earl manually closed the thirty-five-foot floodgates. But it was too late. The damage was already done.

Unknown to Earl, Travis Boston and two other members of Anonymous had been controlling the dam's infrastructure. They hacked into the main computer system and let the water from the reservoir pass through the dam at full capacity. The normal output of Flaming Gorge Dam at this time of year was eight hundred cubic feet of water per second. Now, with every pathway opened through the dam, the water gushed out at thirty-two thousand cubic feet per second—over forty times the normal amount! The rapid and sudden discharge caused a twenty-foot wall of water to race down the narrow canyon.

The immediate area below Flaming Gorge Dam is a blue ribbon trout fishery. People from all over the world visit the region, looking to catch one of the record brown trout on the Green River.

That's exactly what the secretary of the treasury had been doing on his annual fly-fishing trip. Camped on the shores of the river beneath the dam, the small fishing group consisted of the secretary, two of his closest friends, and a bodyguard. Because it was in the middle of the night, nobody had any warning about the impending flood. The swift-moving wall of water ripped through the camp at 3:18 a.m. EDT, destroying everything in its path. Because of the remote location and steep canyon walls, the secretary of the treasury's death wouldn't be confirmed for almost six hours.

WHEN HELEN WOKE up on Thursday, October 28, she had no concept that the day would become an unbelievable succession of national tragedies. Ironically, she had almost begun to believe that the problems of the past week were all behind her. The intelligence briefings continued to implicate the Chiapas cartel in the attack against the vice president, and even Helen was now persuaded of the plot. She looked forward to closing the investigation once Tanner and his team provided conclusive evidence of the cartel's role from the encrypted email messages.

Helen arrived for work at her normal starting time of 5:00 a.m. Hanging up her jacket and checking her makeup, she sat down to finish reading through the Morning Book. The Morning Book was a compilation of intelligence reports and diplomatic cables prepared each day for the National Security advisor. She was reviewing an update on violence in the Middle East when her desk phone blared out. In the quiet early morning hour, the ringing seemed like an electric shock. But Helen was even more startled when she noticed the call came from the secretary of defense.

"Isn't this a little early for you to be at work?" Helen asked Howie.

"Actually, I'm still at home," he said. "I can't figure out how you manage to get into the office so early."

"It comes with age. You'll understand in a couple of years when you can't sleep in past five anymore," Helen humorously said. She was a decade older than him. "So why the early morning call?"

"I just got done talking with some of my people at the Pentagon. They say the EDES phone that we loaned to the secretary of the treasury went offline a couple hours ago," Howie said.

"Is that unexpected?" Helen asked.

"The phone is ultra-durable. The synchronization and GPS signals go over satellite. If the phone isn't transmitting its beacon, it's been smashed to smithereens or a satellite fell out of space."

"Any chance the phone is malfunctioning?" Helen asked.

"That's why the folks at the Pentagon called me. All our other EDES phones check out okay, including the one Tanner still has. And the satellite has passed its operational checks. Something happened specifically to that phone," Howie said with concern in his voice.

"Do we have another way of contacting him?" Helen asked.

"Not that I know of. That's why we gave him the EDES phone in the first place. His fishing trip was out in the middle of nowhere."

"Okay, let's not hit the panic button yet. It's early morning out West, so maybe everyone is still asleep," Helen said.

"Even so, the phone should still be transmitting its status and location," Howie said anxiously. "All our phones use a prototype palladium alloy battery that only needs to be charged every fifteen days. There's no way to power it off. It's an always-on device."

"Let me check in with some folks over at the Secret Service. I'll call you back when I find something," Helen said.

5:30 AM EDT
NEAR WASHINGTON, DC

At his home in the Virginia countryside, Howie remained distressed. He hadn't built a billion-dollar business by making stupid decisions. He lived by the mantra of another famous technologist named Andrew Grove, who coined the phrase, "Only the paranoid survive." After years of negotiating million-dollar business deals in the boardroom, Howie had developed a keen sense for determining when something smelled rotten. Right now, his sense of smell was almost overpowering.

He checked the grandfather clock in his office. His day was full of meetings, the first one starting in less than two hours. His armed chauffeur would soon arrive to take him to work, but Howie felt like he needed to lay low until he found out what exactly happened to the treasury secretary. Acting on his gut instincts, he decided to blow off his morning routine and take his wife to a safe location instead.

6:00 AM EDT
WHITE HOUSE

Helen hung up the phone. Staring at her desk, she thought about what she had just learned from the Secret Service. They had been preoccupied with the death of another high-profile lawmaker. The speaker of the House of Representatives had passed away in his sleep last night. His body was currently undergoing a private autopsy at Walter Reed Medical Center. While it wasn't confirmed yet, the initial reports hinted that he might have died of an accidental insulin overdose.

Helen wasn't one to panic, but she also didn't believe in coincidences. The vice president was killed six days ago. Last night, the speaker of the House died in his sleep. And now, the secretary of the treasury was missing.

Something wasn't right.

She briskly got out of her chair and walked toward the Oval Office. It was just after 6:00 a.m., and she hoped to catch the president before he left for his morning campaign meeting with the attorney general. But when Helen turned the corner to the hallway that went from the West Wing to the Oval Office, she was stopped by Tony Criddle. He was the operations manager on duty that morning in the Situation Room.

"Hey, I was just coming up to get you," he said.

"I need to talk to the president," Helen anxiously replied.

"He's not in his office," Tony said. He leaned in to whisper. "Something happened to the speaker of the House last night. I need you to come with me."

Tony quickly led Helen to an unassuming elevator. Pausing at the opened door, Helen knew this elevator only went one direction—down.

"The president is in the Situation Room?" Helen asked.

"No, he's heading off to someplace safe," Tony said. He escorted Helen into the waiting elevator car and pushed the button to close the doors.

"What about the chief of staff?" Helen asked.

"He's still in New York. You're the most senior official on site," Tony said matter-of-factly. The elevator quickly descended to the Situation Room located underneath the West Wing of the White House.

The Situation Room was staffed twenty-four hours a day by handpicked employees from the intelligence community and the military. The small staff was apolitical—neither Republican nor Democrat. Their sole function was to provide accurate, quick, and concise information to the members of the executive branch. In every way, the employees of the Situation Room were the cream of the crop. From their formal attire to their respectful demeanor, they conveyed complete professionalism.

As soon as the elevator doors opened, Tony escorted Helen to a chair in the Surge Room. This room was part of the greater

Situation Room complex. In many respects, the Surge Room was a high-tech operations center, complete with computers, fax machines, telephones, and overhead monitors.

Helen took her seat. "Thanks, Tony." The Surge Room was mainly for the operations staff, but Helen always preferred to monitor events from in here. As an analyst, she wanted to see the raw data firsthand. "Okay, tell me what's going on," she said. In the background, six staffers manned the high-tech communication equipment.

"First of all, the president is safe. He was on his way to meet with the attorney general when we found out about the speaker's death. With two prominent leaders now dead, the Secret Service decided to secure the situation. They took the president to Camp David. We're going to patch him in on the phone shortly," Tony began.

"Is the First Lady safe?" Helen asked.

"Yes. She's still on vacation in California. The Secret Service has her under tight guard out there."

"What do we know about the speaker of the House?" Helen asked.

"He died sometime in the middle of the night, but nobody noticed until approximately 4:00 a.m. It looks like his insulin pump went haywire, giving him a fatal insulin overdose. But we're waiting for the manufacture to verify that," Tony said.

"Okay, tell me about the secretary of the treasury," Helen probed.

Tony grimaced in a confused manner that made his bald head wrinkle. "What do you mean? We haven't heard anything about him," he said. The other staffers in the room froze when they heard about the unexpected disappearance of another government official.

"Just before I came down here, I got a call from Howie Wiseman. He said the hi-tech phone they gave the secretary of the treasury went offline about three hours ago," Helen said.

Tony turned to his staffers. "See if you can figure out what's going on with the treasury secretary."

Just then a phone rang out. Only one person made calls on this particular line. A communications technician in the center of the room quickly and professionally answered the phone. "Yes, Mr. President. She's here now."

The female technician transferred the call to the phone on the desk in front of Helen. She picked it up. "Good morning, sir," she said.

"Helen, I'm glad you made it down there," the president said. "I told Tony to have you coordinate the events from the Sit Room."

"Thank you, sir," Helen answered, trying to be more formal with the president while others were listening. "It looks like we have an unusual situation developing."

Helen updated the president on what she had learned. She briefly touched on the death of the speaker of the House before mentioning the missing secretary of the treasury, Jim DeRozen.

"Was there anything about this in the Morning Book?" the president asked.

"No, there wasn't anything remotely close to this," Helen said. "Besides some unrest in the Middle East, things are quiet here on the home front."

The president reacted calmly to the situation. "The head agent over my security detail says I need to remain up here as a precaution, but we don't want to cause a panic. The elections are less than a week away, and we can't let anything deter our focus from that."

"Sir, I think you're overlooking something. Do you realize that two of your immediate successors are dead and that another one is missing?" Helen emphasized.

The presidential line of succession was clearly established by the Constitution. After the death of the president of the United States, the vice president would assume control of the government. From that point, authority went in the following order: speaker of the House, president pro tempore of the Senate, secretary of state, secretary of the treasury, secretary of defense, and the attorney general. Following the attorney general, the secretary of the interior, the secretary of the agriculture, and the secretary of commerce completed the first ten people in the presidential line of authority.

"I'm aware of that, but I think you're overreacting," the president told Helen. "We know the drug cartel killed David, and the speaker's death is an accident. While I'm concerned about Jimmy, it's not unheard of him to wander off the grid. He's done it on previous fishing trips. Until we find out for sure what happened to him, let's not do anything irrational. We don't want to upset the upcoming elections."

Helen shook her head in disbelief. The president was completely focused on politics. "As a precaution, I recommend we get some more Secret Service folks to look after your other Cabinet members."

The president let out a small chuckle over the phone line. "That's not how it works, Helen. The Secret Service just protects the president and vice president."

Helen was confused. "Wait, doesn't the Secret Service protect everyone?"

"That's a common misconception, but the cabinet members are each protected by their individual agencies. Diplomatic Security protects Elizabeth, and Howie has folks in the Department of Defense guarding him," the president said.

Helen shook her head. No wonder Washington was such a mess. A dozen different groups were responsible for protecting the nation's most important leaders. "We at least need to get Mike to a safe place. He's the next in line to assume the presidency," she said, referring to the president pro tempore of the Senate. Because of the death of the speaker of the House, Michael Verkin was now the highest ranking official in Congress.

"Mike won't listen. He's campaigning out in Oklahoma, and he won't lie low so close to the election."

"But can't you order the Secret Service to help protect some of these folks in your line of succession? We can't afford to lose anyone else," Helen pressed.

"Okay, I'll talk to them and see what they say," the president conceded. "In the meantime, let's keep our cool. We don't want to cause a panic. I'm hoping to come back down this afternoon, but I want you to coordinate with the other intelligence organizations and keep me posted. In the meantime, the attorney general is on his way up here, and we're going to spend the entire day focusing on the midterms."

"I will. Thank you, sir," she said. Helen ended the conversation and leaned back in her chair. While she was frustrated at the president's apathy for the situation, she also understood his viewpoint. It was inconceivable to think the deaths of the vice president and the speaker of the House were part of some larger conspiracy. After all, the president was still alive, and he was in control of the government.

"We've got a new problem," an operations agent called out, breaking Helen's train of thought. "No one can reach the secretary of defense."

"Wait, I just spoke to him this morning," she answered.

The staffer explained the situation. "His chauffer said the secretary of defense wasn't there when he went to pick him up this morning. The driver rang the doorbell five times and nobody answered."

"Well, call the Pentagon and see if he's there," Tony ordered.

"That's the problem, sir. The secretary of defense never made it to work."

HOWIE WISEMAN NEVER went to the Pentagon. In fact, he headed the opposite direction from the nation's capital on Interstate-66. Taking his wife on an impromptu trip, the couple stopped an hour later near the small community of Strasburg, Virginia. They were now concealed in a private cottage on the north fork of the Shenandoah River, just outside the border of Shenandoah National Park.

The upscale retreat was built by Howie back when he was CEO of his communications company. He occasionally escaped the pressures of political life by isolating himself at his secret home in the famous Shenandoah Valley. The lodge had five bedrooms, each one with its own private bath, and a large kitchen that provided ample space to host up to thirty guests.

The comfortable cabin provided for Howie's immediate need of security, but there was another reason why he had decided to flee to this location. Back when he was a CEO, he had the retreat outfitted with high-speed communication lines and equipment. With several desktop computers and a satellite uplink, the home functioned as a mini-office where he could work in privacy.

"We'll be safe here," he told his wife as they took a seat on the couch in the main family room. "I'm not sure what's going on in DC, but it's best if we keep a low profile for a while."

"Is there any chance they can find us here?" she asked. Her voice had a slight uneasiness to it.

"Nobody knows about this home except a few of our close friends. I'll be able to conduct my own investigation here without drawing any attention to myself," Howie said.

"But wouldn't you be safer at work? There are a lot of military people there to protect you," she said.

Howie always had a bit of paranoia, but he felt more on edge than usual this morning. He decided it was time to confide in his wife. He leaned in for emphasis as he spoke. "The media isn't talking about it, but I think the assassination of the vice president was an inside job. It's one of the theories I was pursuing at work. And now, the secretary of the treasury suddenly goes missing on his fishing trip. I'm not sure what happened, but I wanted to be somewhere safe so I can work without having to look over my shoulder." He paused for a second and then continued. "I'm probably being too suspicious, but I learned in the boardroom never to dismiss a gut feeling, and something definitely feels wrong."

"What are we going to do?" his wife asked.

"Let's spend the day here. You can relax and catch up on your reading while I call some of my friends for information," Howie said. "Maybe they can help me dig up more details on what's happening."

Howie gave his wife a hug. He then stood up and walked to his den. Sitting down in his chair, he took a one-of-kind cell phone out of his pocket. His first call went out to a former coworker who had access to satellite imagery.

"Johnny, this is Howie," the secretary of defense announced after the call was answered.

"Howie! How you doing?" Johnny Lake asked. "You're not

calling to say that you regretted selling out and moving to DC, are you?"

Howie appreciated the humor behind the question. "Honestly, sometimes I do. Especially on days like today," he said. "But do *you* regret leaving?"

Johnny was there at the beginning when Howie formed his wireless communication company. When Howie sold his business years later, Johnny also took the opportunity to cash out and look for new business opportunities.

Johnny laughed. "No way, man. I got fifteen million reasons to have left when I did."

Howie skipped further small talk and got down to business. "Are you still doing satellite imagery for that dot-com?"

"Yeah, I'm just heading into work right now. What's up?"

"I need you to pull up some photos for me."

"Wait, you're the secretary of defense. Don't you have a bunch of spy satellites to do that stuff?" Johnny asked.

"Yeah, but this is a personal favor, if you know what I mean," Howie said. "Something happened out in Utah, and I need you to get some photos of the area without raising any suspicion."

"Whoa, Utah is a big place. You gotta give me something more specific to go on."

"I've got GPS coordinates of the site. Will that work?" Howie asked.

"Sure, can you email me the info?" Johnny asked.

"I'm sending it right now," Howie said. He was typing on his computer while talking on the phone. Using a private and anonymous email, he sent the GPS coordinates of the last known transmission from the secretary of the treasury's EDES phone.

"We've got a satellite that flies over the western US in the next hour. I'll see if I can get you some fresh shots from the next pass-by," Johnny said.

"That's great. Call me back on this number when you have something," Howie said. He disconnected the call and looked at his personal cell phone. It was just like the other EDES phones used by the Department of Defense except for one unique feature. This phone was completely untraceable. Johnny had created the one-of-a-kind device for Howie just before he sold his company. Two special computer chips inside the phone spoofed the device's location on the GPS satellite network, delivering random coordinates.

Howie checked his watch—7:20 a.m. It was still a little early for his next conversation, but he decided to make it anyway. The call went to the chief security officer of a Fortune 500 company headquartered in Denver, Colorado. Once upon a time, Howie was on the board of directors for the chemical company. He had formed a close friendship with Kent Iverson back then. Kent had an excellent reputation for getting information, especially from the local law enforcement agencies. If anything had happened to the secretary of the treasury out in the Rocky Mountains, Kent would be able to find out.

7:30 AM EDT
DRAPER, UTAH

Tanner woke up surprisingly refreshed. Having slept uninterrupted for ten straight hours, he felt ten years younger. He shaved, showered, and got ready for a big day. He was optimistic that the translation process would soon yield positive results, implicating the drug cartel as the masterminds behind the attack on the vice president.

As Tanner stepped into his garage to leave for work, he immediately noticed only one car. The family's minivan was gone, and it suddenly dawned on him that it was still down at Mesa Verde National Park. It hadn't even been a week since the FBI helicopter had interrupted his family vacation, yet Tanner felt like a year had passed. He got into his Honda Civic and drove to work, making a mental note to follow up with the FBI about the whereabouts of his other car.

It was just before sunrise when Tanner arrived at the NSA spy complex on the hillside of Camp Williams. After going through the main doors to the lobby, he walked over to the security checkpoint. The armed guard watched as Tanner placed his personal belongings on a plastic tray. He then pushed the tray along a conveyor belt and into a machine that scanned the items for prohibited communication gadgets. While his personal belongings were being scanned, Tanner swiped his NSA badge and entered a PIN on a keypad. This two-factor authentication method, using a combination of something Tanner owned plus something that he knew, provided extra security from unauthorized access into the ultra-secure building.

Less than a minute later, Tanner entered the large conference room on the first floor where the translation process was taking place. Someone had brought in a radio, and music from a local rock station now filled the room. Fourteen linguists busily worked at their laptops, each copying words from their Bible printouts into their computers. The scene hadn't changed much since Tanner had left the previous night. He walked across the room toward Mel, who was watching two linguists interact with the Cipher. The old man was fully awake and eating breakfast.

"Morning, Mel," Tanner said.

"Hey," Mel replied back. He didn't take his eyes off the old man.

"I see someone got him something to eat," Tanner said. He pointed to the breakfast sandwich in the Cipher's hand. "How's it going?"

"It's been better. I haven't slept in almost twenty-four hours," Mel said. As usual, he was gnawing on a plastic golf tee to counteract his old smoking habit.

"What are they talking about?" Tanner asked. The Cipher was pointing to a sheet of paper that one of the NSA employees was holding. The paper had a bunch of Itza words scribbled on it.

"He's explaining what these words mean. Nobody can figure out the Spanish or English equivalent," Mel said.

"How far along are we?"

Mel turned his gaze toward his boss. He took a deep breath, expressing his frustration at the tedious process. "The last time I checked, we weren't even thirty percent done. I ran a couple of messages through the decryption process on QC, but it still doesn't make any sense. I wish we could just scan in the pages of his Bible and use a computer to do this."

"I know, but none of our tools can recognize the handwritten Itza characters. It's slower going this way, but at least we're confident of our translation," Tanner pointed out.

"Yes, but there's another problem," Mel said. He led Tanner toward a stack of papers on a nearby table. "Here, I printed these off an hour ago. You can see we have a lot of word matches, but they're all worthless."

Tanner picked up several sheets of paper. The first page contained a list of translated words, all starting with the letter "A." He saw the translated Itza word for "apostle" was *bitzchuak*. Flipping to another sheet of paper marked "B," he read that the Itza word for "baptism" was *chu'ltaqwaq*.

"A lot of these words are religious in context," Tanner said.

"That's the problem," Mel replied with exasperation. "It does us absolutely no good to know how to say Jesus in Itza. None of the encrypted emails contain religious words like that. I already checked."

Tanner laughed out loud at Mel's accurate yet sarcastic comment. "Well, I guess it's important if you want to convert Itza speakers to Christianity." He flipped through more sheets of paper, scanning the results.

Mel clearly wasn't amused with Tanner's humor. "See this?" he said, pointing to a column of words on the sheet of paper in his boss's hand. "We've found a lot of other translations, but they're mostly simple words like 'and,' 'the,' or 'when.'"

"Okay, so what are we going to do about this?" Tanner asked.

"Well, we're taking two approaches," Mel said. "Most of the linguists are still working on translating their copies of the Bible.

It's not the most effective, but we get a lucky find every once in a while." He then turned and gestured back toward the Cipher. "We've got two people working directly with the old man. They're going over some of the emails we downloaded and having him verbally translate the words we can't find in the Bible. We're having more success with that approach."

It was then that Tanner fully understood the problem with using just the Bible as a source for translation. "The Cipher must know how to interpret in Itza real time, or at least how to form Spanish words from Itza characters," he said.

Mel nodded his head. "He's having some success in figuring out Spanish equivalents for stuff written in Itza, but we still have to convert that into English," he said. "That's how he decoded the original message about the vice president. Obviously, the phrase 'vice president' isn't in the Bible anywhere. Somehow he has the ability to conjugate Itza words on the fly."

Despite Tanner's best intentions of having a room-full of NSA analysts working on the translation, it was the Cipher who had the most luck in figuring out the hidden messages. "What has he come up with so far?"

"It looks like there's a group of people who are communicating exclusively using the encrypted emails. We aren't sure how many people there are, but it's obvious the leader of the group is some guy named Votan," Mel said.

"I've heard that name before. The Cipher translated it for us in Guatemala," Tanner acknowledged. "What else?"

"Well, it looks like this group appears to be conspiring to do something bad. We aren't sure yet, but they keep talking about change and something about a new leader or king."

"A king?" Tanner asked. "Are they going to kill a king?"

"We just don't know yet," Mel said, throwing up his arms in exasperation. "We need more translated words to make sense of the emails." He handed Tanner a folder. "I've written everything down in here if you want more details. I'm going home to get some sleep."

Tanner put his hand on his coworker's shoulder. "Good work, Mel. I'll take over from here."

"We'll have better success if we keep the Cipher involved. He's worth a thousand translators," Mel said. He turned and walked toward the exit, reaching for the car keys in his pocket.

MOST REBELLIONS START with a defining and public event, like the bombing of Pearl Harbor or the attack on Fort Sumter. The pivotal moment on October 28, however, wasn't a military maneuver. It was a cyberattack against the cellular network in the greater Washington, DC, area. At 8:30 a.m. EDT, the servers that managed the major wireless carriers got slammed with billions of random phone calls. The technology infrastructure of the wireless network wasn't designed to handle the sudden flood of random connection requests. As a result, practically every cell phone user in the nation's capital experienced a busy signal when trying to place a new call.

It wasn't long after that when a member of the Anonymous hacking group called a local TV station, claiming responsibility for the widespread mobile phone outage. He announced the cyberattack was retribution for the government's misguided war against terrorism. The mysterious man further stated that the wireless networks would remain offline until the United States pulled all of its troops out of Afghanistan. Eager to get the scoop, the news channel immediately broadcasted the story. Unfortunately, the TV network never took the time to learn that the demand from Anonymous was completely bogus.

With the inability to communicate using a pervasive technology that so many people depended on, Votan and his group of conspirators created an environment ripe for chaos. In addition to severely crippling a key communication method among government agencies, the massive outage was also the signal for the members in the Order of 28 to begin their evil work. One such event was unfolding at 2201 C Street.

At the State Department headquarters, the deputy secretary of state entered the foyer just outside his supervisor's office. The administrative assistant had gone for her morning break, leaving the executive area momentarily vacant. The deputy secretary moved quickly, taking the opportunity to have a discrete and impromptu meeting with Secretary of State Elizabeth Godfrey.

Stepping inside Elizabeth's ornate office, the deputy secretary of state closed the door and started up a casual conversation. "Did you hear about the phone outage? I guess it's all over the news," he said as he casually walked toward his boss.

"I've been too busy looking at these figures," Elizabeth replied. "Come over and tell me what you think."

The deputy secretary maneuvered around the large desk and peered over his boss's shoulder. He discreetly reached in his right pocket while pretending to look at the computer screen on Elizabeth's desk.

"See these numbers from Europe?" she asked, but she never got the chance to finish her statement. In a quick move, the deputy secretary took a silk cord from his pocket and whipped it around Elizabeth's neck. Forcefully jerking back, he silently strangled the secretary of state as she sat at her diplomatic post. He waited a full minute to make sure his evil deed was accomplished before releasing his hold. Composing himself for a moment, the deputy secretary of state left the crime scene. He nonchalantly walked out of the office and down the hall toward the elevator. Nobody had seen the treasonous act just committed by a member of the Order of 28. Three minutes later, he was driving away from the State Department, never to return again.

8:30 AM EDT
OKLAHOMA CITY, OKLAHOMA

While the deputy secretary of state was carrying out his part of the Order's conspiracy, another attack was happening. Unlike the silent and secret elimination of the secretary of state, the president pro tempore of the Senate was murdered in broad daylight. Michael Verkin had just finished speaking at an early morning campaign breakfast in Oklahoma City. The five-term senator from Tulsa, Oklahoma, would never make it back to Washington, DC. As he walked out of the church where he had just addressed his constituency, a white van pulled up to the curb. The side door flung open, and two men with AK-47 machine guns open fired. The sudden volley of bullets mowed down everything in their path, killing Senator Verkin and his two bodyguards. The expertly executed attack was over in less than ten seconds, and the van sped away before anyone could react.

8:45 AM EDT
OUTSIDE OF STRASBURG, VIRGINIA

At his luxurious lodge on the north end of the Shenandoah Valley, Howie spoke on the phone with his former employee, Johnny Lake. He was looking at the high-definition photos recently taken from a satellite high above Flaming Gorge Dam. The pictures were unbelievable and shocking.

"It looks like a flood. That's the only thing I can determine," Johnny said over the phone.

"Was it a flash flood?" Howie asked.

"Could be. I can see all sorts of debris like fallen trees and rocks, but there's no sign of a camp anywhere. Are you sure these are the right coordinates?"

"Yes. That was the last location we got a signal from," Howie said.

"Well, the damage is very apparent. Whoever was staying there didn't make it," Johnny said resolutely.

Howie let out a sigh. "It was the treasury secretary."

"Whoa, that's weird," Johnny said.

"What do you mean?"

"Didn't you hear about the senator from Oklahoma? It just happened."

"Senator Verkin?" Howie cautiously asked. He knew the president pro tempore was campaigning in his home state this week.

"Yeah, that's him," Johnny said. "I just got a news alert on my computer that says he was killed by a group of gunmen."

As the sixth person in the presidential line of succession, Howie was keenly aware of the frontrunners before him. The leadership of the United States was dwindling rapidly, and Howie was on the verge of panic. "Thanks, Johnny. I've got to run. I'll call back if I need anything," he said.

Howie disconnected the call. He was just about to tell his wife about the news in Oklahoma when his cell phone chirped again. He looked at the caller ID. It was Kent Iverson.

"Hi, Howie," Kent greeted the secretary of defense. "I've got some information for you. It came from the state cops in Utah."

Howie prepared for the bad news. "Okay, tell me."

"There's a search-and-rescue operation taking place right now in Daggett County. The sheriff out there responded to reports of a flood on the Green River, just below Flaming Gorge Dam. Apparently, some of the dam's controls failed and released an unprecedented amount of water," Kent said.

"How sure are you about this?" Howie asked. He didn't want to disclose what he had just learned from the satellite imagery.

"It's solid, but like I said, they still don't know the extent of the damage. The Green River goes through extremely remote parts of Utah. The closest city of any kind is Vernal, and that's at least an hour away."

"That confirms what I heard from another source," Howie said. "Thanks for helping me validate my info."

"I'll call you back if I hear anything new from the search-and-rescue," Kent said.

"Say hi to your wife and kids for me," Howie said. He ended the call and turned on the TV in his cabin, catching the update from the breaking news in Oklahoma. Quickly assembling what he had learned in the past ten minutes, Howie came to a crucial conclusion.

The United States government was under attack.

Pilchwaajads   ʼɛʼlqʼisamduc
hu'ltaqwr   nja;Jumo
xirʼkun   cʰinaq
resadh   adhtz
ihvaralʼ   jovJjir
dikdakila   Jxirikun
achik'axfxAj   aaqresajawi

9:00 AM EDT

WHITE HOUSE SITUATION ROOM

HELEN LEARNED ABOUT the death of the president pro tempore at 8:48 a.m. Ironically, she didn't hear about it through her normal political channels. She was watching a CNN report on the massive cell phone outage when a breaking news logo flashed on the TV monitor in the Situation Room. The news anchor briefly announced what had just happened in Oklahoma City before playing a corresponding video clip, showing the aftermath of the violence. The reporter instantly declared the event a terrorist attack.

Helen hadn't recovered from her shock about the news of the president pro tempore when she received a panicked call from the head of diplomatic security at the State Department. Someone had murdered the secretary of state as she sat at her desk. Unfortunately, none of the security cameras in the State Department had captured the event. The computer systems that recorded the video feeds had been disabled. Someone had hacked into the air conditioning unit for the data center. The hacker remotely turned off the cooling units, causing the temperature in the data center to suddenly spike.

To prevent damage to the servers from overheating, the power was automatically cut to the entire data center. Every computer system, including the one that recorded all the security videos in the building, was rendered useless.

The ongoing, widespread outage of the cell phone network only exacerbated Helen's coordination problems. Many government officials relied heavily on wireless communication, including those at the FBI and the Secret Service. Even most of the folks at the Pentagon preferred cell phones over landlines. A case in point was the secretary of defense, whom Helen was desperately trying to get ahold of right now. "Has anyone been able to find Howie?" she shouted out to the staffers in the Situation Room.

"No, the staff at the Pentagon are going crazy looking for him as well," one of the communication agents answered.

"What about the other members of the cabinet?" Helen asked. "Are they safe?"

"We're still waiting to hear back from them. We're having a hard time getting through to anyone because of the cell network outage," another staffer replied.

Tony Criddle hung up a landline phone and gave Helen an update. "The FBI is on its way over to the State Department right now, but the situation there is spiraling out of control. It won't be long until the press finds out about the secretary of state's death."

A chill again ran up Helen's spine. Elizabeth was a dear friend, and Helen had to use all her willpower to maintain her composure right now. "At least the president is safe," she said, trying to calm her own nerves. The security detail at Camp David was already in lockdown. With a dozen Secret Service agents and over two hundred Marines guarding the facility, Camp David was the ultimate place of refuge for the leader of the free world.

Helen glanced up at the TV monitors on the wall. The murder of Senator Michael Verkin was on all the news channels now. It was the headline on every network, replacing the story about ongoing cell phone outage in the metro area. The attack against the president pro tempore shocked the nation, but they didn't know the other half of the story. It wouldn't be long before the media got wind of the other recent deaths.

"The American public is going to panic," Helen said to Tony. "The death of the president pro tempore is bad enough, but once they find out about the speaker of the House and the secretary of state, everyone will assume the nation is under attack."

"I think that's already evident," Tony said.

A phone rang out in the operations center. One of the staffers answered the call and spoke in a confused tone. He put the call on hold and then turned toward Helen and Tony. "I've got a man calling on an unlisted number. He says he's the secretary of defense."

"Put him through to my phone," Helen said. She privately picked up the receiver in front of her. "Hello," she answered cryptically.

"Helen, this is Howie. I was hoping you'd be in the Sit Room." Even though Helen recognized Howie's voice, the fact that the call came from an unlisted number was suspicious.

"When do we have our weekly meetings?" she quickly asked. It was her simple attempt to verify the caller.

"We eat breakfast together once a week. I called you this morning and told you that we had lost contact with Jimmy out at Flaming Gorge. You'd just gotten into your office."

"Okay, I had to be sure it was you," Helen said. "Where have you been? We've been searching high and low for you."

"After the secretary of treasury went missing, I decided to go underground. I'm about an hour outside of the city, but don't try tracking me down. I'm on a satphone that scrambles its location," Howie said.

"How come your phone isn't affected by the outage?" Helen asked. Talking to Howie helped calm her frazzled nerves.

"It's a special device that I had made for me once upon a time. It uses satellites to communicate," Howie said before quickly changed subjects. "Did you see what happened to Senator Verkin?"

"Yes, but that's not all," Helen anxiously countered. Her voice was a combination of fear and remorse. "Elizabeth is also dead, along with the speaker of the House."

Howie's gulp was audible over the phone. "How did it happen?"

Helen quickly described the events surrounding the deaths of the speaker of the House and the secretary of state. Even as she gave her update, the news seemed unbelievable.

"We're definitely under attack. Someone is specifically targeting our nation's leadership," Howie said.

"I agree. We've got to do something, but everything is happening so fast that I can't think clearly," Helen said.

"Is the president safe?" Howie asked.

"Yes, he's secure up at Camp David," Helen said. "He's staying up there while I figure out the mess down here."

"You can add Jimmy to our list of casualties," Howie said sorrowfully.

Helen gasped out loud. Her head was spinning again from the chaos. "What happened?"

"I asked some of my friends to look into it. There was a sudden flood on the Green River below Flaming Gorge Dam. Someone intentionally released a bunch of water out of the dam, and it wiped out Jimmy's fishing camp. Everything was destroyed," Howie said.

Helen's mind searched for answers. "It could be the cartel. Maybe they have someone on the inside, controlling the dam."

"That's a possibility, but how do we know for sure? Who can we trust?" Howie asked. "We need to isolate ourselves and question everything. As far as I'm concerned, everyone but you is a suspect right now."

"We've got to tell the president," Helen said.

"Of course, but we need to watch what we say," Howie said. His paranoia was clearly at an all-time high.

Helen felt the same way. Until they could get a grip on the situation, it was only reasonable to assume that others besides the cartel were involved. "I'll keep track of the events from here, but I'm going to do it with a small staff that I can trust."

"I've got a contact who works at a medical device company. I'll call her and see if she has any idea if someone could have tampered with the insulin pump," Howie said.

"That sounds good," Helen concurred. "Let's check in with each other first before bringing anyone else into the discussion. We've got to keep our facts from being contaminated. Talk to you soon."

Helen ended the conversation with the secretary of defense and placed the phone back in its resting position. The staffers in the Situation Room looked at her as the National Security advisor, anxiously awaiting her command.

Helen turned toward Tony. "Secure that door. Nobody gets in or out without my approval," she ordered.

"What's going on?" Tony asked.

"Can you trust these folks?" Helen asked, pointing to the six staffers in the Situation Room.

"Yes," Tony replied.

Helen needed more convincing. "Absolutely?"

"I trust them with my life," Tony said confidently.

"Good, because that's what's at stake here," Helen said. "We've been compromised. Someone on the inside is coordinating all these attacks. That's the only logical explanation for how so many leaders can be killed at once."

Helen stood up and walked to the front of the room to address the staffers in the operation center. "We're going into lockdown. Nobody talks to the president but me. If you get a call from someone else, put them on hold and let me speak to them personally." The staffers nodded their heads as Helen continued her marching orders. "We have to sanitize all our communication sources and separate the facts from the fiction. Don't assume anything. Question everyone. Verify everything."

TANNER WASN'T AWARE of the chaos unfolding in Washington, DC. He was fully occupied with the Bible translation, but he now realized that he had made a major mistake. Modern emails used thousands of words and expressions not found in any version of the Bible. Yet somehow the Chiapas cartel had found a way around this dilemma, and figuring out how they did it was extremely puzzling to Tanner.

Sydney walked over to the desk where Tanner studied numerous printouts. "What are you looking at?" she asked.

He didn't glance up from the papers spread out on the table in front of him. "The drug cartel must have a second code key somewhere."

"Like another encryption algorithm?" Sydney asked.

"Kind of, but it's probably more like a dictionary of modern words that they manually converted into Itza," Tanner said. He stopped looking at the papers and focused on Sydney. "The Itza tribe never had words for things like 'computer' or 'airplane'. So the cartel must have formed their own customized Itza words by combining different letters they had translated from the Cipher's Bible," he said.

Sydney was silent for a few minutes. Then her face brightened. "Technically, they wouldn't even have to do that much. Once they found out what the Itza character for the letter 'A' was, they could start using that in all their emails."

An epiphany came over Tanner, and he stood up with excitement. Sydney had just solved his dilemma. "We're doing this all wrong!" he exclaimed. "The cartel didn't translate the Bible and then use those words to communicate. They just figured out the individual characters of the Itza alphabet and converted those into Spanish." He shook his head at the straightforward concept. "It would be simple. Once they understood all the Spanish alphabet equivalents for Itza, they could easily create their own computer program to automatically encrypt the emails for them," he said.

"But some of their homegrown Itza words wouldn't make sense to a native Itza speaker," Sydney pointed out.

"That wouldn't matter," Tanner said. "The cartel isn't trying to craft their emails in a way that a native Itza speaker can understand. They're just trying to obscure it so we can't figure it out."

Sydney enthusiastically completed Tanner's thought process. "That makes perfect sense. We only know of one Itza speaker," she said, pointing to the Cipher sleeping on the couch. "But even he is having problems translating parts of the emails. That's because some of the words aren't truly Itza. They're just the cartel's attempt at encrypting a Spanish word into Itza."

"Exactly!" Tanner shouted again, startling some of the NSA analysts in the room. "There's got to be another key or computer program that has the Itza translation for every letter in the alphabet," he explained in a softer tone to Sydney. "Until we find that second key and convert it to English, we're not going to crack those emails."

Sydney nodded her head. "We still have access to that email server in Mexico. It might be stored on there."

"That's a great idea. I'll call that lieutenant back at headquarters for help," he said. "What's her name again? It's America something." He flipped through the sheets of paper on the desk, looking for her phone number.

Just then, another supervisor burst through the door of the conference room. She was obviously panicked about something. "We're under attack! Someone is killing off the politicians in DC!"

THE GENERAL POPULATION learned about the murder of the secretary of state just before 9:30 a.m. An anonymous tipster at the State Department leaked the information out to the press, and within seconds, every news channel had another breaking story dedicated to the assassination of Elizabeth Godfrey. The death of the secretary of state jarred the entire press corps into action. Even the most novice journalist now recognized a pattern with the recent deaths of the president pro tempore and the secretary of state. Drawing upon what they had learned in their high school civics classes, every political reporter in the country began going down the list of presidential successors, trying to determine the well-being of each leader.

Ten minutes later, Fox News broke another story. The speaker of the House of Representatives had died in his sleep last night, but there was more to the story. A member of the hacking group Anonymous had forwarded a classified memo to Fox News. The memo came from an unnamed source at the White House, suggesting the assassination of the vice president was orchestrated by the Chiapas drug cartel in Mexico. It was an exact copy of the same memo Helen had drafted the previous day for the president and the other members of the National Security Council.

The news channel quickly proclaimed the terrorist attacks were the work of the Chiapas drug cartel, beginning with the murder of the vice president for his opposition for legalizing drugs. The cable network also emphasized that, despite the recent assassinations, the president was still alive and well. Fox News ended their report by saying that the president was aware of the current crisis, and that he would personally address the nation at noon.

At his private location near the nation's capital, Votan watched the news update with delight. His plan was unfolding just as he had envisioned it. The media was accusing the Chiapas cartel for taking out the leaders in the presidential line of succession, overlooking the fact that the Order of 28 was actually behind the attacks.

Votan had planned his takeover down to the last intricate detail. The beginning phase was the assassination of several key Cabinet members, but that wasn't all. The president pro tempore and the speaker of the House also had to die because the entire nation needed to feel threatened, just like they had after September 11, 2001. Amidst the chaos and confusion of the sudden assassinations, Votan would declare the current president unfit to fulfill the duties of his office. With the immediate people in the presidential line of succession dead, nobody would be able to challenge Votan on his claim to rightfully lead the nation.

9:40 AM EDT
WASHINGTON, DC

Sitting in a hotel room on the outskirts of the nation's capital, El Flaco thought about what he had just learned. The secretary of defense never showed up for his morning ride to the Pentagon. The confused chauffer waited for thirty minutes, and then drove around looking for any sign of Howard Wiseman. Unsure of what to do after that, the driver called El Flaco for further guidance. While the chauffer wasn't a member of the Order of 28, he was being compensated handsomely for his small part in the conspiracy. In return for killing the secretary of defense on the way to work, the cartel promised to pay the driver two million dollars.

El Flaco now had a serious problem. The secretary of defense, who was sixth in line to succeed the president, had somehow managed to drop off the face of the earth. If he wasn't located soon, the entire political coup would be in jeopardy. El Flaco immediately began calling his contacts in the government, hoping to determine exactly what happened to Howard Wiseman.

30

IT WASN'T OFTEN that someone put the president of the United States on hold, but that was exactly what Helen had done. She had been delivering an update to the president at Camp David when Joshua Pullman called. Joshua was the head of the Secret Service, and he had recently been ordered by the president to secure the remaining members of the cabinet. Although he doubted the Constitutional legality of his new responsibilities, he wanted to apprise Helen of his efforts to safeguard the remaining leaders in the Executive Branch.

"The president told me to keep you informed," Joshua began, calling over a landline phone. "We have all the other cabinet members secured at different locations throughout the city."

"What about the secretary of the treasury?" Helen asked. "Have you learned anything else about him?"

"We're working with the state cops out in Utah on their search and rescue mission. The flash flood on the Green River caused a big mess," Joshua said.

"When will we know something?"

"It's still early morning out there, so it will probably be another hour until we hear back from them," Joshua said. "The only other person that's still unaccounted for is the defense secretary."

"I hope he's still okay," Helen said, hiding the fact that she had recently spoken to Howie.

Joshua sighed over the phone. "This day is falling apart. The cell phone outage has crippled my team's ability to coordinate. Now, we have a bunch of other VIPs who might be at risk. I hope we don't lose anyone else." His comment was sincere yet unsure.

"I'll tell the president that you've done what he asked you to do. Please keep me informed if you have any changes on your side," Helen said.

"I will," Josh replied as he ended the call.

10:15 AM EDT
OUTSIDE OF STRASBURG, VIRGINIA

Howie couldn't believe how fast the situation was spiraling out of control. The passionate side of him wanted to drive straight to the Pentagon and wage war on the terrorists who had instigated this horrible crisis, but the more logical side of Howie's persona kept his passionate self in check. He recognized that, had he remained in Washington, he would likely be dead now. By fleeing out of harm's way, he was alive and able to serve his country, albeit in a non-traditional manner for the secretary of defense.

Howie was currently trying to determine what had happened to the speaker of the House. All the news channels reported that the speaker had died of an accidental insulin overdose, but Howie didn't buy it. Once again, he turned to his vast network of business associates. He called Maggie Adovnik, a mechanical engineer who he once met at a technical seminar. Maggie designed medical devices, and while she didn't work for the same company that manufactured the insulin pump used by the speaker, she worked on similar products.

"Okay, I got the information here," Maggie said after coming back on the phone. She had temporarily placed Howie on hold while she tracked down the product analysis that her company had done on the type of insulin pump that had been implanted in the politician's abdomen.

"What does it say?" Howie asked.

"Well, this document is a lot more detailed than what you'd find out on the web," Maggie said. "Technically, it's for internal use only. It contains the nitty-gritty on their product."

Howie completely understood what Maggie was inferring. It was common practice in the business world to perform an in-depth investigation on a competitor's product. The analysis was useful in understanding new and upcoming features, as well as any product shortcomings the manufacture didn't necessarily want to highlight. Businesses all across the world, from fast food restaurants to automobile manufactures, engaged in the essential practice.

"We updated our document back in May," Maggie said. She scanned through pages of notes. "It looks like our guys found a potential bug in the wireless communication protocol."

Howie was confused. "The pump has a Wi-Fi connection?"

"Yes. It looks like it has a chipset that conforms to the typical 802.11 standards," Maggie said.

"Why would you put Wi-Fi on an insulin pump?"

"Actually, it's not all that uncommon. More and more medical devices are Wi-Fi enabled. I'm designing a pacemaker right now that has it," Maggie said.

"That sounds like sales fluff," Howie said. As an electrical engineer, Howie had learned firsthand that the sales team in corporations often pushed the engineers for unneeded features to enhance product appeal.

"Doctors love the wireless," Maggie said. "Take this pacemaker I'm working on. The medical team can remotely monitor the patient's heart rhythm or download the device's history when the patient comes in for a monthly checkup."

"Adding Wi-Fi seems like a potential security hole," Howie said.

"That's what our guys in the lab discovered on this particular insulin pump," Maggie said. "It seems this device uses weak encryption on the password that controls the Wi-Fi settings. It's possible that someone with computer skills might be able to hack the device and alter its settings."

Howie quickly made the connection to what had likely happened with the speaker of the House. "Could someone have done this to the speaker's pump?"

"It's hard to say. With *our* medical equipment, we use strong encryption for wireless settings. We also require that one of our tech guys be in the operating room to configure the device when it's implanted. Doctors are smart, but they're notoriously ignorant when it comes to technology. It takes all their brainpower just to keep current on human anatomy," Maggie said.

Howie had heard enough. While he didn't have solid evidence, he recognized a smoking gun in the death of the speaker of the House. "Thanks for your help, Maggie. You're awesome."

"No problem," Maggie said.

"Keep this info quiet for now. I'm not sure if someone hacked into the insulin pump, but I'm going to get to the bottom if it," Howie said.

10:30 AM EDT
WASHINGTON, DC

El Flaco was completely stumped. He had spent the past hour reaching out to various contacts at the Pentagon. Nobody there knew the whereabouts of the secretary of defense. El Flaco had even broken protocol and directly contacted some of the members of the Order of 28 in an attempt to learn if Howard Wiseman was dead or alive. Unfortunately, they were also clueless about what had happened to the leader of the military.

Feeling that the entire plan to overthrow the government might be in jeopardy, El Flaco decided to call his boss for direction. Fortunately, the skinny mercenary had a special cell phone that was immune to the computer virus that was causing the wireless outage across the metro area. In the quiet of his hotel room, El Flaco placed a call to an international number in Mexico. It rang twice before being answered by the man overseeing the entire Chiapas drug cartel.

"We've got a problem," El Flaco said. He didn't need to identify himself to Javier. Few people called the drug lord directly.

"What is it, my friend?"

"I can't find the secretary of defense. I've contacted a dozen different people, and nobody knows where he is. I've even spoken to some of the locals on our payroll, and they are clueless."

Javier was quiet for a moment. "How does this affect Votan's plans?"

"It will be extremely hard for the rebellion to succeed if the secretary of defense is still alive," El Flaco said.

"That puts our business deal in jeopardy. As you know, I don't agree with the Order's ideology. I'm looking at this from a financial perspective," the drug lord said.

El Flaco understood his boss's comment. The cartel had agreed to do the Order's dirty work in exchange for exclusive access to sell their drugs in the United States. But if Votan failed to rise to power, the Chiapas cartel wouldn't make any headway into the lucrative drug trade north of the border. Votan had to become the president so he could turn a blind eye to the cartel's expanding operations in the United States.

"Do you think the secretary of defense is still alive?" Javier asked his lieutenant.

"That's difficult to tell. It's possible that he might have gotten wind of this rebellion and gone underground," El Flaco speculated.

"Is there anyone else we can contact to get more information?" Javier asked.

"Not without exposing our part in the rebellion. If we keep asking questions, it will draw too much attention."

"I don't like the uncertainty of the situation," Javier determined. "How soon could you leave?"

"My plane is at a community airport in Virginia. I could be there in less than an hour if necessary," El Flaco said. He was a certified pilot, frequently using his private Cessna Turbo Skylane to travel undetected. "But if we pull out now, we'll lose all the money we've invested in this operation."

El Flaco highlighted the drug lord's dilemma. The cartel had also bankrolled most of Votan's rebellion, spending nearly ten million dollars buying off informants or employing the disgruntled computer hackers.

"The loss of money would be painful, but it would be nothing compared to being caught in the middle of a failed political coup," Javier said. He paused a moment before giving new instructions "Head out to the airport, but don't leave just yet. You can monitor the situation from there and give Votan a couple more hours to implement his rebellion. If you don't see any progress in determining what happened to the secretary of defense, fly out to our staging grounds in Guatemala and wait there," Javier ordered.

I N THE SITUATION Room, Helen listened to a conference call between the president of United States and the remaining members of his National Security Council.

"I'm addressing the nation in two hours, and I want some solid information to give the American public. We're going to have coast-to-coast chaos if we don't get control of this situation," the president said. He was clearly desperate to stop the crisis, but he didn't know what he was up against.

"We'll reconvene after my speech. Call me immediately if any of you have new information."

Helen ended the conference call. She leaned back in her chair and took a deep breath. While the situation was still dynamic, she had regained some of her composure from just an hour ago. Tony sat on the edge of the desk next to Helen. The duty officer had also been listening in on the conference call with the president. "Why didn't you tell them about Howie?" he asked.

"I will, but for right now, I like the fact that he's presumed dead," Helen said. "It gives me an upper hand in dealing with traitors."

"Because they don't realize that you know that Howie is safe, right?" Tony asked.

"Exactly," Helen said. "I've been listening for anything that might suggest if someone knows that Howie's still alive. If they do, that will help me track down who's behind this mess."

"That leaves the Department of Defense without their leader."

"There are hundreds of generals over at the Pentagon that can carry the load. They'll be just fine for a while," Helen assured the duty manager.

The desk phone in front of Helen blared out. Besides the president, only Howie and Tanner had the direct number to this phone.

"Hello," Helen answered.

"This is Howie. How are things going on your side?"

"It's crazy around here, but I'm getting my wits back," Helen said. "We just had a conference call with the remaining members of the Security Council. Everyone is scrambling to find anything that identifies the terrorists. Right now, all we have is a bunch of speculation."

Howie delivered his update. "I just got off the phone with a friend who works in the medical device industry. She said that the insulin pump used by the speaker of the House was susceptible to a hack from the embedded Wi-Fi connection. It's possible that someone might have remotely logged into the pump's controller and tampered with the settings."

Helen was thrown off by the idea that someone would have intentionally killed the speaker of the House. "How sure are you about this?"

"It's not definite, but look at what else has happened. The dam on the Green River releases a ton of water, causing a flood. Then the security cameras at the State Department don't work because someone pushed up the temperature settings in the data center. And don't forget about this mess with the cell phones in the metro area. Someone with a serious knowledge of computer hacking is spreading hate and discontent," Howie concluded.

"China and Iran both have the ability to launch a coordinated cyberattack, but I highly doubt either one of them are involved. The Chinese government still has egg on its face from their virus attack two years ago. Iran would be foolish to try the same thing," Helen said.

"What about some resentful hackers? Maybe like Anonymous?" Howie asked.

Helen thought about Howie's theory. "From what I learned while I was at the NSA, Anonymous isn't all that organized. There are a lot of bright people in that group, but they all have different agendas."

"Maybe some hackers teamed up with the cartel. I know there's a faction of Anonymous that just wants to create anarchy," Howie said.

"That sounds more realistic. It would be easy for the cartel to buy the services of professional hackers," Helen said.

"I agree, but there's something else that's still gnawing at me, and it goes beyond hackers and cyberattacks," Howie said.

"It's what we talked about at breakfast, right?"

"Yeah, I just can't shake the feeling that something bigger is going on. I can see the argument that the cartel has a reason to cause problems, but how does this help them? Killing off our leaders would only justify us declaring an act of war. There's no cartel on earth that can stand up to our military. They'd lose everything," Howie said.

"Yeah, something isn't right, but nobody around here can put their finger on it. Everything is cloudy right now," Helen said. She suddenly thought about Tanner and his work on translating the Itza Bible. "I'm going to call the team out in Utah. Maybe they've found something to help point us in the right direction."

11:15 AM EDT

NSA DATA CENTER, UTAH

Tanner was in his office at the Bumblehive. He had stepped away from the translation work to check in with Megan and the kids. He was relieved to know that they were safe, staying with his parents in southern Utah until things settled down. "I'll call you later on tonight," he told his wife.

"I love you," Megan said over the phone.

"I love you too." He ended the call and got ready to return to the conference room downstairs. Suddenly the secure "gray" desk phone blared out. He checked the caller ID. It was coming from the Situation Room.

"I'm surprised you called me. I thought you'd be overwhelmed with the crisis back in DC," Tanner said.

"Honestly, I was pretty frantic an hour ago. But I've got my game face on now, and I'm doing better," Helen admitted. "What's the mood like out there?"

"People are obviously shocked, but nobody is panicking. Everyone is cautiously going about their daily business. It kind of reminds me of how people went to work on 9/11," Tanner said.

"It's definitely worse out here on the East Coast. There are reports of people stockpiling up on food and supplies. A lot of people have gone home for the day," Helen said. "The only thing preventing an all-out panic is the fact that the president is still alive and running the country."

"The news reports say that Anonymous is claiming responsibility for the phone mess. Does that correlate with what you know?" Tanner asked.

"Yes, but we're still trying to confirm that. The outage is making everything worse. We're having a hard time coordinating everything," Helen said. "But if you've got a minute, I need to throw a couple of things at you."

Tanner listened as Helen delivered a brief summary of the hacking incidents regarding Flaming Gorge Dam, the air conditioning units at the State Department, and the insulin pump. As his previous boss, Helen knew about Tanner's former hacking lifestyle. He knew she completely trusted him, and she felt that he would give her the best answers, especially when it came to computer vulnerabilities.

When she finished, Tanner let out an audible sigh. "That's hard-core hacking, going after SCADA controllers and embedded chips like that," he said. "Pulling that off is way beyond script kiddies."

"What about the drug cartel? It's obvious that the hacks were used in conjunction with the assassinations," Helen said.

"I doubt they have anyone with the skill set to do that, but the cartel does have a lot of cash. For the right price, they could hire someone to do the hacking."

"Like someone from Anonymous?" Helen asked.

"That would be a good starting point," Tanner said. He paused and then expounded on his idea. "Actually, that would make the most sense. Not even the crazies in China would want to do hacks like those. I mean, killing the speaker of the House by hacking into his insulin pump is just the same thing as killing him with a bullet. It's an obvious act of war."

"But Anonymous isn't a nation, they're just a global organization," Helen said. "They're even more elusive and secretive than al-Qaeda."

"Right," Tanner said, completing Helen's line of thought. "So the cartel employs a few hackers from Anonymous to help with the killings, knowing it would be practically impossible for us to track them down and bring them to justice."

"Is there anything in those emails that shows the cartel is working hand in hand with Anonymous?" Helen asked.

"We ran into a problem while decoding the messages," Tanner said. "Our translation process is producing mostly religious words. We think there has to be another key somewhere, correlating modern words with the Itza language."

"Can't the Cipher figure out the emails?" Helen asked.

"He's helping the best he can, but we have thousands of messages to decode. He can only go so long before he needs another nap."

"Pump him full of some coffee," Helen said. "I need those messages decoded immediately, even if it means kick-starting the Cipher with copious amounts of caffeine."

"I think I've got a better solution," Tanner replied. "I just spoke with the person at Fort Meade who originally broke into the backup computer system and downloaded the encrypted emails. She's getting me access to the server so I can see if there's another encryption key hidden on there somewhere."

"Tanner, I need you to push everyone and get those emails decrypted today. I'm going to tell you something that you can't repeat," Helen said. Her voice dropped down to a hushed tone. "From my point of view, this appears to be bigger than just the cartel or some angry hackers. I think someone on the inside has to be involved, and I'm betting it's someone at the top. I'm counting on you to deliver a miracle."

Tanner felt overwhelmed at the increased urgency of his assignment. "I guess this investigation has moved beyond Bibles and ciphers."

"Way beyond," Helen said.

TANNER AND SYDNEY sat down at the operations desk for QC. Using the secret user account and password that Lieutenant Sakamoto had given him, Tanner logged into the backup email server in Hermosillo, Mexico.

"I hope you can still remember how to do this sort of thing," Sydney said.

Tanner chuckled. "Fortunately, successful hacking is more about process and methodology. I remember that much better than my diminishing technical skill set," he said.

Tanner began his task by writing and executing a simple shell script. The customized computer program searched the entire file system of the email server. Linux servers had thousands of files, the vast majority of them legitimately required to operate the computer. He was prepared for this condition, however, and programmed his script to look only for hidden or oddly named files—a trick that hackers often used to conceal a file from prying eyes.

The program ran for forty minutes before Tanner noticed something unusual. Buried way down under the Tomcat file structure, the script found a hidden directory. Because of his vast experience exploiting servers, Tanner quickly realized that the directory was not part of a normal web server installation. Navigating into the hidden directory, he uncovered several binary files and a single text file.

"Look at this," he said. "There's a text file called 'dictionary.' I found it in a hidden location with other binary files called 'encode' and 'decode.'"

"Wow, those names seem kind of obvious," Sydney said. "Why are they in English? I thought they would be in Spanish."

"The owner most likely speaks English as a first language. He probably didn't think that naming these files in English was a problem, seeing that they are in a hidden directory."

"What's in that dictionary file?" Sydney asked anxiously.

Typing on the keyboard, Tanner quickly opened contents of the online dictionary. The document had a simple layout. A column on the left listed every letter in the English alphabet, and the column on the right contained the corresponding character in Itza.

"Jackpot!" Tanner shouted, pumping his fist in the air.

"That's it," Sydney said. "But doesn't that seem too simple?"

"Why complicate something that doesn't need to be?" Tanner asked. He quickly typed a command to download the hidden files that he had uncovered. "I'm going to run this decode routine against the encrypted emails and see what it does."

Sydney leaned in for a better look. "It's show time," she said.

The computer program sprung to life. It began by queuing up the Itza emails in batches of ten. Then ten separate status bars flashed up on the screen, each one estimating the conversion progress as an email message was translated from Itza into English. The quantum computer tore through the correspondences with ease. When a status bar reached one hundred percent complete, it scrolled off the screen and a new status bar appeared. Soon, the computer screen flashed wildly as hundreds of status bars rapidly scrolled by. Things were moving so fast now that neither Tanner nor Sydney could visually keep track. A minute later, the program abruptly ended. A summary screen popped up on the monitor, showing the total number of email messages decrypted: 12,569.

"Let's see what we've got," Tanner said enthusiastically. He opened up the folder where all the output was stored. Immediately, he saw the fruits of success—rows and rows of email messages, all converted into English.

"Way to go!" Sydney exclaimed, giving her boss a congratulatory slap on the back.

Tanner paused for a moment. "Before we claim victory, let's verify our results using a quick pattern match against the translated words from the analysts downstairs. We can't afford to be wrong about the decryption," he said.

Sydney nodded her head. "Good idea."

While the linguists hadn't translated everything in the Bible, the words they had determined were already uploaded into QC. Tanner wrote another simple script to compare the words from the linguists against a few of the emails they had just decoded. The results matched perfectly.

"We did it!" Sydney said.

"But now it's time for the hard part. We've got to sort through all these emails and find the most pertinent ones," Tanner said. "Let's save all this information. Go get Mel and the rest of the team. We'll need everyone working together on this."

12:00 PM EDT
CAMP DAVID, MARYLAND

A T NOON ON October 28, the president of the United States briefly and solemnly addressed the nation.

"My fellow Americans, I speak to you from the peaceful surroundings of Camp David. Yet, today, many of our fellow citizens are experiencing turmoil and grief. Once again, we find ourselves the victims of despicable acts of terror. Our freedom and our way of life are threatened by these evildoers. Their acts of murder were intended to weaken our nation's leadership, but they have failed. America is bigger than just an individual man or woman, or a single title or rank. We are a great country of many, and we cannot, and will not, be intimidated or threatened by heinous acts of violence.

"The terrorists who attacked our nation are members of the Chiapas drug cartel. They are led by a criminal named Javier Soto. Our intelligence reports indicate the cartel assassinated our noble vice president, David Torres, for his fierce opposition to illegal drugs. As a doctor, David completely understood the danger and destruction caused by drug abuse. He devoted his entire life, both as a doctor and then as a politician, to prevent the toxic chemicals from overtaking our society.

"The Chiapas cartel didn't stop with just the murder of the vice president. They came to our homeland and intensified their violent attacks. By assassinating important leaders in our capital, they hoped to cast our nation into chaos. They have failed. We will not panic. Our nation is strong. Our military is powerful. And the functions of our government continue without interruption.

"As Commander in Chief, I have directed that all measures be taken to bring the criminals to justice. They will be accountable for their evil acts. Today is a day for every American, from every walk of life, to stand united. We have overcome tragedy before, and we will do it again. Thank you, and may God bless America."

Like millions of his fellow Americans, Votan watched the brief presidential address. But he wasn't listening to what the president had said. Votan was paying attention to the Commander in Chief's body language. Despite being advised to prerecord his address, the president had decided to give it live. As a result, the stress of speaking at a time of crisis was apparent to the entire nation. The president looked haggard and confused. He attempted to appear calm, but Votan knew the president was terrified. That's because Votan had spent the entire morning with the Commander in Chief at Camp David.

It was time for Votan to make his final move. The isolation and secure confines of Camp David provided the perfect location for his political coup. The lead Secret Service agent on the president's security detail, who was also a member of the Order of 28, had staffed the rest of his team with agents who were loyal to Votan and his cause. Nobody would come to the president's defense, not even the military, which was leaderless at the moment. The final step of the coup would be quiet and quick. When Votan addressed the nation at 9:00 p.m. tonight, he had no doubt that he would be the nation's new leader.

1:00 PM EDT

NSA DATA CENTER, UTAH

TANNER AND HIS team began their ominous task. Every decoded email had been printed off, forming a massive stack of papers in the center of the conference room table. All the members of the QC team were present, including Mel and Rachel, who had been summoned back to work after just a few hours of sleep.

"Okay, here's the plan," Tanner said. He stood before the group seated around the conference room table. "We need to read through all these messages and sort them into three piles—urgent, important, and minor. We've got to quickly determine the underlying context so I can call Helen back with some solid facts."

"It would probably go faster if we threw all these emails in a database and wrote some code to do this for us," Rachel said.

Tanner shook his head. "We have digital copies of the emails stored on Sydney's laptop, but the data is too raw to do anything without creating an effective program. We're just going to have to do this the old-fashioned way and analyze the data as we sort it."

"Why are just the five of us working on this?" Kevin asked. "Wouldn't it be better if we had all those interpreters helping us out?"

Kevin had a good point, but Tanner had a better reason to keep only his team involved. "Helen thinks the killings are probably just the tip of the iceberg. Someone higher up in the government is likely helping the cartel," he said. "There might be a traitor in our midst, so that's why I'm only letting people that I completely trust look at these printouts."

"What are the Cipher and the other linguists doing downstairs?" Rachel asked.

"They don't know that we've found another key and cracked the emails, so let's just let them keep plugging along with their translation," Tanner said. "In the meantime, we'll quietly sort these messages and call Helen directly when we find anything."

The group got to work. Each member of the team grabbed a handful of papers and started skimming though the messages. Some of the emails were brief, containing trivial information like flight schedules or weather reports. But there were other emails that were blatantly more scathing in their context, talking about rebellion and assassinations. The analysts worked quickly and quietly, sorting the emails into different stacks according to their importance.

"I think we should have someone summarize the context of these critical emails on the whiteboards as we sort through them," Sydney said. "That way, we don't have to wait until we're all done to start seeing a trend."

"Good idea," Tanner said. He stood up and walked over to one of the large whiteboards on the wall. "Shout out when you put something in the urgent pile. I specifically want to know if you find names or details about the assassinations."

As the QC team read through their emails, Tanner jotted down the key points from the messages. On one side of the whiteboard, he started a column with the names of important leaders. The first name Tanner wrote down belonged to the president of the United

States. While the president was mentioned in a good portion of the emails, there were also messages about the vice president, the secretary of state, the speaker of the House, and several other leaders killed during the past 24 hours.

It also became clear that the conspirators used aliases when talking about themselves. So Tanner started another column on the opposite side of the whiteboard, listing pseudonyms like Votan, Mulac, Yaluk, Cizin, Akbul, and Tohil. "I think it's safe to assume all the bad guys have aliases," he said.

"That makes sense. The targets are clearly identified by their real names, like Elizabeth Godfrey, but the bad guys conceal their identities with code names," Kevin said.

"I've been searching the Internet for some of those aliases. They're all different Mayan gods, like the god of fire, the god of lightning, and the god of darkness," Sydney said, reading from her laptop.

"If anyone can find a message that links the aliases with actual names, that would be huge," Kevin said

Rachel spoke out from the far end of the table. "Let's start another column that lists the major plot elements. I'm finding an awful lot of messages talking about getting rid of the Constitution and scary stuff like that," she said.

Tanner wrote "Plots" as a new heading on the whiteboard and listed "no more Constitution" underneath it.

"I'm seeing a lot of references to something called the Order of 28. It sounds like a secret society or group," Mel said.

"I bet that's what they call themselves," Tanner pointed out. He wrote "Order of 28" in big letters at the top of the whiteboard.

"I've only found a couple of emails talking specifically about the drug cartel. Is anyone else seeing more than that?" Sydney asked.

"That's a good point," Rachel said. "I'd expect more information about the cartel, but I've only found a few messages mentioning them."

"I'm not seeing much either, but I'm finding a lot about this Votan guy. From what other people are writing, I'm thinking he's the leader of the Order of 28," Kevin said.

Tanner took a red dry-erase marker and circled the name Votan on the board. Ever since he heard that Votan was the Mayan god of war, Tanner had speculated that he was the instigator.

The team continued their work for another twenty minutes. They shouted out key words for Tanner, and he recorded them under the appropriate column on the whiteboard. The analysts worked diligently, but with over 12,000 emails, the process was painfully slow.

"I think I'm seeing another pattern develop," Kevin said. He stood up and walked over to the whiteboard, pointing to a long list. "We've got a bunch of names here. Some of these are well known, like Howard Wiseman or Elizabeth Godfrey, but look at these other names. I've never heard of these people."

"Maybe they're trivial players. It's possible that small guys in the conspiracy didn't get code names. If we look at the list of aliases, I only see twenty-eight names," Rachel said.

"I bet those aliases all belong to the Order of 28," Kevin stated resolutely.

Tanner pointed to his writing on the whiteboard. "Let's break down these names into two groups," he said. "One list will be important figures like Howard Wiseman, and the other list will be these unrecognized people."

Tanner walked over to another whiteboard on a different wall. He started copying all the unrecognized names. As he wrote a name, Kevin erased it from the list of more prominent leaders. After a few moments, the analysts saw the unexpected results.

"Except for the president, that list of important people basically names everyone that has been assassinated," Sydney said.

Tanner studied the list, yet something didn't seem right. He turned his gaze from the whiteboard to Sydney. "Pull up a browser and search for the presidential line of succession. I want to go through the whole list," he told his coworker.

"Okay, I've got the information," Sydney said.

"Start with the president and go down the list from there," Tanner said. He prepared to write the titles on the board.

Sydney listed off the leadership positions in the line of succession. "The president is first, then the vice president, the speaker of the House, president pro tempore, secretary of state, secretary of the treasury, secretary of defense, attorney general, secretary of the interior, secretary of agriculture, secretary of—" She was cut off by Tanner.

"Okay, that's enough. We've got emails mentioning all these guys down to the attorney general," Tanner said. "Has anybody found an email mentioning the secretaries of interior or agriculture?" he asked.

"No," Rachel said for the rest of the group.

Tanner quickly crossed out the names of the leaders who had been killed. The remaining list now contained just four names: the president, the secretary of the treasury, the secretary of defense, and the attorney general.

"How come you didn't cross off the treasury and defense secretaries?" Rachel asked.

"We still don't know if they're dead or not. The press is just reporting that they are missing right now," Tanner said.

"But we know that the attorney general, the secretary of interior, the secretary of agriculture, and the others down on this list are still all alive. The media confirmed that just after the president's speech at noon," Sydney said.

"Right, so something is going on right here," Tanner said. He drew a bold line between the secretary of defense and the attorney general. "Let's say the treasury and defense secretaries are truly dead. That leaves the president and then this huge gap of dead leaders down until we get to the attorney general. At that point, all the remaining successors appear to be alive."

"Yeah, that's weird. Why hasn't the cartel gone after the president?" Kevin asked. "That's the obvious question."

"And why stop at the attorney general?" Rachel added. "If the cartel truly wanted to target our nation's leaders, why would they stop at Rodney Groth?"

Rachel's observation caused a shock to run up Tanner's spine. "Wait, what did you just say?"

"I said, if the cartel really wants to take out our leaders, why stop at Rodney Groth?" she repeated.

"His name isn't listed on the board," Tanner said. Adrenalin rushed through his body. "The name Rodney Groth isn't listed anywhere on the board," he re-emphasized with excitement. "Look, we've got the real names for everyone else in the line of succession. We've got David Torrez, Elizabeth Godfrey, Howard Wiseman, and all the others," he said, circling several names on the board. "We have emails that mention all these leaders by name, but when we get down to the attorney general, nobody has found the actual name of Rodney Groth in any of the messages."

"He might be mentioned in some of the other emails. We're only about one-tenth of the way through this stack," Mel said, pointing to the unread messages on the table.

Tanner turned again toward Sydney. "Do a simple search of those emails you have stored on your laptop. See if any of them contain the name Rodney Groth."

Sydney ran a quick "grep" command on all the emails stored in a directory on her laptop. A few moments later the results came back. "His name isn't mentioned in any of the email texts," she said.

Tanner drew a star next to the title attorney general on the whiteboard. "We need to focus here. Something about Rodney Groth doesn't seem right."

"I'm going out on a limb here, but could it be as simple as the attorney general is involved in all this?" Sydney asked.

Mel let out a sarcastic laugh. "Right, he's murdering all his fellow politicians."

Tanner stood back from the whiteboard for a better look at his chicken scratch. "Don't laugh, Mel. I was thinking the same thing."

"That's insane. The media, and even the president, say the drug cartel is behind this," Mel countered.

"Yes, but Helen says it's more than that. She's pretty sure

someone at the top is involved, and the attorney general is someone at the top," Sydney said.

"I can't believe you're seriously considering this," Mel argued. "That's treason we're talking about. The AG would be out of his mind to do something that stupid."

"I agree with Syd," Rachel said. "It's obvious the folks above the attorney general were intentionally assassinated."

"Of course that's true. Nobody is *unintentionally* assassinated. That's why it's called assassination and not manslaughter," Mel said. His normal pessimistic nature was on full display. "And not all those people were murdered, remember? One died of an accidental insulin overdose, and two are still missing."

"Whatever," Rachel shot back at Mel. "Someone is behind all this, and from these emails, it looks like it's someone that has more knowledge and influence than a bunch of drug runners in Mexico," she shouted.

"Easy," Tanner said. He motioned for the members of his team to calm down. "We're brainstorming here. Every possibility is on the table right now."

Mel took a golf tee from his shirt pocket and put it in his mouth. "Okay, I'll play ball," he said, leaning back in his chair. "Let's say that the AG is behind all this. Doesn't that seem far-fetched to you? Killing off all these leaders just so he can become the president?"

"He doesn't want to be president. He wants to be a supreme leader or king," Kevin corrected. "We've seen dozens of emails that talk about getting rid of the Constitution and setting a new government."

"Okay, so he wants to be the man in charge," Mel said. "This is nonsense because it will never happen. The president is alive, and he's still running the country. The AG would have to kill the president, and there's no way he can do that with the increased security now."

"Yeah, tell that to the vice president or the secretary of state," Rachel said with frustration. "Someone was able to get to them."

Mel's tone became empathetic. "Hey, I agree. It's a tragedy that the vice president and those other leaders are dead, but killing the president of the United States is on a completely different level. Let's be honest, the Cabinet doesn't run the country. It's the president, and he's alive and well."

"For now, but who knows how long he'll be alive," Rachel pushed back.

Mel threw his arms up in mock surrender. "Okay, okay. I give in. Rodney Groth is Votan, and he's determined to be the new president," he said flippantly. "But even if the AG somehow manages to get past all the Secret Service agents and kill the president, it wouldn't work," he said. "There would be a national uprising. Nobody would follow Rodney once they learned that he killed the president."

Sydney looked up from her laptop. She had been quiet during the rest of the discussion. "Maybe he doesn't have to kill the president."

Tanner turned to look at Sydney. "What do you mean?"

"What if the attorney general just claims the president is somehow incapacitated and can't lead the nation during this crisis? According to this website, there's a weird part of the Twenty-fifth Amendment that says Rodney might be able to do just that."

The NSA analysts thought about what they had just heard. It seemed like Sydney might have stumbled upon something. But once again, Mel threw cold water on everything. "This is getting way too complicated. It sounds like a topic for one of those conspiracy theory shows on cable TV."

"Maybe not," Tanner said. "Rodney is the nation's head lawyer. He probably knows more about the Constitution than anyone else. Maybe he found a way to manipulate it for his gain." Tanner quickly erased one of the whiteboards to illustrate his theory. "Give me five minutes to tie this all together, and then tell me that it's *not* possible for Rodney to pull off a coup of this magnitude."

2:30 PM EDT
NOKESVILLE, VIRGINIA

It was just after 2:30 p.m. when El Flaco started up his Cessna Turbo Skylane. With the fuel tank topped off, the single engine airplane could make the nonstop trip to the drug cartel's staging ground in Guatemala. He taxied across the tarmac of the small community airport in Virginia and prepared to takeoff.

Despite spending the past five hours playing detective, the cartel's lieutenant still couldn't determine what had happened to the secretary of defense. Howard Wiseman had vanished, and it was infuriating to El Flaco that he couldn't get any reliable information from his contacts scattered across the capital city. To complicate matters further, El Flaco couldn't call Votan and inform him about the defense secretary's status. The members of the Order of 28 were under a strict communication blackout until Votan addressed the nation later that evening. The situation had clearly deteriorated, and El Flaco was now doubtful that the coup would even succeed. But there was another, more serious problem looming for the Order of 28 that El Flaco understood better than anyone else. As a former Army Ranger, he knew that every member of the armed forces swore to "defend the Constitution of the United States against all enemies, foreign and domestic." El Flaco lived in absolutes. If the secretary of defense wasn't dead, he was still alive, and the military would always follow their designated leader when he showed up to take command.

As the Cessna Turbo Skylane lifted off into the sky, El Flaco felt a wave of relief. He was in over his head, and getting out of town was the right move. At some point, the secretary of defense was going to resurface. When he did, there was going to be an ugly showdown between Howard Wiseman and Votan.

THE QC TEAM in Utah was finally ready to call Helen with a synopsis of the emails. Analyzing the other printouts took a while, but Tanner and his team wanted to make sure they had solid evidence to back up what they were about to tell the National Security advisor. Leaning toward the speakerphone in the middle of the conference room table, Tanner punched in the number for an extension in the Situation Room. Five rings later, Helen answered the call with a wary hello.

"Hi, Helen. This is Tanner. I've got the rest of the team on the line with me, and we've got to talk to you right now." The urgency in his voice was unyielding.

"Have you decoded the emails?" she asked.

"We cracked them about two hours ago. I won't bore you with the details, but we found a separate key that completed our Itza-to-English dictionary," Tanner said. His heart was pounding as he prepared to deliver the shocking information. "I assume you're on a private line?"

"Yes. I'm the only one," Helen said, ready to receive the update.

Tanner briefly described the initial process of sorting the messages into different categories. He then explained some of the preliminary findings, including the fact that there seemed to be a group of conspirators working together. From the emails, Tanner said his team had concluded that the Chiapas cartel was working hand in hand with other conspirators in killing off the nation's leaders.

"So you think there's a group of insiders that are helping the cartel?" Helen asked.

"It's more than that. We think the cartel's involvement is just a business arrangement," Tanner said. "It's this higher group of conspirators that really seems to be calling the shots."

"Okay, who's in this group?" she asked urgently.

"From what we can tell, there are twenty-eight people in the inner circle. They call themselves the Order of 28. Unfortunately, they all refer to each other by code name in their emails, so we don't know who they are exactly. But from the tone of the emails going back and forth, these individuals are movers and shakers in the government. We're talking big time players back in DC," Tanner said.

"Who's leading them?" Helen asked.

"Somebody named Votan," Tanner said before pausing. His stomach knotted up as he prepared to implicate the attorney general of the United States in high treason.

"You hesitated," Helen said over the phone. "What are you holding back?"

"First, I want you to know this is just a theory, okay?" Tanner said, preparing to deliver the outrageous news. "We think Votan is the attorney general."

"Rodney Groth?" Helen said in shock.

"I know, it's crazy," Tanner said. "Even some of the team here thinks I've lost my mind."

"What evidence do you have for this accusation?" Helen asked.

Tanner took several minutes to tie the plot together. "It all started with the assassination of the vice president in Panama.

Everyone believed the cartel was responsible for the murder because of the vice president's opposition to illegal drugs. Even our initial intelligence reports implicated the cartel," Tanner began.

"That's right. I've got a memo from the CIA affirming that," Helen said.

"But the decoded emails say it's all a ruse. Rodney is using the cartel to systematically eliminate people to achieve his ultimate goal," Tanner said.

"What's that?" Helen asked.

"He wants to take over the government," Tanner said.

Tanner heard Helen gasp over the phone line. "How come we haven't heard anything about that?" she asked.

Rachel entered the conversation. "There are literally hundreds of people involved in this conspiracy besides the Order of 28. They're scattered across all parts of the government, working together to keep the president and his advisors in the dark."

Sydney added her sentiments to the conference call as well. "The attorney general is seventh in line for the presidency. We think he's using the cartel to assassinate the people before him. Once they are all gone, he only has to remove the president. At that point, Rodney is legally the next in line to be in charge."

"But how can he kill the president without being held responsible?" Helen asked.

Tanner paused a second before answering. "We haven't figured that out yet. But we're thinking that Rodney might not need to kill the president. According to some ambiguous language in the Constitution, he might just be able to declare the president unfit to discharge the duties of his office. We all saw how distressed he looked during his speech."

Tanner wrapped up the elaborate theory and was greeted by silence on the other end of the line. After a few moments, he called out, "Helen, are you still there?"

"I'm here," she answered in hushed and serious tone. "I need you guys to lock yourselves in that room and stay out of sight. Don't talk to anyone about this. You got me?"

In just a microsecond, it became absolutely clear to Tanner and the other members of his team that their theory wasn't just speculation anymore. "What's going on?" he asked.

"Things are a lot more tenuous here than the media is reporting. The nation is in a leadership vacuum with Congress at recesses. And when the attacks started this morning, the director over the entire Secret Service helped us round up the remaining cabinet members. They've all been taken to safe houses in different locations. The executive branch is spread out everywhere, except the attorney general and the president. The two of them are alone up at Camp David."

"Rodney could make his move right now," Tanner said with exasperation. "He probably timed the attacks so he could be isolated with the president."

"Exactly," Helen concluded. "I'll call the secret service immediately and have them detain Rodney."

"Wait, that might not be a good idea," Tanner interjected. "The conspirators have penetrated all parts of the government. We've found several emails suggesting that even some of the president's bodyguards might be involved."

"If that's true, then who *can* we trust?" Helen said.

"What about the military? Aren't there some troops at Camp David?" Rachel asked.

"Yes, but the military patrols just the perimeter of the facility. Indoors, a small group of Secret Service agents still run the show," Helen said.

"You've got to warn the president somehow," Tanner shouted. "Even if we're completely wrong, call and get someone to protect him."

"I'll will, but Rodney is also at Camp David. I've got to let the president know he's in danger without tipping off anyone," Helen said.

"Whatever we do, we've got to move fast. If we're lucky, we might be able to stop this uprising in its tracks," Tanner said.

36

3:10 PM EDT
CAMP DAVID, MARYLAND

SIXTY-TWO MILES NORTHWEST of Washington, DC, is a military complex called the Naval Support Facility Thurmont. For the vast majority of the world's population, however, the private retreat in the Catoctin Mountains is simply known as Camp David. The exclusive facility is one of the few places on earth where the president of the United States can find solitude and tranquility. Completely off limits to the public and press, Camp David is the president's private abode away from the White House. The complex spreads out over a wooded area of 120 acres. It is comprised of a dozen separate cabins, a recreation center, and even a chapel.

While Camp David is first and foremost a presidential retreat, it still contains all the necessary accommodations for the Commander in Chief to lead the country. The main structure at Camp David is the Laurel Lodge, where the president keeps his finger on the nation's pulse. The building has a presidential office, several conference rooms, and a small TV studio where the president can even address the nation.

The current president was meeting with the attorney general in the main room of the Laurel Lodge. The comfortable living area had several high-back chairs and a leather couch that sat across from a two-story brick fireplace. The two politicians were discussing the recent terrorist attacks and how to move forward despite the chaos.

"I need to show the American people that our nation is still in good hands," the president said. He got up from his chair and walked toward the large windows that looked outside upon the colorful fall foliage. "I need to get back to the White House as soon as possible and meet with the rest of my Cabinet."

"That might create unnecessary risk," Rodney advised the Commander in Chief. "Besides, you're safe up here. With Congress at recess for the elections, there's no reason to rush back. You can manage the events from here."

"Except that staying here makes me look like a coward," the president said. He turned around to face his attorney general. "Did you see the video from my speech?" he asked rhetorically. "I looked like a disaster. If I can get back to the White House and regroup, I can address the nation from the Oval Office tonight. That will instill confidence that I'm in charge and there's no need to fear."

Rodney got out of his chair and moved toward the president. The two men were alone in the quiet room, allowing them to speak frankly and openly. "I strongly advise you not to do that. Stay a couple of days up here and let the situation stabilize."

The president looked up at the taller man. "What's going on, Rodney? You've never been one to back down from the spotlight."

Rodney took a step closer to the Commander in Chief. He was less than an arm's reach away now. "I can't let you go back down there," he said with an icy stare.

The president arched an eyebrow in bewilderment. "If I didn't know better, I'd say you were giving *me* an order."

"Let me be perfectly honest," Rodney said. His face was set like stone. "You've lost control of the situation. It's time for someone else to call the shots."

"What are you talking about?" the president asked. He seemed genuinely confused. But Rodney didn't answer the question. Instead, he turned and briskly walked toward the rear of the lodge. He opened the door and let four Secret Service agents into the room. Together, the five intimidating men marched toward the Commander in Chief.

"I'm relieving you of your command, effective immediately," Rodney said with authority.

A chill ran up the president's spine. "What's the matter with you?"

Rodney didn't flinch. "I'm acting president now. I am in charge."

The president didn't exactly understand what was happening at first. Then a horrible realization washed over him. The recent assassinations and violence were Rodney's doing. It was all an elaborate political coup to seize control of the government.

"You can't do this! We're friends!" the president shouted.

Rodney's resolve was unshakable. "I *am* doing this."

"You traitorous snake!" the president shouted. Rage exploded across his face as he lunged toward his two-timing attorney general, but the head of the security detail had already anticipated the impulsive reaction. He quickly sidestepped the president and smashed the barrel of his H&K MP5 submachine gun into the back of the president's head, causing him to tumble to the floor. Rodney picked up his large foot and forcefully pinned the president's head against the carpet.

"Good, you're learning how to submit to your new leader," Rodney said with an evil laugh. "I'm running the country now! Got that?"

With a quick move, Rodney kicked the face of the most powerful man in the world. A sickening "crunch" sound filled the room, signifying that the blow had just broken the president's nose. He moaned out in pain, but Rodney ignored the injury. Instead, he turned toward the Secret Service agents and issued his first order as the new Commander in Chief. "Lock him up in the conference room."

Two Secret Service agents sprang to action. They grabbed the president by his arms and dragged him across the floor toward one of the smaller conference rooms in the Laurel Lodge. Throwing the president into the windowless room like a useless bag of trash, the two agents quickly locked the door behind them and stood guard.

Rodney turned toward the chief bodyguard. "What about the rest of his personal staff and assistants? Did you round them up without suspicion?"

"Yes. They're at the Aspen Lodge and completely isolated from everything. I've got two of my best men guarding them," the agent reported.

While the Secret Service agents at Camp David were completely loyal to Rodney and his cause, the contingent of Marines and Navy personnel at the presidential retreat were not involved in the conspiracy. As a result, Rodney had to move about Camp David with extreme caution. Taking the other two Secret Service agents with him, Rodney exited the Laurel Lodge and discreetly walked down the forested path toward the communications facility. Along the way, he met up with two additional agents, doubling the number of his small posse. The traitorous agents followed Rodney as he strode toward the communications center. When the group arrived, the four Secret Service agents quickly burst into the facility with their MP5 submachine guns drawn.

"Everybody get on the ground!" Rodney ordered. Caught completely off guard, the four unarmed Navy communication specialists did as they were instructed. Two Secret Service agents kept their submachine guns pointed at the frightened Navy staffers while the other agents quickly went to work. They gagged and bound each Navy technician before locking all of them in an adjoining closet.

Rodney dished out his commands to the remaining Secret Service agents. "I want this place to be a black hole of communication. Lock everything down. Nobody calls in or out until I give the word!"

Confident that all communication ties to Camp David were now severed, Rodney left the building and headed back up the hill toward the Laurel Lodge. None of the military forces at Camp David had any clue what had just happened. The first step in his takeover had been completed without a single shot being fired.

37

HELEN SAT ALONE at a desk in a small break-out area of the Situation Room. She had just finished her private phone call with the NSA analysts, and had come in here to think. Putting her head in her hands, she massaged her temples and pondered what to do next. Her upcoming actions might very well save the nation or disgrace her from public service.

She picked up the phone and dialed the president's office at Camp David. The phone rang endlessly for nearly a minute. A wave of nausea overcame Helen, and she literally had to use all her willpower to keep from having a panic attack. Stumbling out of the break-out room and into the adjoining operations center, she called out, "Get me the president, immediately!"

"What's wrong?" Tony asked. He rushed over to help Helen sit down in a chair.

"The president is in danger. Someone on the inside is after him," she exclaimed.

Tony was confused. "Who is it?"

"Rodney Groth," Helen said.

"Impossible. He's with the president right now," Tony said.

"That's the problem. The president was taken to Camp David for protection, but that isolation has now made him vulnerable to an inside attack," she observed.

"I can't get through to Camp David. Nobody is answering," a staffer shouted out.

"The backup communication link is also down!" another operations officer added.

"Get Josh Pullman on the line." Tony ordered, referring to the head of the Secret Service.

"Wait!" Helen shouted. "Don't do that."

Tony turned and looked at the National Security advisor. "Why?"

"I'm not sure his organization can be trusted."

"You think Joshua is involved in this?" Tony asked. "No way. He helped us secure the other members of the Cabinet this morning."

The initial wave of nausea had passed, and Helen was getting her faculties back. "I doubt that Josh is involved, but someone in his organization has to be."

"What evidence do you have for this?" Tony asked.

Helen briefly explained what she had learned from the NSA analysts in Utah. She touched on all the main points, including how there had to be more than just one group involved in the conspiracy. She concluded by emphasizing that it would be impossible to pull off a coup of this magnitude without a traitor or two on the president's protection detail.

"There are over four thousand sworn agents in the Secret Service," Tony said. "That's a big group to accuse."

"You're thinking too large. Look at how the terrorists got to the vice president. I bet you someone on the protective detail team has turned and is working directly with Rodney," Helen said.

"I see your concern, but I just can't buy the fact that the attorney general is leading a rebellion at Camp David," he stated.

"That's why it's possible. It's so insane that nobody even considered a coup was happening until we figured out the contents of those emails," Helen said. Suddenly, she figured out how Rodney was going to accomplish his coup. "He's doing the exact same thing the Soviets tried to do with Gorbachev back in '91!"

"What?" Tony asked.

Helen took a couple of breaths, trying to organize her thoughts. "I remember it well because I was working on the NSA's Eastern European team at the time. The Communist hard-liners had grown weary of President Gorbachev's reform programs. They planned a secret coup to coincide with his vacation to the Crimea Peninsula. The hard-liners cut all of Gorbachev's communication links back to Moscow, and put him under house arrest using just a handful of conspirators."

Tony seemed confused. "But Rodney can't do that. It's illegal. The American public wouldn't stand for it."

Helen shook her head. "What happened to Gorbachev wasn't legal either, but it almost worked. After isolating Gorbachev, the hard-liners got on TV and told the Soviet public that the president was on his deathbed. Then they implemented martial law to maintain order in the capital. Because they controlled the flow of information, the public was forced to believe what they were being told."

Helen watched as Tony's face turned white. "Rodney could do the same thing here. With the president out of the loop, he could declare a state of emergency and take control of the military."

"Exactly," Helen said.

"Let's call the Pentagon and send some troops to Camp David!" Tony stated enthusiastically.

Helen shook her head. "That's the wrong move to make right now. We have no idea how far or wide this conspiracy goes. We can't call out the cavalry until we know who we can trust."

"But we can't just sit here on our hands," Tony said.

Helen agreed, but she had a better idea. "Let's call Howie. He'll know someone in his organization that can help."

3:20 PM EDT
OUTSIDE OF STRASBURG, VIRGINIA

Howie's prototype satellite phone chirped to life. He answered the call. "Hello."

"Howie, this is Helen. We've gone to Defcon One."

The military analogy hit Howie hard. "What's going on?"

"I just spoke with my former team out in Utah. They finally decrypted all those emails, and they found out this mess is a lot more than just some rogue drug cartel operation," Helen said.

"That's what I've said since the beginning. I knew someone on the inside had to be involved."

"Yes, but did you think it might be the attorney general?" Helen asked.

"Rodney?" Howie said, his voice trailing off. He was shocked speechless.

Howie listened as Helen expanded on what she had learned. She spoke for several minutes, weaving all the disparate and confusing facts into a comprehensive quilt. She told Howie that the president was currently alone with the attorney general at Camp David, and that nobody could get through to the communication center up there. The ongoing cell phone outage enhanced the president's isolation, exposing him to further risk. She concluded that, if Rodney had succeeded in converting several Secret Service agents to his cause, he could easily make his move right now at Camp David.

"Of course," Howie said. "Rodney could say that he's taking charge because the president had a nervous breakdown or something. With the secret service agents on Rodney's team, who would be around to stop him? The rest of the executive branch has been decimated."

"And we know that Rodney's extremely charismatic. With all the violence from the drug cartel, the American public is looking for leadership right now. The nation just might follow Rodney if he says that he can effectively stop the cartel and end the crisis," Helen added.

"So what do we do now?" Howie asked. "If Rodney is really behind this, we can't allow him to claim the presidency."

"We've tried getting hold of the Marines up at Camp David, but it's like that place has fallen off the map. Is there anyone in your organization that we can trust to send up there?" Helen asked.

"Not after all the stuff that's happened today. In fact, the only person I can completely trust right now is you," Howie said. Then he had a wild idea. It wasn't foolproof, but it just might work in this situation. "Hey, I'm about forty minutes away from Camp David," he said. "I know my way around up there as well as anyone else. I'll leave immediately and rally the local troops, somewhere out of sight of the Secret Service. We'll find the president and get him to safety."

"That's a bad idea," Helen said. "If the president dies, you're in charge. We can't jeopardize the leadership of the nation by having you lead the charge on Camp David."

There was a pause on the line as Howie thought about the ramifications of Helen's comment. "I have no desire to be in charge. I just want this mess resolved, and there's nobody in a better situation to do that right now than me."

"I don't like it," Helen countered. "You're our wild card to trump Rodney's plans."

"We're running out of time," Howie said, growing more anxious. "We've got to move now if we want to stop Rodney from pulling off his coup. This is our best alternative given the mess we have right now."

"Okay, I see your point. How much time do you need?" Helen asked.

"I'll take this phone with me. If I don't get back to you in two hours, call the press and tell them everything you know. Then call General Neville at the Pentagon and have him launch a full-out assault on Camp David," Howie firmly said. "In the meantime, find a way to get the remaining Cabinet members back to the Situation Room without tipping off anyone. If things go south at Camp

David, we'll need whoever is after me on the list of successors to run the government."

"I'll call Director Baldwin at the CIA and get his help in gathering up the remaining Cabinet members," Helen said. "He and I don't always see eye-to-eye, but maybe that will work to my advantage. If he seems too eager, then we'll know something is also wrong at the CIA."

"Don't tell him about me. Just say that you need his help getting people back to the Situation Room," Howie said.

"I will," Helen said. "Good luck."

"You too," Howie replied.

38

IT WAS SHORTLY after 4:00 p.m. when Howie approached Camp David. Although he had visited the site many times before, today he wasn't coming through the front gate on official business. Instead, the secretary of defense approached a smaller gatehouse on the north side of the complex. This entrance wasn't as well known and wasn't as likely to be compromised by Rodney or his conspirators.

Driving slowly up the road toward the checkpoint, Howie intentionally made sure not to startle the Marines patrolling the area. The secretary of defense stopped his red Buick Lacrosse at the gatehouse and rolled down his window.

"This area is closed. You'll need to turn around," a guard said. When Howie handed his military ID to the sentry, the young Marine did a double take before snapping to attention.

"I'm sorry, sir. I thought . . . ," the Marine stumbled.

"Thought I was dead?" Howie asked.

"Yes, sir. I'm sorry, sir."

"No need to apologize. It's been a crazy day for all of us," Howie said. "What's your name, solider?"

"Lance Corporal Klossen, sir," the Marine answered.

"Corporal, I'm going to get out of the car, but I don't want you to report that I'm here. I need to speak to your team first," Howie said. He slowly and deliberately got out of the car. He even raised his arms, showing that he was willing to submit to a pat-down.

"No need for that, sir. I'm sorry I didn't recognize you earlier," Lance Corporal Klossen said.

It soon became clear to the other four Marines patrolling the entrance that someone significant had just arrived. They quickly huddled together at the checkpoint to see what was happening.

"Gentlemen, I need your help. It's crucial that nobody knows that I'm alive but you. Is that clear?" Howie told the five Marines that circled around him.

"Yes, sir," they called out in unison.

"Who's the commanding officer up here?" Howie asked.

A young Marine eagerly replied. "Captain Davidson, sir."

"Okay, I need you to escort me to Captain Davidson without anyone noticing," Howie said. "Can you give me a ride in that?" He pointed toward a Humvee behind the gatehouse.

"Yes, sir," Lance Corporal Klossen said. "Right away, sir."

The Marines helped Howie push his sedan off the road and hide it in the trees. Then two soldiers quickly loaded him in the back of the Humvee. A few minutes later, the Humvee cruised past the Buckeye Cabin, heading toward the barracks.

"I need to get inside without causing a commotion. Can you drop me off somewhere that I can sneak in?" Howie asked.

"Yes, sir. There's a loading dock in the rear. We can get you in that way," Lance Corporal Klossen said.

The Humvee emerged into a clearing and stopped at the Marine barracks. The two Marines got out of the Humvee and motioned for another pair of Marines to come over. Together, the four soldiers formed a makeshift circle to obscure the secretary of defense as he quickly made his way into the building. Once inside the large lodge, they escorted Howie down the hall toward Captain Davidson's office.

Lance Corporal Klossen snapped to attention after stepping through the door. "Sir, we've got a special visitor."

Captain Davidson was in his early fifties with salt-and-pepper hair. He was sitting at his desk and looked up just in time to see the secretary of defense step in before closing the door behind him.

"Good afternoon, captain," Howie said to the shocked officer. Captain Davidson quickly stood up and saluted, knocking his coffee across his desk in the process. "Sir, we received word that you were likely dead."

"Not yet," Howie said, "but for the next hour or two, it's imperative that everyone still thinks that I am." He quickly closed the shades on the window, obscuring the secret meeting.

After the coffee was cleaned up, Howie took a seat across from the captain. The secretary of defense explained the urgency of the situation, highlighting what he had learned from the National Security advisor. He emphasized a political coup was likely occurring at that moment at Camp David.

"None of my men are involved. I personally guarantee it," Captain Davidson said confidently.

"We think that some of the Secret Service agents in the president's protective detail have been compromised. We need to round up your men and go rescue the president," Howie said.

"All my guard units have radios. I can call out to them and get an update on the president's whereabouts," Captain Davidson said.

"Can you do that without alerting the Secret Service?" Howie asked.

"We have multiple frequencies. I'll call out on a channel that's only used by the military units up here."

"Do it, but don't sound the alarm. Just make it a casual inquiry if anyone has recently seen the president," Howie ordered.

Howie remained hidden in the office while Captain Davidson left to get a situation report. Ten minutes later, he came back into his office. He was visibility worried about something.

"The last time anyone saw the president was three hours ago when he walked into the Laurel Lodge," Captain Davidson said.

"That's not unusual, seeing that he's got an office in there. However, I can't get through to my guys at the communication center, and that is completely abnormal. They never leave their post."

"Okay, that's what I figured. They've taken out the communications link to isolate the president," Howie said.

"I've got a company of a hundred and fifty Marines up here, and another company is just an hour away," Captain Davidson said. "Give me the word and I'll call them up."

Howie shook his head. "That's too clumsy. We need a small strike team to rescue the president, not a thousand Marines storming a castle. Too many troops will cause confusion."

"I've got two 14-man squads that are specifically trained in hostage rescue," Captain Davidson said.

"That's perfect," Howie said. "We'll split them up. One squad will go over and reestablish control of the communications facility. The other unit will go see if the president is at the Laurel Lodge."

"I'll call them up immediately," Captain Davidson said. He picked up his desk phone to issue the orders.

"One more thing, captain," Howie said. "Get me a weapon and some fatigues. I'm going with you."

4:30 PM EDT

CAMP DAVID, MARYLAND

I T TOOK ABOUT thirty precious minutes to get everything organized. Captain Davidson activated his specialized Marine squads that were qualified in hostage rescue. They had trained to help rescue the president if he ever fell into enemy hands while at Camp David. Today, however, the Marines wouldn't be going after some unnamed terrorist group. They would be battling expert bodyguards, assigned to protect the most powerful man in the world.

With the hostage rescue teams now ready, Howie and Captain Davidson reviewed their hastily arranged plans. While they would have loved more time to prepare, they realized that each minute they postponed rescuing the president, the more likely they wouldn't get to him alive. Dressed in matching camouflage, Howie privately briefed roughly two dozen men that comprised the elite rescue squads. "I need to reiterate that we aren't sure what we'll find, so nobody is allowed to fire until they are fired upon. Is that clear?"

"Yes, sir," the men replied in unison.

"These are fellow Americans that we're talking about, and we aren't even sure how many are involved in the conspiracy. Exercise extreme judgment before you shoot. The best possible scenario is that everyone, including Rodney Groth, comes out of this alive," Howie said.

Captain Davidson added his two cents to the briefing. "The secretary and I will go with the squad to the Laurel Lodge. When we find the president, we'll escort him to the rendezvous point. Good luck," he said, dismissing the troops.

Howie and Captain Davidson monitored the situation on a radio as the Marines carried out their orders. The soldiers, however, didn't all rush out of the barracks in unison. Instead they left at different intervals, maintaining the illusion that nothing out of the ordinary was happening. The squad's snipers were the first to go, one of which was Lance Corporal Klossen, the same Marine who had initially greeted the secretary of defense at the north entrance to Camp David.

"The snipers are now in place. One is on the hill overlooking the Laurel Lodge, and the other is down at the communications center," Howie heard over the radio.

After the snipers were in position, the remaining members of the hostage rescue squads followed, each taking an indirect route to their target. These Marines were armed with both an M4 Carbine machine gun and a 9mm Beretta pistol. Every solider on patrol at Camp David had similar firearms, and the casual manner in which these Marines walked two-by-two suggested they might be on their way to relieve their peers of duty.

The hostage rescue squads had coordinated their operations to begin at precisely the same moment, converging upon their targets from opposite directions. One fireteam would go in through the front door of the building while another unit attacked from the rear. A third fireteam would secure the perimeter of the lodge with a sniper providing cover from a distance. With this setup the Marines hoped to quickly and professionally take control of both their targets.

Howie and Captain Davidson gave the squads ample time to get into position before moving out. The two leaders then left the main barracks and strode toward the Laurel Lodge, taking a direct path toward the cabin. Their arrival at the building was the signal for the other Marines to spring into action. In an instant, eight Marines appeared out of nowhere, overpowering the Secret Service agents guarding both the front and rear entrances. Their spontaneous action caught the traitorous agents by complete surprise.

"Where's the president?" Howie bluntly asked. He directed his question toward the Secret Service agent who was now lying face down on the cement path. Two Marines held the traitor in place, pressing their knees into his back. But the agent didn't say anything. He only stared off in the distance, expressing his defiance in silence.

"Let's go in," Captain Davidson ordered. Preparing to storm into the Laurel Lodge, the Marines in the first squad suddenly stopped when they heard the sound of gunfire off in the distance.

Down the hill at the communications center, things had just turned deadly. The second squad of Marines had run into trouble. Their surprise assault was discovered by a double-crossing Secret Service agent patrolling in the nearby woods. He was a hundred and fifty feet from the rushing troops when he drew his weapon. Despite his rigorous training, the agent's Sig Sauer P229 pistol, like all handguns, wasn't very accurate when fired at such a great distance. Only one of the agent's ten shots hit its target, wounding a Marine in his left leg.

With shots now fired by the conspirators, it was okay for the Marines in the second squad to shoot back. The soldiers dropped to the ground and returned fire. Outnumbered three-to-one by trained Marines with automatic rifles, the Secret Service agent in the woods quickly met his fate.

Back up at the Laurel Lodge, Captain Davidson swore out loud. "Our secret is out. Let's move now!" he shouted.

The squad's leader radioed the order to the other members around the cabin. They lined up in formation and prepared to storm into the building from both entrances. A Marine then launched a flashbang grenade through a side window into the lodge. It exploded in a deafening flash that temporary disoriented the traitors to the inevitable assault.

Having been forewarned by their fellow conspirators at the communications building, the six Secret Service agents inside the Laurel Lodge were ready for the attack. Barricaded behind desks and couches, they immediately began firing their weapons as the Marines charged through the front door. The lead Marine was hit in the head and fell dead to the ground. The second Marine through the door was hit in the stomach, but he managed to get off a quick shot, skillfully killing the conspirator who had just mortally wounded his teammate.

The remaining Secret Service agents continued their counterattack. While they were exceptional when it came to protecting and shielding a single individual, they lacked the advanced combat tactics that made a Marine a Marine. With one fireteam coming through the front door and another fireteam flanking around the rear entrance, it was only a matter of time before the conspirators were overpowered. When the last Marine fired his weapon, six Secret Service agents were dead with only one Marine killed in action.

"What's the situation?" Captain Davidson asked into his radio. He was waiting outside the lodge with the secretary of defense.

"We have six dead combatants, sir," the squad commander radioed back.

"What about our causalities?"

"We have one man down, and two injured," came the response.

Hearing the volley of gunfire, Howie watched as additional Marines rushed across the meadow toward the Laurel Lodge. The hostage rescue squad assigned to guard the exterior signaled their peers to stand down and help secure the building. Too many Marines inside would complicate the rescue.

"Have they found the president?" Howie anxiously asked.

"He's not in the main area," Captain Davidson said. "They're going to check the rest of the building before letting us in."

With a medic helping the injured Marines, the rest of the hostage rescue squad went to work. Starting in the kitchen, they checked for any sign of the president or attorney general. The last room they approached was the president's private office.

It was a fitting location for a final showdown.

As two Marines opened the door to the room, they halted in shock. The president of the United States was blindfolded and gagged, sitting behind his desk in his custom leather-backed chair. He was completely tied down, preventing his movement in any direction. Blood covered the front of his shirt, and his chin was pressed against his chest, holding something in place. It took the lead Marine just a second to determine the object was a hand grenade.

Kneeling directly behind the president's large office chair was the attorney general. He was positioned in such a way as to be completely shielded by his hostage. The only exposed body part was the attorney general's arm, pressing a Secret Service pistol into the side of president's head.

"Gentlemen, you've come at a bad time." Rodney laughed from behind the chair. He shoved the gun against the president's head. "Put down your weapons," he ordered.

The Marines' guns were drawn, but they had no clear shot. The president was at least twenty feet away, giving the attorney general ample time to pull his trigger before anyone could get across the room. For a few awkward seconds, nobody moved. Then Captain Davidson and Howie showed up, witnessing the standoff firsthand.

"Rodney, this is insane. It's time to stop," Howie shouted from the doorway.

"Howie, is that you?" Rodney asked in shock from behind his human shield. "It's disappointing to hear that you're alive and well. I really needed you to be dead right now," he said sarcastically.

"We've retaken the communication center. It's over," Howie said. His voice was resolute.

"It's not over. The revolution is just beginning!" Rodney shouted defiantly.

"Everyone's dead. You're all alone," Howie said.

"No, I'm not. I've got hundreds of people dedicated to me. We're going to succeed!"

Howie checked his watch and then quietly whispered something to Captain Davidson. The captain nodded his head and left the building. Howie then ordered the Marines guarding the room to lower their weapons. As the soldiers relaxed, he stepped into the office with his arms raised, showing that he was unarmed.

"What's this all about?" Howie asked.

"It's about a better future," Rodney said. He slightly rotated the president's chair toward Howie as he spoke, giving himself improved coverage. "The government is broken. The Constitution is outdated. We need a powerful leader, someone who has full control to fix our nation's problems."

Howie slowly moved counterclockwise, sliding his back against the opposite wall of the room as he spoke. "What about Congress?" he asked.

Rodney instinctively moved the president's chair further away from Howie. "Congress is the problem. They get in the way of everything. We need a new government with just one leader making the right decisions."

"That sounds like a dictatorship," Howie said. He glanced at the small window high on the wall. A few more tiny steps and Rodney would be in position.

"Call it what you like, but the revolution has already started. You're too late!" Rodney shouted back.

Perched on a small hill overlooking the Laurel Lodge, Lance Corporal Klossen saw his target move into view. While the office window was much too small for a person to enter, it was ample enough space for a 7.62mm bullet. Looking down through his high-powered scope, the sniper now had an unobstructed view of the back of the attorney general's head. Holding his breath, the Marine fired his M40A5 rifle.

Inside the Laurel Lodge, the sound of shattering glass caught everyone off guard. The attorney general, who had been focused on Howie, failed to realize that he had inadvertently positioned himself in a direct line of sight under the small window. The sniper bullet hit Rodney in the back of his head, killing the traitor instantly. Unfortunately, the impact of the bullet also pushed his body forward, jarring the president's chair in the process. The Commander in Chief lurched, releasing the grenade that was tucked beneath his chin.

The explosive tumbled across the desk and onto the floor. "Grenade!" Howie shouted. Lunging with all his might, he threw himself on top of the explosive. The Marines in the doorway instinctively ducked for cover, anticipating an ear-splitting explosion. It never happened. They looked up in time to see the defense secretary roll over onto his back, holding the grenade in his hand.

"It was a bluff. He never took the pin out," Howie gasped. He took a couple of quick breaths to calm his nerves. "Get over there and help the president."

Pllchwaajpds
hu'ltaqwr
xiɪ'kun
resadk
ihvaraly
dikdaklla.
achik'axlxÅj.

'ᵱ'q'lsamduc
aja'Jnmo
'ɕhinaq
.adhtz
jövJjir
Jxiᴿikun
.aqɾesajawl

5:00 PM EDT
WHITE HOUSE SITUATION ROOM

ELEN NERVOUSLY ANTICIPATED an update from Howie. He had
called from Camp David just before he headed out with the
Marines to reclaim the Laurel Lodge. But that was almost forty
minutes ago, and Helen was increasingly worried that something
bad had happened. Suddenly, a phone rang out in the Situation
Room. She said a silent prayer, hoping it was positive news.

"It's from Camp David. The communications are back up," a
staffer eagerly said. She answered the call and then put it on speaker
for the entire room to hear.

Howie's voice rang out from the speakers embedded in the ceiling. "Helen, are you there?"

"Thank goodness you called. Tell me the president is okay,"
Helen said.

"He's alive and safe. The medics are checking him out at the
Aspen Lodge right now. It looks like he has a broken nose, but he'll
be fine," Howie said before continuing. "The situation is stable up
here. We lost a couple of Marines in the firefight, but the good guys
are fully in control now."

"What about Rodney?" Helen asked.

"A sniper bullet got him, but he was definitely our bad guy. We found him with a gun pointed at the president's head. It was a little dicey there for a moment, but the Marines saved the day," Howie said.

"What about the other conspirators?" Helen asked.

"We took out six Secret Service agents during a counterattack at the Laurel Lodge, and four more down at the communications center," he said. "We've rounded up the rest of the president's security detail and locked them up, but we aren't sure who's involved because they're not talking. It's going to take some time to sort this all out."

"Have you accounted for everyone else up there?" Helen asked.

Howie answered quickly. "Yes. The president's staffers are shaken, but they're okay." He switched his focus back to the conspirators. "But we've got another problem. Rodney claimed he had hundreds of people working with him."

"The decrypted emails definitely point to that," Helen said. "Unfortunately, the only other conspirator that we can positively identify right now is Javier Soto."

"I've been thinking about that," Howie replied. "Once the president gets settled, I'm going to suggest that we send someone after Javier. I've got SEAL Team Four training right now at Mac-Dill Air Force Base just outside of Tampa, Florida. I've already called and put them on standby. They could be in Mexico in just a couple of hours."

Helen instinctively checked the clock on the wall of the Situation Room. It was 5:10 p.m. "I like it. If we could get Javier to talk, or at least get some information off his computer, we might be able to positively identify the remaining traitors."

"What about the other Cabinet members?" Howie asked. "Did we get them to safety?"

"The CIA is rounding them up right now. I anticipate their arrival here shortly," Helen said.

"I wonder why Rodney didn't go after the other members of the Cabinet?" Howie asked.

"We might never know for sure, but I think that killing the rest of them wasn't worth the risk. By focusing on the people ahead of him in the line of succession, Rodney eliminated the most powerful people standing in his way," Helen answered.

"We're not out of the woods yet, but it sounds like we're moving in the right direction," Howie said. "Once the president checks out, we'll set up a conference call with you and the remaining members of the Cabinet. Hopefully, we'll be able make some sense of this mess before 9:00 p.m. That's when the president wants to address the nation again."

Helen sensed a problem with the president's tight schedule. "Then we've got to move fast and identify the other conspirators. When the president shows up alive and well on TV, the rest of the traitors will disappear into the night," she said.

5:30 PM EDT
NSA DATA CENTER, UTAH

It had been over two hours since Tanner and his team had heard from Helen, but they hadn't been idly waiting around. Using charts and tables drawn on every square inch of available whiteboard space, the team diligently analyzed the rest of the decrypted emails. They had made good progress in their work. Even Mel, with his pessimistic disposition, could now see how the collaborators were planning their coup.

"We know there's a secret group called the Order of 28 that is behind all this. Votan is running the show, and we're highly confident that's the code name for the attorney general, right?" Mel asked.

Kevin answered. "That's correct. The attorney general contracted with the Chiapas cartel to assassinate key leaders in our government."

Sydney continued the team's reasoning. "Besides eliminating the other key leaders, the cartel's terrorism accomplishes two important things. First, it creates a nationwide panic. And second, with so many people dead, it casts doubt about who is actually in charge of the government."

"That's also right," Tanner answered. "Unfortunately, we don't know for sure how Rodney plans to side-step the president on the way to the top. But it looks like he has a lot of powerful friends who are going to support his claim to be the new president."

"I think that is the key point," Rachel said. "It looks like there are several judges and even some members of Congress who are part of the Order of 28."

"The emails clearly point that out, but we still need a specific message or file that positively identifies every member of the Order of 28," Sydney said.

Just then, the phone on the conference room table blared out. Tanner stepped away from his notes on the whiteboard and answered the call.

"How's the work coming out there?" Helen asked her former team.

"We're making a lot of progress on the email messages. We think we know the basics of the coup," Tanner said.

"The situation has dramatically changed since we spoke last," Helen said. She quickly explained what had happened up at Camp David. She finished by highlighting that the immediate threat to the president had been eliminated.

The NSA analysts were dumbfounded when they heard that the attorney general was indeed the ringleader of the coup. Tanner was the first of the stunned analysts to speak. "I can't believe it. Rodney almost succeeded with his insane plan."

"There are only a handful of people outside of Camp David that know what I just told you, so keep it quiet," Helen said. "And this isn't over yet. We've got to move fast to track down the rest of the people involved."

"What do you want us to do?" Tanner asked.

"Who else have you identified that is part of the Order of 28?"

"It's hard to know for certain because they all use code names for each other, but we know that several people in the Secret Service are involved. There are also several judges and members of Congress in on the plot. And we're pretty certain that a higher-up at the State Department might have actually killed Elizabeth Godfrey."

Helen paused at the new allegations. "Have you found anything in the emails about Javier Soto?"

"Yes. We know that he is involved. His cartel made a business deal with Rodney to get him into power," Tanner said.

"We've got to track down Javier immediately," Helen said urgently. "The CIA says he lives in southern Mexico. They have a photo of him, but they don't have an exact location of his whereabouts. So I need you to look through those emails and see if you can find anything that will help us positively determine his location."

"We could probably track him down by IP address," Tanner said. "We'd just need to crosscheck the IP address on his email headers with our list of Internet service providers in Mexico. We could pull a physical address from that."

"If you can get me his location within the hour, that would be extremely helpful," Helen said. "We've got a team of Navy SEALs preparing to go after him."

"There's a list of people here we don't know anything about. These guys aren't using aliases, so we think they're just minor players in the plot. You should probably have someone check them out also," Rachel said over the phone.

"Send me that list right away," Helen said. She then added some additional details before ending the call. "Chances are that you're going to get a boatload of information here shortly that you'll need to quickly decrypt and analyze. So fire up QC and get ready. We're not to the finish line yet."

A
T 6:00 P.M., Navy SEAL Team Four took off from MacDill Air Force Base. Flying in the back of a retrofitted Boeing C-17, the forty-man unit was led by a lieutenant commander who had spent several years serving in both Iraq and Afghanistan. Every member of the elite team was combat tested. When they weren't fighting for their country, the SEALs trained nonstop, perfecting their special ops expertise.

While SEAL Team Four didn't have any advanced warning for their mission, they eagerly anticipated their assignment. Their plan was straightforward. Using an HAHO (High Altitude High Opening) approach to prevent enemy detection, the elusive troopers would parachute from the C-17 cargo plane at an altitude of 25,000 feet. They would silently glide on their parachutes for half an hour, eventually landing under the cover of darkness at the hacienda owned by Javier Soto. The SEAL team would then quickly neutralize any opposition before capturing the drug lord and taking him back to the United States.

The strategy loosely followed what their counterparts in SEAL

Team Six had done when they went after Osama bin Laden. Instead of arriving by helicopter, however, SEAL Team Four was limited by time constraints and had to implement a HAHO assault. Jumping out of airplanes was inherently illogical, but jumping out of a jet cruising at the same altitude as a commercial airliner was insane. Nevertheless, every member of SEAL Team Four had performed the HAHO jump before, and they had complete confidence in doing it again.

After nearly two hours in flight, the green light in the rear cabin of the C-17 flashed. It was time to go. Following their training protocol, the special ops warriors plunged off the rear-loading ramp of the C-17. Guided by the supplied GPS coordinates, the SEALs steered their parachutes toward their destination. Floating in the night sky, they noticed lights on the distant horizon. Their objective was in sight, but the special ops warriors didn't land directly on the hacienda's property. Instead, they landed on the sandy beach several hundred yards away on either side of their target. With the crashing waves providing background noise, the SEAL team's arrival was virtually silent. They swiftly gathered up their black canopies, checked their weapons, and moved out to capture Javier Soto.

The special ops warriors were split into two 20-man units. One group approached the hacienda head-on from the beach, while the other unit flanked around to the front. Because of their limited intelligence on the compound, the SEALs weren't sure of what resistance they might encounter. The CIA estimated that Javier Soto had a dozen guards armed with AK-47s, but the actual amount could easily be twice that number. Such uncertainty was why the SEALs trained as hard as they did. They had to be able to adapt and gain control of any situation they came across.

The first unit approached the magnificent home from the rear. Moving up from the beach, the men with black camouflage clothing and black face paint blended into the shadows of the night. Up ahead, an armed guard rested by a palm tree near the pool. He lit a cigarette—a classic mistake. The SEALs all had night vision goggles, and the glowing cigarette sang out like a diva at the opera. The lead SEAL quickly fired two shots with his suppressed HK-416 submachine gun. The faint "pop-pop" noise was barely audible, but the result was still lethal. The guard slumped down in a soundless death.

Like a small colony of deadly fire ants, the SEALs swarmed the hacienda from opposite directions. They moved with precision and poise, eliminating the armed guards with ease. While it was true that Javier Soto had over a dozen men defending the perimeter of his hacienda, they weren't trained soldiers. They were nothing more than hired thugs, who woefully lacked the skills to match one of the finest military forces in the world.

The SEALs successfully secured the exterior of the building, but moving out of the night shadows and into the well-lighted home presented obvious challenges. To gain the upper hand, the SEALs cut the power to the complex. The entire house went dark, accompanied by shouts of confusion from the staff. Suddenly, several loud explosions went off as numerous concussion grenades were tossed into the mansion. The SEALs stormed in from all angles, taking advantage of the darkness and smoke. Quick gunfire was exchanged, and then everything went silent. Five more mercenaries were dead.

The SEALs skillfully moved up the grand staircase to the second floor. After subduing several members of the house staff, they finished their search of all the rooms, but the drug lord was nowhere to be found. A SEAL who was fluent in Spanish questioned the staff. Javier had gone for a drive in his BMW Roadster convertible and was anticipated to return at any moment. Calling on his radio, the lieutenant commander updated the members of SEAL Team Four. He told the perimeter unit to take up defensive positions and be on the lookout for an approaching vehicle. While the troops outside prepared for the imminent arrival of the leader of the Chiapas cartel, the SEALs inside scoured the hacienda for information. They found two laptops and several cell phones. They also located a hidden safe in the office that was easily compromised by several well-placed explosives. Unfortunately, the safe yielded few interesting articles. It was mostly full of US currency and fake identification papers.

Confident that they had all the information they could find, the SEALs tied up the house staff and hid them far off in the jungle bushes. Eight agonizing minutes later, a silver BMW roadster turned off the highway and headed down the long dirt road. Javier Soto was on his way home.

As he slowed down for the final approach to his villa, Javier was ambushed by four Navy SEALs. They dragged him out of his convertible before it even came to a complete stop. The ops warriors threw a dark canvas bag over their captive's head and then handcuffed his hands together. Escorting the bewildered drug lord through the mansion and out the back, the SEALs quickly reassembled on the beach. The sound of approaching helicopters was heard off in the distance. Less than three minutes later, all forty SEAL team members and their prized prisoner were boarded onto three Knighthawk helicopters, heading out to sea.

8:15 PM EDT
WHITE HOUSE SITUATION ROOM

Javier Soto's capture was witnessed in real time via live satellite link back to both Camp David and the Situation Room. The members of SEAL Team Four had performed their mission flawlessly.

"How long until they get back to the ship?" Helen asked over the video-conference monitor. The communication system linked the Situation Room with Camp David.

"Twenty minutes," Howie said. "The ship has an interrogation room set up and ready to go."

"And there's someone on board that can quickly copy the hard drives and send the contents to the NSA folks in Utah?" Helen asked.

"Yes, the Navy techs have already established the link. They'll start uploading the data as soon as possible," Howie said.

Helen checked the clock on the wall—8:15 p.m. "That's cutting it awfully close. Hopefully we'll have enough time to get some solid facts from Javier or his computers before the speech."

8:35 PM EDT
GULF OF MEXICO

The three Knighthawk helicopters landed on a Navy ship in the middle of the Gulf of Mexico. The rotors on the lead helicopter hadn't even stopped spinning before two SEALs jumped out onto the flight deck. They grabbed their blindfolded hostage and quickly escorted him away from the aircraft and toward an elevator. He was on his way down to the interrogation room.

While Javier Soto prepared to experience innovative and effective interrogation methods, his two laptops were taken to another area on the ship. A Navy electronics technician quickly pulled out the hard drives from the laptops and connected them to a device that copied all the data, bit-by-bit. The technician didn't worry about the fact that the contents of the hard drives were encrypted because he had been assured by the NSA that it wasn't a problem. The specialist quickly went about his work, streaming the copied data off to the NSA. After bouncing across two different satellite uplinks, the information arrived at a nondescript building in Utah.

8:45 PM EDT
NSA DATA CENTER, UTAH

"Here it comes," Tanner said. He and the other members of his team were huddled around the console of the quantum computer. They had been expecting the incoming data stream, which arrived just before 8:45 p.m. EDT.

"It's encrypted?" Sydney asked. Her statement wasn't so much of a question as a statement of observation. The analysts had fully expected the data to be encoded. They just didn't know which encryption cipher it used.

"Yes," Tanner said. He typed a few commands on the keyboard. "But we're in luck. It looks like its standard AES."

Few people in the federal government knew about the QC team's exceptional code-cracking abilities. With the help of their quantum supercomputer, Tanner and his team had cracked AES, one of the most widely used encryption methods in the world. As a result, the NSA could read practically any encoded message sent across the Internet. Tanner kicked off a batch routine that began decrypting the data as it arrived. The plain text output of the hard drive's contents began filling up another folder on the super computer.

Had Tanner and his teammates known the data was streaming from a Navy ship in the Gulf of Mexico, they would have been surprised. But if they knew the files were from the personal laptops of a famous drug lord, apprehended by elite Navy SEALs less than an hour ago, they would have been astonished. But that was how modern warfare had evolved. Information had to be captured, decoded, and analyzed instantaneously to keep one step ahead of the bad guys. For that exact reason, the NSA had spent billions of dollars developing its PRISM spying program and associated data center in Utah.

Even though it took some time to download the full contents of the hard drive, Tanner didn't wait to start the investigative work. Navigating into the folder where the plain text files were stored, he looked for anything that might be a clue to the identities of the members of the Order of 28.

"What's that?" Rachel asked. She pointed over Tanner's shoulder to a file that just finished the decryption process.

Tanner located the file that Rachel had referenced. It was simply called "names." He opened up the newly unencrypted file and gasped. It was a list of every member involved in the conspiracy.

TANNER DIALED THE extension for the Situation Room. Helen answered the call just after one ring. "Hi, Tanner," she said. "I've got you on speakerphone with the president at Camp David and the remaining members of the Cabinet here at the Situation Room."

Tanner was caught completely off guard by the unanticipated audience of the three-way phone bridge. He wasn't sure if he needed to formally acknowledge the president in such a setting. Fortunately, the Commander in Chief made the first move.

"Go ahead and tell us what you found on the laptops," the president said.

"Thank you, Mr. President," Tanner said. He decided to give a quick update before delivering the shocking news. "I'm not sure where we got this data, but it obviously came from a source inside the Order of 28. Everything corresponds to what we've found so far in our email investigation. I consider the information to be extremely accurate," Tanner said. He moved on to the most important revelation. "There are a lot of facts here that still need to be dissected, but the greatest discovery we found is a list containing the members of the Order of 28."

"Who's on the list?" Helen asked. Her anxiousness was apparent in the way she blurted out her question over the phone bridge.

Tanner decided there wasn't any point in softening the blow, so he began at the top of the list and started reading out names. The first name belonged to Rodney Groth. That information wasn't all that shocking since everyone on the call already knew about the man who had tried to kill the president. However, the names of the traitors that came next were unbelievable: the deputy secretary of state, the ambassador to the United Nations, the head of the DEA, the lead Secret Service agent on the president's security detail, the associate deputy director of the FBI, the director of the ATF, the solicitor general, the commissioner of the US Customs Service, and the deputy administer of FEMA. The list also contained over a dozen different congressmen and a handful of federal judges. A prolonged silence occurred as the remaining leaders of the United States digested the information. The president was the first to break the awkward silence. "How confident are you about the names on this list?"

"Sir, I'm not sure about the source of this data, but I'm absolutely positive that those names were part of the encrypted information that we received," Tanner answered clearly.

"Did you find mention of anyone in the armed forces?" Howie asked.

"No," Tanner said. "Everyone on the list appears to be a Washington insider."

"Excellent work, but we need everything on those hard drives," Helen said. "Hurry up and finish your analysis. Call me directly if you find other pertinent information."

"We will," Tanner said.

The president didn't think twice about how abruptly the NSA analysts had left the call. That was the least of his concerns. With a list of two dozen known conspirators, the president had to focus on apprehending the traitors while assuring the rest of the nation that everything was going to be all right.

"I've got my speech in ten minutes, folks. How do we proceed?" the Commander in Chief asked his remaining Cabinet on the conference call.

"I noticed there wasn't anyone on that list from the military. We can probably assume that my department is relatively clean," Howie said.

"We can't have the military going around arresting Americans. That's against the law," the secretary of Homeland Security said.

"On the other hand, we can't trust the FBI either. One of their top people is listed as a member of the Order of 28," Helen said.

"Maybe we can get the local cops to go after these traitors," said the secretary of the interior.

"We'll use the military," the president said. "We can arrest the conspirators under authorization of the National Defense Authorization Act. That allows us to go after terrorists on American soil and detain them indefinitely."

"Sir, you know I'm not one for politics. But if you do that, you'll face incredible public opposition," Helen said.

"That doesn't matter. We're a nation in crisis. Congress is out for the campaign season, and I've got to establish order to resolve this mess," the president said. He addressed his secretary of defense. "Howie, it's time to come out of hiding. I want you to call up the Pentagon and tell them that arresting these remaining traitors is their top priority."

"Yes, sir," Howie said.

The president then spoke to Helen. "I want you to coordinate with Howie on tracking down the rest of the conspirators. In the meantime, I've got an off-the-cuff speech that I've got to deliver."

9:07 PM EDT
CAMP DAVID, MARYLAND

THE PRESIDENT'S PRIME-TIME address started seven minutes late. Forgoing his normal preparation and makeup routine, he appeared on national TV with only a fresh set of clothes. The blood on his face had been cleaned off, but his broken nose was obvious to the entire nation. Despite his exhausted appearance, the president appeared more organized and more focused than he had been earlier in the day. With only a sheet of scribbled notes as his guide, he started his national address from the small TV studio at Camp David.

"My fellow Americans, today the foundation of our nation was shaken to its core. The terrorist attacks by the Chiapas drug cartel were part of a larger conspiracy to overthrow our government. A secret society called the Order of 28 was responsible. These cunning and devious individuals orchestrated the chaos. They turned their backs on freedom and liberty. The rule of law meant nothing to them. These traitors only cared about putting themselves into positions of power. Working hand-in-hand with the Chiapas drug cartel, the members of the Order of 28 were determined to pull down the Constitution and set up a supreme leader. Miraculously, their evil plans were thwarted at the last minute.

"The leader of this secret society was the attorney general, Rodney Groth. Plotting with other evil leaders in the nation's capital, he executed his plan to become a president for life. He arranged the assassinations of the presidential successors before him, and he even attempted to eliminate me. But he failed. The Marines at Camp David responded courageously and killed Rodney and several of his conspirators just as they were implementing their political coup.

"Unfortunately, the treachery goes far beyond the attorney general and his secret council. I've ordered the members of our armed forces to find and arrest all the conspirators. We know who they are, and we are bringing them to justice. Right now, Javier Soto, the head of the Chiapas drug cartel, is on his way to stand trial in the United States. The other collaborators will have to answer for their crimes. We will move past this national tragedy. Order will be restored, and peace will prevail. Good night, and may God bless America."

10:00 PM EDT
NSA DATA CENTER, UTAH

Tanner and his team didn't watch the president's impromptu speech. With the full contents of Javier Soto's hard drives now decrypted, the NSA analysts in Utah discovered a wealth of information. They knew all the details about the Order's evil plans. The information was absolutely astonishing and completely condemning.

The members of the Order of 28 were all handpicked by Rodney Groth. Using flattery and twisted logic, he had convinced his fellow conspirators that the Constitution was obsolete. He preached the need for a supreme leader, a single ruler to fix the problems facing the nation. He created his secret society as a way to accomplish his misguided vision.

The Order of 28 was comprised of power hungry, mid-level administration officials and judges. In return for selling out their country, the members of the Order of 28 were guaranteed powerful leadership positions once Rodney became the nation's first king. All the members of the Order of 28 swore an oath to support Rodney and his claim on the presidency.

Rodney and his followers formed an alliance with Javier Soto, who was trying to become a big time player in the illegal drug market. Javier was promised exclusive access to the US drug trade in return for killing key leaders and causing a general panic. The sinister arrangement was perfect. Javier would get to expand his drug operation by doing the dirty work of the Order of 28. And by outsourcing the killings to the cartel, the Order of 28 planned to maintain their innocence.

There was also another side of the conspiracy that Tanner and his teammates hadn't known. The decrypted data elaborated on a unique cyberattack coordinated by the Chiapas cartel. They had secretly employed the services of members of the hacking group Anonymous to carry out the attacks. The cyberattacks were directly responsible for the death of the speaker of the House and the treasury secretary. The hackers had also disabled the security cameras at the State Department, allowing the deputy secretary of state to go unnoticed when he murdered Elizabeth Godfrey.

Finished with their analysis, Tanner and his team updated Helen on their discoveries. While they didn't know it, all the information they provided was substantiated by Javier during his ongoing interrogation process. Helen compiled the data from both sources and forwarded it to Howie, who used the information to rapidly track down the conspirators. Working with local law enforcement agencies and the National Guard, the military quickly arrested over two hundred people in what would soon become one of the largest nationwide dragnets in history.

OCTOBER 29
WHITE HOUSE, WASHINGTON DC

IT WAS JUST after 11:00 a.m. Helen sat alone on a couch in the Oval Office, waiting for the president's return from Camp David. While she had been in the famous office nearly a thousand different times, today her visit seemed more solemn. She pondered on Rodney Groth's failed attempt to overthrow the government. He had come frighteningly close to pulling off a political coup of epic magnitude. Her head spun as she recounted the chaotic events of the past thirty hours. It seemed like it had been an eternity since she was unceremoniously whisked down to the Situation Room after learning about the death of the speaker of the House.

In her hand, Helen held three finalized reports for the president. One was from the medical device company that created the insulin pump used by the former speaker of the House. An analysis by the manufacture concluded that someone had exploited a vulnerability in the wireless protocol, gaining full access to the pump's controls. The hacker remotely altered the pump's settings, giving the politician a fatal dose of insulin while he slept.

The second report also involved a bizarre computer hacking

incident. Out on the Green River in Utah, the controls for the floodgates on Flaming Gorge Dam had been compromised. The hackers overrode the operator's computer, releasing a tremendous amount of water into the narrow canyon below the dam. The instantaneous flood killed the treasury secretary, along with a dozen other innocent victims.

The third and final report was from the mobile communication providers in the metro DC area. While cell phone service had been restored to the nation's capital, the report summarized some obvious security weaknesses with the computer systems that managed the wireless networks. All three major cell phone providers had implemented an ad-hoc fix to restore service, but the report emphasized that other unknown vulnerabilities likely existed in the cell phone network.

In the silence of the grand office, Helen turned her thoughts to the assassination of the vice president. His murder was the catalyst for Tanner's journey to find the mysterious Cipher. At the time, nobody expected that a single, strangely worded message would end up being the critical clue to uncovering one of the largest conspiracies of all time.

Once again, Tanner had proven to be more resourceful than anyone could have possibly imagined. While he was still three years shy of his fortieth birthday, Tanner had been responsible for exposing two of the greatest plots against the United States in recent history. Of course, as an NSA analyst, Tanner's accomplishments would never be publicly acknowledged, but Helen knew he liked it that way. He'd rather stay off the radar, quietly serving his country while others stood in the spotlight. As Helen thought about her former employee, she had a strange thought. *Would Tanner ever consider being a National Security advisor?*

The east door to the Oval Office flung open. The president quickly strode in, followed closely by Howie. Helen stood up to greet the Commander in Chief. "Helen," the president said. Instead of shaking her hand, however, the president moved in and gave her a strong hug. Helen returned the gesture, recognizing that something was different about the president. He seemed more genuine. Maybe it was the attempt on his life, or the fact that the nation he loved had almost fallen into ruin. Either way, the president was now visibly a changed man.

The president stepped back, allowing Howie to give Helen a similar hug. "I'd be lying if I didn't say I thought I might be dead today," Howie said.

"Me too," Helen said. Information contained in the decrypted emails showed that Howie's personal chauffer was involved in the conspiracy. The driver was supposed to have shot Howie on his way to work yesterday.

The president sat down on the couch, inviting his two trusted advisors to take a seat across from him. Helen noticed that the president was avoiding his usual seat behind the Resolute desk.

"Here are the details on what happened to the speaker of the House and treasury secretary," Helen said. She handed the president the three folders with "Top Secret" stamped on the cover. He quickly skimmed through the information.

"This verifies what we learned from Javier and his laptops, right?" the president asked.

"Yes, all the evidence points to the cartel working with members of the Anonymous hacking group," Helen said.

The president leaned back on the couch. "Should we go after these guys?" he asked, referring to the Anonymous hackers.

"I don't think it would be worth it. First of all, it's doubtful that we'd ever find them. They may not even be Americans. And second, I think it distracts from our efforts to track down the main conspirators. Going after the hackers right now would make it look like we were on a witch hunt," Howie said.

"I agree," Helen said. "We'll find the hackers later on. Right now, we need to focus on bringing the members of the Order of 28 to trial. They're the primary people responsible for this mess."

The president nodded his head. "We've arrested all those folks, except for this mysterious El Flaco person. Do we know anything else about him?"

"Unfortunately, we don't. Even Javier doesn't know his real name. He just goes by El Flaco," Helen said.

"Can we find him?" the Commander in Chief asked.

"Javier told us about the cartel's staging area in Guatemala. Earlier this morning, we launched a Reaper drone out of Cannon Air Force Base. It should be down in that area of the jungle any moment now. We'll try and get some high-res photos and determine if El Flaco is there," Howie said.

"If you find him, take him out," the president ordered. "Don't wait for me to give you the green light."

Helen was puzzled by the president's decisive action. "Sir, what if he's an American? Shouldn't we bring him back to the United States?"

"He's not on American soil. As far as I'm concerned, he's an enemy combatant," the president said resolutely.

"What about Javier Soto?" Helen asked.

"He's clearly not an American, so lock him up at Guantanamo. He can rot with the rest of the scum down there."

Helen noticed something unusual about the way the president was giving such succinct orders. "What's going on?" she asked. "You're acting like you're getting ready to check out for a long vacation."

The president glanced at the secretary of defense. Howie took a sheet of paper from his folder and handed it to Helen. It was the president's resignation letter.

Helen was dumbfounded. "You're quitting?!" she asked in shock.

"Not quitting, resigning," the president said. "Howie will be running the show through the midterm elections. Once Congress reconvenes and chooses a new speaker of the House, he will become the acting president and fulfill the rest of my term."

Helen turned and glared at Howie. "When did you agree to do this?" she asked with irritation.

"Just before we left Camp David, but it wasn't my idea," Howie countered.

"He's right. It was my idea," the president said. "This is what's best for the nation. The Order of 28 had their hands in everything. We've arrested the ringleaders, but the corruption goes farther than we know. My opponents will inevitably say the entire mess is my fault because the scandal happened on my watch. They'll demand a Congressional hearing, and that will turn into a fiasco that this nation hasn't seen since Watergate," the president said. Then he paused, becoming more introspective. "That's not what we need right now. We need to be unified, not divided. My resignation will be an act of good faith, showing the country that I'm committed to clearing out all the corruption."

"We're already missing half of the nation's leadership. We can't afford to have you gone too," Helen said.

"Hogwash," the president said. He sat up straight and stared intently into Helen's eyes. "I learned something up at Camp David. The nation is bigger than me. It's bigger than any single person . . . or president. The Founding Fathers knew this, and they put all the necessary safeguards in the Constitution to keep this country running. If we follow the Constitution, we'll be okay," he said.

Helen had heard the president give hundreds of speeches to people all over the world, but none of them compared to the impromptu address he had just delivered on the couch of the Oval Office. Patriotism radiated from the president. He wasn't a politician anymore. He was a true leader.

Tears welled up in Helen's eyes. "We're going to miss you."

"It's going to be okay. I'm absolutely confident that Howie can keep the country on track for the time being," the president said. He turned and checked the time on the magnificent grandfather clock against the wall. "I'm announcing my resignation to the nation in less than an hour, but I still have one more thing I have to do as president."

The Commander in Chief stood up and walked over to the historic Resolute desk. He opened up a drawer and removed a pre-printed sheet of paper. Taking a pen, he filled in a few parts of the form before scribbling his name on the bottom. He handed the document it to Howie.

"Make sure he gets this," the president said.

Helen leaned in to read the paper. It was an official presidential form, recommending that Tanner Stone be awarded the Presidential Medal of Freedom for his "especially meritorious contribution to the security or national interests of the United States."

"I think there are only two or three people that have ever received that award more than once. Tanner definitely deserves to be part of that exclusive group," the president said. He gave a half-salute to Helen and Howie before leaving to clean up for his final press conference.

THE WHITE HOUSE press room was buzzing with anticipation. Upon hearing that the president had come back from Camp David, the news correspondents assigned to the White House flooded the briefing area to get the first update. The address they were about to hear would make history.

The president entered the room just after 12:00 p.m. The Commander in Chief wasn't dressed in his normal suite and tie. Instead, he wore a cleanly pressed white dress shirt and dark blue slacks. He had taken a shower and cleaned up, but it was still obvious that he had been assaulted during his hostage incident at Camp David. The area around his nose and under his eyes was black-and-blue. Interestingly, there was something else that was different about the leader of the nation. The president moved with purpose. He seemed confident and determined. Even before he uttered a word, the seasoned press correspondents felt that this speech was going to be monumental.

The president spoke extemporaneously from his heart. He began by delivering an update on the search for the members of the Order of 28. The traitors had been captured, and they were being held in separate federal facilities as they awaited trial. The president also mentioned that the corruption went far beyond the main conspirators. Over four hundred people had been arrested so far. He stated that these individuals were smaller players in the plot, each carrying out acts of violence or aiding the Order of 28 in their evil plan. The Commander in Chief then clearly stated that everything was under control. He confidently iterated that the worst had passed, and that the American people need not fear about their future.

The president paused before continuing on to the next part of his address. Cameras clicked away as his face became emotional. He described in full detail what happened at Camp David. He told the nation how his former friend and confidant, Rodney Groth, was a man blinded by power and ambition. The president described his last moments with the attorney general. The president said that, for a brief moment, he experienced pure and unrestrained evil. The nation had come perilously close to collapse. He admitted that even he had been scared. Not only afraid for his own life, but for the lives and future freedom of Americans everywhere.

At his darkest moment, when the attorney general had a gun pointed to his head, the president had thought about the Founding Fathers. He remembered the Constitution, and how it was more than just a legal document that spelled out the workings of the government. The president said the Constitution stood for freedom, and as long as the Constitution was upheld, nobody could take away the nation's liberty.

The Commander in Chief then shocked the press correspondents and the entire world. He announced that, effective immediately, he was resigning from the office of the president of the United States. He explained that his resignation was necessary to ensure that a new administration, free of corruption, could be established as quickly as possible. Citing key points of the Constitution and the Presidential Succession Act of 1947, the president said that the secretary of defense was both legally and deservedly the best person to lead the nation. Howard Wiseman would be the acting president until the midterm elections were over. Then the majority party in the House of Representatives would quickly reconvene and choose a new speaker of the House, who would immediately resign and becoming acting president. That acting president would then serve two years until the next scheduled national election.

Before closing his historic address, the president again spoke of the Constitution. He reiterated that the Founding Fathers had provided a way for the nation to get through this difficult time of transition. The path was clearly marked by the Constitution. The president promised the nation that it could, and would, heal from the tragedies of the past week if it embraced the inspired document.

GUATEMALAN JUNGLE

As the president finished his passionate and patriotic address, an unmanned aerial vehicle, or UAV, arrived at the Petén region of Guatemala. The MQ-9 Reaper drone scouted the dense jungle area described by Javier Soto. High resolutions photos taken from the initial flyover positively identified a Cessna Turbo Skylane parked in the middle of a small clearing. The tail number on the plane corresponded to a similar aircraft that had taken off yesterday afternoon from a municipal airport in Virginia. On a subsequent flyover, the drone photographed several people at the site, including a fair-haired, light-skinned person believed to be El Flaco. The discovery was relayed via satellite link from the drone back to the ground control station at Cannon Air Force Base. The flight unit at Cannon Air Force Base then notified their leadership at the Pentagon. They quickly replied, informing the UAV flight crew that the Commander in Chief had already made the call—take out the compound.

Two minutes later, the Reaper drone dropped a five-hundred pound bomb on the Chiapas cartel's staging grounds. The massive blast destroyed everything on site, including a rare second copy of a Bible that contained a translation from Spanish to Itza. The drone's final flyover verified that nobody had survived the blast.

DECEMBER 8
ANAHEIM, CALIFORNIA

THE FIRST PART of December was a perfect time of year to visit Disneyland. The crowds were small, and the warm California sun was a welcomed contrast to the cold and snowy weather back in Utah. The trip to Disneyland seemed extra special for Tanner and his family. Maybe it was how the amusement park was uniquely decorated for the upcoming holidays. Or maybe it was part of a greater feeling that things across the nation were finally getting back to normal.

Tanner leaned up against a handrail, watching his wife and Sara circle around on a carousel. In her arms, Megan held their not-so-small-anymore baby. Glen and Julie Holland were also present, receiving compensation for their interrupted vacation back in October. They sat on a nearby bench, enjoying an ice cream with their newly adopted family member—a hundred-year-old Guatemalan known only as Miguel.

Tanner let his thoughts drift off. It was hard to believe that the midterm elections had been held just last month. Somehow, the nation made it through the complex transition process and was now moving forward. Congress helped ease the changeover by quickly naming a new speaker of the House, who immediately vacated his position to become the acting president. It was the first time in the history of the United States that three different people held the title of president in one month.

The trials for the members of the Order of 28 dominated the daily news. It was pretty much a forgone conclusion that the conspirators would all be found guilty of high treason, but due process had to be administered. Unlike the rest of the nation, Tanner didn't follow the legal proceedings. He had seen all of the evidence firsthand, and he wasn't interested in listening to a bunch of news pundits, speculating on what had happened between Votan and his followers.

A cell phone chirped to life, bringing Tanner out of his thoughts. Reaching into his pocket, he removed the wireless device. It was the same EDES cell phone he had used in Guatemala, and there was only one person that knew the number.

"Hello," Tanner cautiously answered. Things had gotten crazy the last time Helen called while he was on vacation.

"I see that you still have my phone," Helen said. She let out a small laugh.

"I figured I'd keep it safe until someone asked for it back," Tanner said. He had left his personal phone at home, but had taken the specialized government phone on his trip, just in case something came up.

"I hear you're in southern California," Helen said.

"Yeah, we're making up for our rudely interrupted trip back in October," Tanner said. His response was part joke and part accusation.

"You must have gotten your minivan back."

"We did, but we decided to fly down for this trip. It's kind of a quick vacation."

"Good for you. If you can take some time off, I guess that's the ultimate sign that life is normal again," Helen said.

"What about you? You're due for a vacation," Tanner said. He knew Helen had been working overtime, providing continuity in the Executive Office for the acting president.

"Didn't you hear? I'm retiring in March. I'll have tons of free time for a vacation after that."

"No, I hadn't heard," Tanner said. "You've decided to call it quits on government service?"

"The last six weeks have been brutal. I'm completely burned out, but I'm sticking around a little bit longer to make sure the transition stays on track."

"What about Howie? I heard he's thinking about going back to the private sector," Tanner said.

"He is. Two weeks as acting president showed him that he had no stomach for professional politics," Helen said. "What about you? Are you staying with the NSA forever?"

"Probably. Why do you ask?"

"Have you ever considered living in DC?" Helen asked, ever so slyly.

About the Author

EW PEOPLE UNDERSTAND the terrifying, yet realistic, threat of computer hacking like Denver Acey. Denver has spent his entire professional career in the information technology industry where he has witnessed and even thwarted actual cybercrime. From his top-secret job working for the US government to securing computer networks at Fortune 500 companies, Denver is personally familiar with hackers and their unscrupulous activities.

But over the years, Denver has become increasingly frustrated with Hollywood's inaccurate portrayal of cybercrime. Hackers are more intelligent and more sophisticated than simple teenagers who guzzle down Mountain Dew while playing video games. Cybercrime is a billion-dollar business that encompasses organized crime and foreign governments. For these elite hackers, the fruits of success are iconic trademarks, innovative patents, and government secrets.

Because of his unique background, Denver decided to write novels to dispel hacking myths while highlighting the tenacity of cybercriminals. Utilizing actual computer hacking concepts and scenarios that he has experienced firsthand, Denver illustrates—in a simple way for even the non-techie to understand—how vulnerable we all are to cybercrime.

SCAN TO VISIT

WWW.DENVERACEY.COM